THE A

The Archivist

DAVID POWNALL

QUARTET

First published in 2010 by
Quartet Books Limited
A member of the Namara Group
27 Goodge Street, London W1T 2LD

A catalogue record for this book
is available from the British Library

ISBN   978 0 7043 7200 9

Typeset by Antony Gray
Printed and bound in Great Britain by
T J International Ltd, Padstow, Cornwall

FOR RAFFI

History advances in disguise; it appears on stage wearing the mask of the preceding scene...

RÉGIS DEBRAY

CHAPTER ONE

As the hymn *All people that on earth do dwell, sing to the Lord with cheerful voice,* came towards its close, Daniel Rogers had to let go of his treble part. It was not a high note troubling his voice, but a strange, presageful crackle in the middle registers. Turning his body away from the congregation he groped under the surplice, putting pressure on his groin in the same way an accordion-player might squeeze his instrument, in order to make a tonal adjustment.

His voice plunged, veering into another key, then disappeared altogether.

This could be it, he thought.

It would have to happen in church.

But he couldn't be sure. His tendency to day-dream while singing tunes he knew too well could be responsible. His mind had drifted away from the job in hand. While thinking about something else his voice and brain had separated.

He tried again, producing a squeak that turned into a croak.

Goodboy Bluit picked up the dissonance. Peering across the aisle he raised his eyebrows, corrugating the dome of his bald head, and gave Daniel a stern look. Goodboy's duties as choirmaster sometimes sat uneasily with his job as assistant bursar of Lord Mendora Land College. He had been thinking about the cost of the hundred yards of elastic rope for launching the Combined Cadet Force's glider when the disharmony came out of Rogers. He frowned. It was a bit early to lose the boy.

The organ was given a final hefty pump by the veteran tenor Mr Groom, head of a local yeoman family with a tradition of service to the church that went back centuries. His extra-long surplice had been handed down to him by his father who had been a much taller man.

Two hundred and twenty boys sat down making a thunder in the wooden pews.

Manhood may be about to happen, Daniel told himself as he gingerly lowered himself into the choir stall. I can't wait to get through to the end of all this.

From recent experience, he knew the voice would return – probably in time for the next hymn. That's how it went – up and down, up and down. But this fracture had been a deep one, distinctly threatening.

He watched the vicar as he clambered up the five wooden steps into the pulpit to give his sermon. Daniel was glad to shift his thoughts to this man, a big influence on his life, someone he believed in. Henry would take his mind off the gathering storm of hormonic change. Daniel knew of no other boy who listened as closely to the words of the Reverend Henry Long as he did. He was a fan club of one. His attitude was – if I don't pay attention to what this experienced and inspired old man is telling me, my hours imprisoned in this ancient pile are wasted.

The vicar's right hand shot out and grasped the brass candlestick on the ledge of the pulpit. He pulled himself into his accustomed oratorical stance, great white-haired head thrust forward. He surveyed his audience from under bushy eyebrows and breathed a little in short gasps. Before speaking, he licked his lips.

He always breathed a little in short gasps and licked his lips after grasping the brass candlestick, winding himself up.

Then he always swayed once to the left and once to the right before the first word came out.

And that first word was always *no*.

This morning, February 7th, 1950, he said: *No matter what we think* . . .

Last Sunday had been: *No man is an island* . . .

And the Sunday before that, which was the Feast of the Conversion of St. Paul: *No one in their right mind* . . .

The Sunday before that occurred in the school holidays but

even though Daniel was at home two hundred and fifty miles away he could bet his life Henry had kicked off his sermon with another *no*.

He was right.

No wonder was Henry's starter that Sunday.

On the endpage of *Hymns Ancient and Modern* Daniel had a list of options he could supply if Henry ran out of no's.

No sooner . . .

No hiding place . . .

No thought . . .

No charge . . .

No better than . . .

No doubt . . .

But he hadn't thought of *no wonder*. That was a masterstroke. After *no wonder* you could say anything.

Once again, the vicar had demonstrated his power to rise above any attempt to foretell or outguess him. Why couldn't other people see his genius?

Henry got stuck into his audience. His subject was the futility of arguing with the divine will – submission is everything, he said, the word *Islam* means just that and we need something in collective Christianity to represent that important concept. If the military have quite finished with it, we could rescue *unconditional surrender* and adapt it to our religious purposes. Then he moved swiftly into sectarian wrangling, then back to his main theme via mushroom clouds, and the theory that the three-part unity of God was unfissile, his divine nature only found in unsplit atoms.

With an effort, anyone who read the newspapers and listened to the BBC could follow all the connections, but the mind and ear needed to work fast. Daniel struggled to relate a digression, an unconnectable aside really, that lasted less than five seconds when Henry smiled mysteriously and let slip that his favourite French word was *d'ailleurs*.

The soporific effect Henry's style had on the congregation of grey-suited boys upset Daniel. To reject the best entertainment school life had to offer seemed perverse. Henry was better than the films, better than the radio. But even the sixth-formers looked blank as the vicar shared the best of his intellect with them – and their minds were supposed to be working at a very high level in order to pass exams.

Daniel watched Henry's right hand closely as it worked on the candlestick, thumbing and fingering. Hours of enforced contemplation in the choir-stalls had trained the boy's observatory powers. He could concentrate on a small item for a long time. At harvest festival last year he had gone through the entire service without taking his eye off a big rat replete with fruits and produce it had gnawed its way through, dozing between the feet of a pregnant village woman. She couldn't see below her bulge and the rat knew it.

Rule one of Henry's sermon technique was: never let go of the candlestick.

It was the anchor, the Aristotle by his side. To release his hold meant the argument was lost and, once more, nothing, nothing, had been changed by words.

Over the years, the place on the shaft of the candlestick where Henry's grip was exerted had been worn into a softer tone, more old gold than brass. Daniel loved that colour even more than the light from the stained-glass windows slanting onto Henry's superbly laundered surplice. His wife washed all the surplices of the choir every fortnight, but Henry's was done every week and boiled twice in starch. This gave him the look of a giant frost crystal.

There was something about that handspan width of wear on the candlestick that moved Daniel to the depths of his being. When the old clergyman was excited by a revelation bursting out of the carapace of his reasoning he would grip the candlestick so hard the pulpit shook.

At that moment his priesthood flamed up, he had a strangle-hold on the throat of sin. Little snarls came from his trembling lips. Sometimes there was foam in the corners of his mouth.

But as all things have their time, Henry's freely roaming rampage across the minds of dreaming boys had to end each Sunday, (his average sermon was thirty-two minutes long) and his power drain away at the appointed hour. Daniel had to watch as the fire died in the vicar's blue eyes, the crystal points of the starched surplice melted from their frosty sharpness, and the sadness come into Henry's expression as he watched the grizzling, grey-suited horde drift out of the church unmoved and unchanged yet again.

Every Sunday a powerful argument was put with passion and completely ignored.

Because no one ever listened, it could not even be claimed that Henry's sermon had its moment but then shared the fate of so much human thought in being forgotten.

Indifference.

This was the killer.

As Henry raged in the damp chill of the church Daniel some-times had the vision of him in one of his wilder sermons tearing the candlestick from its mounting and brandishing it aloft – an Anglicised version of the Statue of Liberty. Oh, then they'd pay attention! The congregation would laugh their heads off, enjoying Henry's humiliation.

To prevent this ever happening, Daniel gave himself the job of regularly tightening the screws at the base of the candlestick. Every Monday straight after school he walked the mile down from the Junior House to the village shop, bought a tin of condensed-milk, crossed the street to the church, took a screwdriver from the organ tool-box and did the maintenance on the candlestick, then put two holes in the tin of condensed-milk with the screwdriver and sat in the vestry sucking out the nectar.

The jumbled flow of thought in his mind tended to become an inundation as he sat there, preoccupied. Most of the items he thought about alone in the gloom were skimpy, trivial, mere flotsam on the flooded stream.

The label on the condensed milk tin said: *Unfit for Babies.*

He always dwelt on that.

Following a Sunday when Henry had not been on top form, Daniel kept the empty tin of condensed milk and offered it to Henry as the basis for a sermon.

'Why are you waving that tin at me, Rogers?' the vicar said.

'The world is a tin of condensed milk, sir? Unfit for Babies?'

'Indeed.'

'You could take it into the pulpit with you, sir. That would make them sit up.'

'It's so good of you to think about me, Rogers.'

For Daniel, Henry was the only man, the only authority, who could enfold the world's craziness into his thinking, which was why he always started with *no*, a coded rejection of the horrors of the destruction-drunk twentieth century.

Daniel did his weekly job on the candlestick and paid homage to the vicar's wide-winged theology because the boy was possessed of a powerful sense that he had lived in a sane land before his life began, and Henry might have been there.

At birth they had both been ushered into a madhouse.

His first memory was from when he was two. His family were crammed under the stairs at his grandparent's house during an air raid on Liverpool. He was in his mother's arms, watching the filament of a clear light bulb tremble with the percussion of the bombs raining down on the docks. In pauses between the waves of bombing his grandfather could be heard drunkenly raging and swearing from his armchair by the fireplace. There wasn't enough room for him under the stairs and he had to be a man, for once. As the raid came nearer, Daniel's twelve-year-old aunty broke into screaming hysterics and had to be slapped by his grandmother. That moment had entered the boy's bones. He could still feel his mother's arms steeled round him.

Daniel felt the vicar was in contact with the peace of pre-natal sanity. If he could fully understand what the man was saying, this could save him from all the trouble he was in at school.

The benign curve of the vicar's character was an arm around Daniel's shoulders. With Henry close by in thought he was never completely alone. A clergyman has a presence in a community. He need not be seen at all times, but the knowledge he's there is like time, air and the police force, something that can be depended upon.

Also, Henry was a war that had never happened. He was connections that had never been broken. With him everyone was alive who had ever been alive, including Daniel's father.

And Henry never cared about making a fool of himself. He was a holy fool of the best kind. That was another reason his sermons were worth listening to. He would say anything that came into his head. He was not afraid to show his confusion. He did not pretend to have certainties.

He rambled.

As John the Baptist and Jesus did in the wilderness, he rambled.

In the choir for six months, Daniel still thought it strange no one suggested he be taught music. Goodboy Bluit had picked him out while walking up and down the rows of new boys singing the school hymn at their first assembly, ears cocked. That afternoon Daniel was recruited into the church choir at three shillings a term, sixpence extra for weddings. When he pointed out that he couldn't sight-read, Goodboy told him it was unnecessary. He would pick everything up from singers on either side.

The entire choir couldn't sight-read.

They all only listened to each other.

When it came to the Easter cantata it had to be practised hundreds of times so they knew it by heart.

Daniel was an eleven-year-old who never wasted his time intellectually, even though the progress of his mind could be laboured. The hours he was forced to spend in the church each week were put to good use. The poetry of the Book of Common Prayer, the hymns and psalms, flowed through the boy's mind and he sought meaning from them amongst the violent pubescent uproar of a daily twenty-four hours penned in a secular monastery for juveniles. The church did have a sort of independence from the regime of Lord Mendora Land College. It was the right place to wonder about existence; to wonder about Hitler's war, which was hardly over; to wonder about rage; to wonder why his grandfather at home had to be drunk every single day; to wonder why his widowed mother wouldn't look at another man; to wonder why this small early English church was the only refuge for his soul.

Henry's theme this week was redemption. He used a cricketing analogy for the soul. God was a slow left-arm spin bowler. He could turn a ball on the deadest of wickets, which was most people.

'Let us not forget the importance of a good groundsman,' Henry said, pointing to Mr O'Leary, keeper of the school's twenty acres of sports fields, sitting with his family. 'Skill with the earth, seeding and nurturing, when to cut, when to use the heavy roller, can make such a difference.'

Mr O'Leary was pleased to be mentioned, but his eyes were glazed. A friend of the vicar for many years, he had to admit that once Henry got into the pulpit all was lost.

Henry plunged on to the googly, most deceptive of balls.

Daniel watched the headmaster's face to see how he was taking the sermon this week, hoping he had already switched off. The Old Man, as he was known, habitually wore a frown, but that frown could get worse. Lately, Henry's rhetoric had been pushing the Old Man's frown into the hinterland of a scowl.

Henry was skating on thin ice these days. The Old Man's ambition was to steer the ex-orphanage towards full public school status. The original charitable foundation had been twisted out of shape during the Depression – the Jewish banker's bequest

16

to create the best orphanage in Britain based on a modern interactive farm now had to be supplemented by fee-paying pupils. The Old Man wanted a seat at the Headmasters' Conference – to be up there with Winchester and Wellington. The school had no chapel or hall so the village church had to do as the place of worship and morning assembly up at the main school took place in the gymnasium under ropes hanging from the rafters like the hangman's nooses at Nuremburg.

For the school of the Old Man's dream, the vicar should be a top man, an up-and-coming serious cleric bound for a bishopric, not someone who punished boys for horsing around in Scripture lessons by beating them with his trilby hat.

Henry was afloat on a major digression – the power of the contrite, disciplined soul. Bee keeping came into it, somehow, via Samson, the carcase of a lion and tins of Tate & Lyle syrup, (maybe a cross-reference to Unfit for Babies here). There had been a side-thrust at Belsen and the disrespect shown to human bodies by bulldozing them into mass graves, the driver having to wear a mask over his face, like this – here Henry put the hem of his surplice over his mouth and breathed in stentorious blasts. *Our cruelty to each other is a stench in the nostrils of God,* he bellowed, as he tore away the mask, following this up with the approaching demise of steam on the railway, from thence into a Humphrey Bogart film about transporting nitroglycerine.

Daniel found himself floundering in spite of his expertise in following the complexities of Henry's redemptory logic. It upset him when he failed to make all the connections. Before he could bring the loose ends together, Henry had left Hollywood and found an autobiographical route to his personal best bowling figures. Playing for Hampshire in 1910 he had taken five wickets for nineteen runs against Somerset at Taunton. This was a great gift from above, and a blessing, certainly not a triumph of the individual, he insisted. I would never quote the statistic in pride or vanity but simply to make the point.

There was always at least one sublimely human moment for Daniel in Henry's sermons and this was it. The boy's eyes pricked with tears and he had to lower his head.

When he was back in control of his feelings, he looked up to check how Henry was being received this Sunday by Moira, the Old Man's tall, grey wife. Although she often suffered the rasp of the headmaster's sardonic tongue in front of the boys, Daniel thought she must have some influence useful to Henry. Yes, she was smiling indulgently. And it wasn't her customary high-table rictus. Daniel counted her as a fan of the vicar because she liked the theatre and Henry was the nearest thing to it in the hermetically sealed world of the school. The Old Man himself had switched off, perhaps, but his eyes were hard. As Henry slid from cricket into why there were no games in the Bible, *God never plays games* he declared, wrenching at the candlestick, Daniel experienced a second strong upsurge of emotion that took him by surprise.

Henry could do this to him so easily – catching him unawares even when he hadn't quite followed the plot.

This was worrying. He couldn't go on being so vulnerable to one man, especially a man so out of touch with everyone else. A boy must respond, be critical, make sense without being taken over – even a boy short of a living manhood model of his own blood.

Henry had hardly ever noticed him. He didn't notice boys, which was why he was so popular. The masters who noticed boys were dangerous, especially in the bathrooms.

Helpless in the stream of puberty, awash with dissolving loyalties, cut off from his family, persecuted by his own voice, scarred by fights and beatings, overwhelmed by Henry's cloud-minded glory, Daniel decided he must find help from somewhere.

He would go back to the text.

There and then he vowed to read the Bible right through.

He would make up his own mind.

When the service was over, Daniel cornered Henry in the vestry and asked what *dailleurs* meant.

'*Besides,*' Henry replied. 'No other word means so much.'

Daniel extracted the correct spelling from him and retreated with the precious ambivalence. He held it in his mind like water cupped in the hand of a thirsty traveller.

He sat on the bench under the hooks where the cassocks and surplices hung, and concentrated.

Henry was right. Given thought, *besides* was quite a word. Below the surface it had several richer meanings. Why had he never picked the power of that word out for himself? Words were pouring past him out of reach.

All that must change.

The church had emptied by now. Daniel went and checked the big Bible on the brass eagle lectern in the chancel, turning over the pages.

When he came to the end he looked at the black number printed at the bottom of the page.

One thousand two hundred and seventy.

Reading through that lot would keep him going.

Having been told time after time that his free education at Lord Mendora Land College was the best chance he'd ever get to rise in the world, he had to do something to make it feel that way.

Here were one thousand two hundred and seventy pages that had been scanned and sifted for centuries. The countless eyes that had passed over the words had left a deposit on the paper, a sheen.

'If our religion is true it must be everything,' Henry had said during an Advent sermon hurled at the boys, 'which is how we know there have never been any real Christians,' following this up with one of his pearls: 'If you have to live in an asylum the best place is near the door.'

The elegant Mr Pacey opened the cupboard and gave Daniel the choice of sticks. There were seven of them in a rack like rifles in an armoury. Some were bamboo, some were willow, one was long and flat like a weaver's rule, another curved and knobbly.

'Take your pick, Mephistopheles,' the young housemaster drawled, film-star aquiline features relaxed in a smile.

Daniel noted the plum-coloured smoking-jacket, the claret cravat and the embroidered Persian slippers. Pacey had been reading a book before the condemned arrived.

It was in a foreign language.

His place was marked with a lace handkerchief.

Pacey was the idol of the matrons and maids.

The boys knew he was in hiding at the school, probably from a woman whose life he had ruined, or several of them.

He was a very good golfer and tennis-player, a *bon viveur*, a playboy, an occasional actor and a sadist.

This was to be Daniel's third beating in a week.

During the previous term he had broken the school record – ninety-two strokes in twelve weeks – an average of one point zero nine a day. In the end-of-term report sent to his mother the Old Man had said he wasn't quite happy about Daniel's standard of behaviour.

'What's all this about, son?' she'd asked, following it up with a second question he couldn't find the means to answer. *'Aren't you doing as well down there as I might have hoped?'*

The punishment at the expert hands of Pacey was for dawdling back to Junior House after church, lost in a dream. The first beating of the week had been for fighting, the second for getting four out of ten in a French vocabulary test.

Daniel chose the thinnest stick, which was contrary to the best advice. But he knew what he was doing. Pacey daren't lay on too hard with a whippy weapon in case he cut the flesh or curled the stick round the hip to damage the genitals. A month ago Mr Hyman the handicrafts master had bloodied his overlong favourite willow round the loins of Rawlins of 3B who'd subsequently complained to his father. Mr Rawlins had removed his son from the school. From the bursar's office had come the rumour that a full year's fees had been the price of the parent keeping quiet. Now Mr Hyman suffered the humiliation of being banned from using any kind of corporal punishment and being called Pussy ever after.

Pacey ordered Daniel to take down his trousers and bend over facing the door, which he opened.

'May I have the door shut, please, sir?' Daniel asked respectfully. 'I don't want people watching.'

'I'm going to propel you into the corridor, Mephi. Keep your legs together and pull your testicles forward if they've dropped. I musn't hit them' Pacey said nonchalantly. 'Mephi, dear renegade, dear tormented, irreconcilable idiot, what d'you deserve for the heinous crime of being late back from church?'

'Oh, one, sir . . . at the most . . . half a one would be fairest.'

'I think it has to be four. You were obviously up to no good.'

'How about two, sir? I lost track of time. I was thinking about something.'

'That's a lie. You are incapable of thought.'

The first blow hardly shook Daniel. But Pacey was teasing him. The second doubled the first, the third doubled the second, and the fourth sent the boy flying through the door into the corridor. An Italian maid was polishing the floor outside. As Daniel struggled to pull up his trousers in front of her, she burst into tears.

When he told the story in the dormitory after lights-out he said Francesca, the squint-eyed Italian maid, had only wept because she'd been hanging around outside Pacey's door for hours hoping to catch sight of him. When Daniel came flying out she'd looked straight through him into the eyes of her dream and he'd slammed the door in her face.

Daniel's backside had been studied by boys in the ablution block after the beating. In accordance with ritual, he'd shown his weals to everyone, and said *feeble*. Pacey's skill in not quite breaking the skin was admired. The masters all had different

21

punishment signatures. Some used the gym shoe, some the strap, some rubber-tubing from the labs, there was even a rope's-end wielded by a master not long out of the Navy.

Beating was a cult amongst the live-in bachelor staff, a source of clubbish humour, a trial of staff-room strength, a witness to adult power and the inconsequentiality of pain, and a test of personal vagaries in sexuality. In school slang the word for masturbation was *flogging*.

Mule was the senior housemaster. He had other names, names his parents had given him, names his enemies had stuck on him, names the Army had given him, but Mule was the one he embraced. That night he was on the prowl with a cushion tied to the end of his artificial right leg so he could move soundlessly along the cork-floored corridors. He was in a foul mood because damp had got into one of his butterfly collection cases, making the wings of thirty-six tiny brown fritillaries droop, never to rise again. He listened outside the A dormitory door and identified Daniel's voice, helped by the Liverpool accent. Entering at the charge he snapped on the lights, pounded down to Daniel's bed, yanked back the covers and dragged him to his feet.

'Will you never learn, you impossible lout?' he roared. 'How many times must you be punished?'

Daniel said nothing. The warm pains round his buttocks were still there. Mule never made a boy take down his trousers like Pacey did. Should he ask for a day's delay of execution so his backside could settle down?

But Mule had gone silent, staring in disbelief.

'What's the Bible doing in your bed?' he demanded.

'I'm reading it, sir.'

Mule picked up the black book. He could see a torch half-tucked under the pillow. 'Reading after lights-out is less of an offence than talking after lights-out, but it's still an offence.'

'Sorry, sir,' Daniel offered.

'You've already been beaten once today I understand,'

Mule said, having enjoyed Pacey's amusing account over tea. Picking up the torch, he continued: 'I'm confiscating this but the good book has saved you from what you deserve. Get back into bed.'

Daniel was enough of an actor to seize this opportunity to consolidate a very rare good impression. Picking up the Bible he held it with both hands against his heart and lay down, eyes closed, leaving the covers as they were when Mule had torn them back. Mule paused, unsure what he should do. Then he grudgingly leant forward and pulled the covers over the unfamiliar spectacle of a first-form boy in the thrall of piety.

After Mule left on his cushioned foot there was a pregnant, thoughtful quiet. This was not a precaution against the housemaster coming back but a genuine silence of the bewildered. There were other torches under other pillows in A dorm, but they were for illuminating the improbable fornications to be found in the books of Hank Jansen, the popular sage of sex.

Daniel was aware that he had become a mystery to his equals. Before he fell asleep with the Bible clutched to his chest, he heard a whispered question circling the dormitory as nineteen other very young minds pondered:

How the fuck did he get away with *that*?

When he had got through the books of Genesis and Exodus – which astounded him with their supercharged suggestiveness – Daniel asked Henry for a personal interview in order to talk about the Holy Spirit and a few other things.

After Matins the following Sunday the vicar asked Daniel to remain behind.

They sat side by side on a bench in the vestry.

Three big bells stood on the floor opposite. They had been there since the Great War, waiting to be re-hung in the tower.

On the biggest of the bells was an archaic inscription: *Hail Mari ful of gras*. No matter how often he saw it, the inscription always made Daniel smile. For luck, every time he entered the vestry and every time he left, he ran his fingers over the word *gras* and whispered: *grace really.*

'What's on your mind, Rogers?' Henry asked.

The task Daniel had set himself in reading the Bible from one end to the other was explained and Henry had to admit that not only was he taken aback, but made to feel guilty.

'Even I haven't read the whole thing through,' he confessed. 'I should have done, but I haven't.'

Daniel didn't like the idea of making Henry feel guilty.

Henry went on in chattier mood to muse aloud that his own days as a theology student at Oxford would have been an appropriate time to read the whole Bible, but he had been very busy.

'I expect you were busy playing cricket in those days, sir.'

Henry nodded. 'Amongst other things,' he sighed. 'It seems to me, that I never took life seriously as a youth. It was all pleasure, pleasure, pleasure.'

'Perhaps that's what I should do, sir?'

'It would be wrong of me to give you that advice, Rogers.'

'Sir, I hadn't realised that the Bible is just a history book about the Jews. Even the Creator was a Jew.'

'Does it say that anywhere?'

'I looked up Jerusalem in the atlas. It's a long way from here. Did we take on the history of the Jews as our own history?'

'Look, Rogers, I can only give you five minutes,' Henry said. 'We've got people coming to lunch.'

'What was on God's mind when he told Abraham circumcision would be the sign of His covenant with the Jews?'

'Why ask me!' Henry snorted, getting up to tap his pipe out on the tenor bell.

'What a place to have a sign!' Daniel insisted.

Henry gave him a probing glance. 'What would you suggest? A ring through the nose? Perhaps there was a health reason. These were desert people living side by side with their animals. Don't take it too seriously. It was a long time ago.'

'Sir, how can you, of all people, tell me not to take the Bible seriously? It's your life, isn't it? Will you tell me a few books I can skip, sir? I'm getting lost and I've only done two. There're sixty-four more to go.'

Henry declined the request. 'I'm far too busy to think about it.' he said. 'This is a challenge you've set yourself. You can always drop it.'

'For instance, sir, Lot's daughters got him drunk and went to bed with him to preserve his seed. What's going on there?'

'I really must be getting home, Rogers.'

'Please help me, sir.'

'I'm not prepared to explain all the inconsistencies in the Bible. It would take me the rest of my life.'

Daniel pulled a face. 'I need something to hold onto, sir,' he said darkly. 'There's no one else I can talk to about this. If I write questions down as they crop up, may I have five minutes with you after Scripture each week?'

'Please don't write too much down about Lot and that kind of thing,' Henry urged. 'You must always keep Scripture in balance with your other subjects. If you must carry on with this project I think the sooner you get into the New Testament the better. The story-line is a lot simpler.'

By the end of the next week Daniel had filled two exercise books with queries. When Henry cast an eye over them, important and valid to an eleven-year old boy seeking manhood, he found his inability to provide answers painful, and doubted the value of his ministry amongst the unhearing horde.

CHAPTER TWO

The craze housemasters had for beating boys reached its height in the summer of 1950. The craze amongst the boys at this time was firing paper pellets at each other with elastic bands. At times the air of the common-room was white with whizzing paper. When the craze of the masters collided with the craze of the boys and the latter were beaten for hitting someone in the eye with a pellet, a special energy of warfare was released. Visitors to the Junior House picked up this excitement and decided it must be the ongoing spirit of the place.

With its lacerations and personal dramas, beating outmatched other punishments in the thrills it provided. Giving lines to write out, *raking,* in which the master plays no part, except to throw the completed punishment into the waste-paper basket, was considered lame and unmanly. The few masters who avoided the use of corporal punishment – family men who had houses on the school estate and were not affected by the passion for beating – found themselves dealing with requests for lines to be converted into strokes of the cane. The married masters discussed this phenomenon amongst themselves. They decided it might be a symptom of addiction to pain which could lead to full-blown masochism. When they took the problem to the headmaster he called them boneheads.

'You should know by now that hard cases always prefer to get things over quickly,' he said. 'Double the lines every time you get asked.'

This reduction in the power of pain to control behaviour had several consequences; one was an even greater use of the stick in an effort to assert the authority of suffering. A temporary housemaster made the point in a staff meeting that, taken to its logical conclusion, this policy could lead to the introduction of capital punishment in schools. As a result of this exaggeration he found himself paid off and waiting for the bus to Basingstoke.

His intellectual legacy emerged in staff meetings afterwards when the stick was referred to as the ultimate deterrent – a cut-back version of the hydrogen bomb.

The married masters formed a splinter group. Although they weren't prepared to jeopardise their jobs, and knew specific protest to the Old Man was pointless, instead of joining the flagellators for coffee at morning break, they brought their own in thermos flasks and met in the Chemistry lab store. Another manifestation of these strange spiritual-cum-political twists and turns, more subtle and complex, was an outbreak of thieving in the Junior House.

Mule's response was to intensify the beatings. He made sonorous orations about honesty to the Junior House boys at meal-times. The result was a further increase in thefts. Soon theft between boys was as common as conversation. Mule decided to enlist the support of the victims themselves as vigilantes. Everyone was being stolen from and everyone might be guilty so everyone was to keep an eye on everyone and report suspicious behaviour.

As an ex-Army officer, Mule should have known that *splitting* was more of an offence than thieving, so he was told nothing. The problem worsened until thieving was a craze. Whatever respect Mule's authority had in the Junior House drained away and he was left helpless, stick in hand.

As the housemasters continued flailing away that long summer, the thieving escalated. It appeared to be an intuitive general redistribution of wealth, a share-out amongst fellow-sufferers. Nothing was overlooked. Any item was worth stealing, including things previously treated with contempt like socks or hairbrushes. Finally, a meeting between a deputation of boys and Mule took place. He confessed to being at his wit's-end, which the boys found easy to imagine. Asking the local constabulary to intervene had been considered but the Old Man had ruled it out. The school must regulate itself. He had instructed Mule to establish an action group of suitable boys to police the Junior House from within with power to investigate and punish.

There was no need for this group to refer to higher authority. The stealing must be stopped by the boys themselves.

This group, when formed, was called the Cosh Gang.

There was a judge, a prosecutor and an executioner.

Two systems of summary justice ran side by side without overlapping. No boy was ever handed over by the Cosh Gang to the masters for punishment, which did away with splitting, and the masters never passed a culprit discovered by them on for the boys to deal with, which disguised the abdication of their authority. If a master on his rounds came upon a trial or a beating in progress, he turned his head and went his way. Even the matrons in surgery desisted from questioning boys about injuries received at the hands of the executioner (who always worked on the head and upper body) – a lesson in keeping mum these women had learnt from bathing the rodded backsides of boys with camomile lotion and stemming their tears after the masters had been at them.

On 6th June, four months after starting out, Daniel finished reading the Bible. He declaimed the final section of the sacred text out to A dorm at half-past ten, long after lights-out:

And if any man shall take away from the words of this book, of this prophecy, God shall take away his part out of the book of life, and out of his holy city, and from the things, which are written in this book. He which testifieth these things saith, Surely I come quickly (cheers from the audience), *Amen. Even so, come, Lord Jesus. The grace of our Lord Jesus Christ be with you all, Amen. The end.*

Daniel had earned useful kudos on all sides by sticking to his great reading task – respect from the masters for his diligence and determination, and respect from the boys for his magnificent discomfiture of Mule on the night he was caught in bed with the Bible. While on dorm duty one night Pacey drawled that having to stand by and actually watch Mephistopheles reading the good book gave him vertigo.

Because of his relationship with the Bible, on which oaths were taken at the Cosh Gang trials, Daniel rose to the position of prosecutor. He was feared by all thieves in the Junior House. Nevertheless, the criminals remained active, as if helpless and beyond reform, driven by the streams of warped, unnatural energy loose in Junior House, reminiscent of the manic atmosphere of prisons. Queues of boys waiting for trial in the corridor outside the ping-pong room sang sad, muted blues melodies. As the condemned were thumped by Brotherton, the executioner, there was applause from those who would shortly be suffering the same fate themselves.

During the holidays, his drunken grandfather had been enthralled by the sight of Daniel sitting beside him ploughing through the book of Numbers. He told his grandson several times, man to man, that although he, himself, was often called Manny, his full baptismal name was Emmanuel, which means *God with us,* bestowed by his Ulster fundamentalist father, a man who had always carried his Bible with him, even to the pub. There was obviously a rebirth of ancestral character here, and the workings of an atavistic power. Another memory Daniel's marathon of reading invoked in his grandfather was of visiting the mosque of St. Sophia in Istanbul when he was part of the occupation force in the Great War.

'First it was a Christian church,' he said, tapping the ash of his Capstan full strength onto the carpet and spitting a huge blob of yellow phlegm over the grate, 'then they changed it to a mosque, but it's still a church underneath. Changed my life being there with the Turks. I liked them. They're a proud nation, even in defeat. The call to prayer is what we need back in this country.'

29

Daniel was a successful prosecutor. His weighty accumulation of knowledge on all forms of human transgression and divine retribution gave him confidence to attack the small crimes of his weaker fellows. The list of offences was extended beyond theft to include unpopularity, odd behaviour (nervous tics, jaw-clacking), lachrymation after corporal punishment, refusing to fight and bed-wetting. There were no sexual misdemeanours recognised by the Cosh Gang court. In the hurly-burly of group pubescence anything in that line was permissible. The ghost-faced extreme wankers were comic heroes who received respect. They gave shows and demonstrations, an advance guard pushing the frontiers of self-abuse forward until full knowledge of the mystery of manhood arrived.

When Swilly Gropius stood trial in the ping-pong room for unclean personal habits, before his interrogation could proceed, he had to swear an oath. Daniel put a piece of cardboard on top of the good book to protect it from germs. Swilly, with the defiance of the damned, cursed Daniel for his cruelty, swept the Bible aside and stamped on it. He was felled on the spot by the executioner. As he lay groaning on the wood-block floor Swilly espied Rhino Harrison under the ping-pong table with his shorts round his ankles, beaming over his inflamed *brute*.

The school lay in the diocese of Winchester. Using the good offices of his opposite number at the famous public school of that city, a fellow Scot he was cultivating, the Old Man was able to persuade the bishop to send someone to listen to one of Henry's sermons undercover. The spy turned up for Pentecost.

Celebrating the descent of the holy dove and its miraculous giving of tongues to the apostles had the effect of lifting the Reverend Henry Long out of a bout of despondency. When he entered the pulpit and grasped the candlestick with his right hand, with the left, from under his surplice, he produced a racing pigeon and tossed it into the nave.

The condensed milk tin had done its work.

Daniel had persuaded Henry to try out a visual aid.

The spy's report to the bishop is still in the archives of the diocese of Winchester. In it is a condensed version of Henry's Pentecostal sermon which contained strong criticism of the squadron-leader of Vampire night fighters from a nearby RAF aerodrome for flying his planes low over the village and school on return to base at three-twenty every morning and waking everyone up.

As night after night crockery and porcelain shook on the Welsh dressers of his parishioners, who could forget the wanton destruction of Dresden?

And, like the good news of the Christian message, to what land did those pilots fly night after night, coming back empty-handed from the depths of darkness, scarred in the eyes by stars, their faith in the future of humanity undermined by going round in circles to no good purpose?

What on earth are we doing to our young men, both in the air and on the ground?

When Henry was given early retirement a month later, he chose to remain in the village, renting a workman's cottage, where Daniel was able to visit him. His replacement, the Reverend Michael White, was in place before the end of the summer term.

The school trustees discussed Daniel's case on many occasions, aware of the difficult family background. Goodboy Bluit, who had visited the house of Daniel's grandparents to interview him for the free scholarship, and met the family, had provided an analysis of the applicant's life at home.

His mother and grandmother are decent but uneducated women of the working-class, anxious that Daniel should be removed from the bad influence of his grandfather, who is the head of the family in name only. His uncontrolled drinking causes them continual embarrassment and shame, which they loyally endure because that is their tradition. While I was in the house, the

man tried to force rum on me and used obscene language,
completely ignoring the importance of my visit. Mrs Rogers
would trust LMLC to provide the good examples Daniel would
have been given by his father had he survived the war.

Aware of this reasoning, Daniel had never bothered to run away, as many other new boys did. There was an escape committee that met in the Anderson shelter and some made it home on platform tickets, but Daniel knew there was no point. He accepted that the school was the best deal his mother could find for him and he had to stick it out.

If he had ever run away, he would have been brought back, flogged and lectured *ad nauseam,* (which would be far worse than the flogging), and, worst of all, his bed would have been double-checked every night to see if he'd done a flit.

The judge in the Cosh Gang was Sidney Bryant, one of the smallest boys in the Junior House. Nevertheless, he was gifted with a certain knobbly, ghoulish intelligence and a genius for telling horror stories. His knowledge of Nature, Red Indians and the Age of Reptiles offset his dwarfishness and odd, morbid looks. The boys accepted that the head of the Cosh Gang had to be a top brain.

Bryant invited Daniel to spend half-term with him at his uncle and aunt's flat in Highgate, London, so they could go to the Natural History Museum, the Science Museum and the Bow Street Magistrate's Court to see prostitutes.

On the train to Waterloo Bryant opened up about his stepfather – a refugee Pole who had fought alongside the British and was now running a second-hand car business in Nottinghamshire.

'When the Russians invaded Poland in 1939 they shot his brother. I wish they'd shot him as well,' Bryant said with a queer gleam in his eyes that Daniel had noticed over the pingpong table whenever a judgement was being delivered.

'He's a brute. I can't understand my mother at all. They're

coming down for Founder's Day. It will be hellishly embarrassing for me.'

A stepfather's better than no father at all, Daniel thought to himself.

'He's taken all her money,' Bryant continued, 'and bought an old tumbledown priory and filled the grounds with wrecked cars and lorries, and he's forcing her to run a flop-house for all his Polish mates working in the coal-mines,' Bryant continued bitterly. 'You should see them drink the hard stuff!'

They discussed alcohol for a while, aware of its power.

'Does your stepfather give you a grim time personally?' Daniel asked, thinking Bryant's set-up sounded rather good. The idea of a house full of proper men rather than warped teachers attracted him.

'When I go home no one takes any notice of me,' Bryant complained. 'And the Pole has a huge family back there and he'll bring them all over to live with us, you'll see. He's got his own son by his first marriage, who he thinks is perfect, so what hope have I got?'

Daniel got up and opened the carriage window. 'D'you know anyone with a normal family?' he asked.

The question was ignored as irrelevant. 'My mother does everything he tells her.' Bryant declared. 'She never talks about my father at all. It's as if he had never lived.'

The visit to the public gallery of Bow Street Magistrate's Court put the museums into the shade. They counted fifty-two prostitutes being processed through the system. They all pleaded guilty and were fined forty shillings by the magistrate for soliciting. The variety of women dumbfounded them – it went from grey-haired female tramps to beautiful creatures in sun glasses and smart suits.

'What d'you make of them?' Daniel asked as they sat in a café nearby where several of the guilty were relaxing after their disgrace.

'Could be anybody,' Bryant muttered. 'One of them reminded me of my mother.'

Daniel could never have had that thought. His mother was part of the pre-natal Utopia he sensed in his memory, happy here on earth when her man was alive, dancing with her and in one piece. His father had been a god of the dance, loved by all, so he was told. The man had no faults his mother could remember. Even now, she couldn't bear to talk about him as dead. At no time before Daniel went away to school had she told him directly that it was so.

Daniel saw her grief, her imprisonment, her beauty, the impossibility of a life bound to a myth. Whenever he went home for the holidays he went in his mother's bedroom while she was at work and his grandmother was out shopping with his little brother, took the box out of the bottom of the ottoman and looked at all the photographs, documents, and letters that had any reference to his father. One picture showed his first grave in the cactus grove at Baharine Farm, Madjez-el-Bab, Tunisia, with six names on the cross. A lorry-load of land-mines his father's platoon had been unloading close to the front line had exploded. It might have been a mortar hit, or someone had dropped a mine. All the fragments of the men had been put in the same grave. Another photograph was of another grave in a big war cemetery, with an individual place of burial for his father's remains, and a headstone, but Daniel knew that this was just for show. The Army couldn't possibly have known which bit belonged to which man when they reburied them. After the enormous blast they must have all been left hanging indiscriminately on the cactus. He prized the first photograph. In his heart he would rather they had stayed where they were, together.

There were several letters from his mother to his father stamped: *It is regretted that this item could not be delivered because the addressee is reported deceased.*

There were short letters from his father, written from the line to his mother stamped *Passed by the censor* and dated by the Army Post Office after his death. He imagined his mother receiving these missives from the dead – warm, affectionate notes signed off *Sonny with love,* and love sent for Daniel, himself.

There was a letter of condolence from his father's lieutenant, and his mother's reply, blazing with grief and indignation, begging for more information. That had also been returned with *the addressee is reported deceased* stamp on it because he'd had been killed in the interim.

From this cache of writings and pictures he knew the truth his mother had not been able to tell. His grandfather, even in the drunken depths of his own endlessly repeated war memories, never mentioned Daniel's father, his son-in-law. His bitter, drink-loosened mouth was kept shut on that subject. For him Sonny was taboo because the women wouldn't stand any further violation of that life. When his grandmother did talk about Daniel's father it was always with pleasure, in praise of his looks, his skill on the dance-floor, his good appetite for her cooking, and the perfect sweetness of his nature, and how he had been reborn in the person of Daniel's brother, John.

During his last leave before embarking for North Africa with the First Army his mother had asked for another child. The last ascertainable words of his father spoken in his homeland were: 'I'll give you one for your birthday.'

And so, six months after the man had been blown to bits, he was miraculously reassembled, born again on his woman's birthday, keeping his name John, keeping his character and potential. This meant that he was not dead, which she had known all along, and continued to know, though their life together was a secret in her heart.

One day when Daniel had the contents of the box spread over his mother's bed, he looked up and saw his grandmother in the open doorway. She had come in without being heard while he was engrossed in reading. He saw the fear in her eyes, followed by concern and hesitation – then she silently closed the door and left him to it.

The best time in Daniel's early boyhood was brought to a close by his grandmother's cry for help, calling her daughter back from two years in the Cheshire countryside where she had been taken on as a trainee cook by a family of gentry straight after the war.

Experienced servants were difficult to get in those days. The advertisement in the *Liverpool Echo* asked for a smart young woman who could be taught to cook. His lordship was an ex Indian Army colonel. Being a war-widow with two boys to bring up gave Daniel's mother an advantage with him. In spite of the obvious inconvenience of having a seven-year-old and a two-year-old running around the place, he persuaded his wife to accept the applicant.

The gardener had fallen in love with her.

In his vague way, his lordship had fallen in love with her.

All the members of the Cheshire Hunt had fallen in love with her.

But she would have none of them.

These days often came into Daniel's mind while he was enduring the dark night of the Junior House. His mother must love again – get married – maybe to one of the bachelor masters who could be saved from himself by becoming a family man.

The history master, the rope's-ender, was a prospect.

In spite of being infected with beating mania, he was gentle at heart and could be normalised, changed by the love of a good woman, and maybe taught the quickstep.

Because the school was a world of it own, for the boys it was effectively the real world. Even on holiday it remained a strong shadow in their heads. Lord Mendora Land College was sold to them by *all* adults, *all* relatives, as a better place with better opportunities. It was better organised, better disciplined, promising success in the world – an everyday world the boys knew less and less about by being away at school. Nevertheless, they were assured, when you grow up, you will come to dominate your times by not being part of them.

Marcus Oliphant, the buzzing ginger PT master, was the dynamo at the centre of the school's sport and fitness machine. He ran and bounced everywhere on tapered, hairy legs, controlling his breathing, wiry body trembling like that of a newborn faun, a faery creature.

While in conversation he would fall forwards to the ground and do press-ups, speech unhindered. Walking along the box-hedged path to the administration block he might suddenly do a scissors high jump. Every lunchtime he leapt the seven steps leading to the dining-hall.

Oliphant was looked upon with fondness by the boys. In spite of being the master most involved with the corporeal dimension, he never beat a boy. In many ways he was a secular version of Henry Long, but had no church to defend or betray him. Once he had been a Scottish Calvinist but the importance of physical fitness had driven spiritual concerns from his mind.

He put enzymic Bemax on his porridge so he would never die.

Mule, who was another émigré Scot, put salt on his porridge until it was white. This was his only kindness to the boys since it meant he might die early.

Pacey looked upon porridge with an Englishman's profound contempt, and never ate breakfast anyway.

Oliphant measured and weighed every boy every year and kept records for the Old Man to study so he could build a top-class rugby side that would win him a seat at the Headmasters' Conference. Fifteen man-boys, strong, courageous and fleet, scrummed and winged through a dream in the Old Man's mind. It was no accident he hailed from Edinburgh – the city of body-snatchers. With Oliphant's statistics he worked out what was coming through the school years in physical power, planning how a great team of maximum strength could be put together. They worked on an annual mathematical model constructed from data and observations.

In 1950, the year the Cosh Gang began, the Old Man's dream became a reality. Fifteen very strong, hardened, proven rugby-playing boys emerged in the sixth form, all emotionally steady within a public-schoolish arrogance, well motivated and full of imperial self-confidence. Coaching his team towards triumph over every public school in the south of England took all the Old Man's attention. He had no time for anything else.

When concerned individuals tried to tell him what was going on in the Junior House he called them boneheads.

It was Founders Day. The prize-giving and speeches were held in a marquee erected on the rugby pitch where the 1st XV had completed its clean sweep of the English public schools in the south and south-west. Although the Old Man had not yet received his invitation to join the Headmasters' Conference, he was confident the school's starry reputation on the rugby field predetermined the issue.

The seventy boys of the Junior House sat in the front rows with their parents and listened to the headmaster's report to the governors as rain hammered on the canvas above and a wind off the downs shook the marquee.

Behind them sat the senior school and their parents.

In the hands of the Old Man, Founder's Day had become a misnomer. The founder was never mentioned, or his ideas for creating the best orphanage in Britain. The real history wasn't recalled, only the fantasy of creating another academy for the replication of the rich.

Fantasy of a different kind was personified in the first appearance of Mrs White, the new vicar's wife. After her entrance into the marquee no male in the audience paid attention to anything else. She burned bright in the grey-toned, heavy air. Boys called up to receive prizes from the chairman of the board of trustees stumbled because they weren't looking where they were going, their eyes latched onto Mrs White's beauty.

When her husband took the prayers, droning away with her standing beside him in her glory, masculine electricity full of resentful envy flashed through the humid air. How had such a nondescript man got his hands on such a woman?

Daniel looked at her hard. Behind her black-eyed dazzle sat all the matrons and assistant matrons in their best. The contrast was cruel. It was as if some artist had designed this vision for him to look at with a question in mind.

It had been a very good year, the Old Man reported, a year of progress and achievement on all fronts. Proof of academic excellence is going hand in hand with evidence that the dedicated school health regime is being successful. Reynolds got into Oxford . . . the shooting eight won a third in the .22 at Bisley . . . the Young Farmers Club a first for Large White gilts at Andover . . . as for the rugby team . . . well . . . The Old Man's stiffness of manner relaxed, his voice became warm, and his eyes glowed.

Stanislav, the burly, balding Polish second-hand car dealer stepfather of Bryant was sitting at the end of the front row. After several pints of beer at the Cock and Dolphin beside the school gates and neglecting to urinate before entering the marquee, he was uncomfortable. Imagining sex with Mrs White helped him forget the pressure on his bladder but there was a long way to go. Out of a sense of responsibility he tried to listen to the headmaster drooling over his rugby team. Stanislav had heard it all before in eastern Silesia, only there it wasn't sport that was worshipped but intellect. Which was why every boy who'd won a prize at his school had been shot by the Russians in their purge of Polish home-grown talent – including his brother. Stanislav had been spared because he was reckoned to be slow and stupid. Now, as he let the Old Man's paean of praise wash over him, he couldn't help but wonder if the Poles now suffering under Soviet domination would be better off idolizing a ball game above the workings of the brain.

Mrs White crossed her legs and the great tent filled with a sigh that could have been the wind through the guy ropes. The eyes of the Old Man's wife narrowed as she heard the sound. There was something ridiculous and gross about males yearning for that kind of thing *en masse*. The downfall of empires made a sound like that. Mrs White seemed unconscious of the impression she'd made, there was an innocence there, but the Old Man's wife noted the cut of her clothes, especially her sapphire-blue high-heeled shoes, that had not been idly chosen.

After the speeches in the marquee, Dawn, Bryant's mother, led Stanislav around the school displays of work like a performing bear, clarifying his broken English to anyone they happened to talk to. They were outlandish as a couple. She was correct, well-spoken and precise while he remained in the work place, down to earth, coarsely humoured in an invisible cage of half-adopted English manners. But they seemed indivisible to Daniel. She was a low-paid librarian from a small mining town who had lost her husband and needed a man to work on. She had taken a decision to love her lumbering bear with all his faults and vulgarities. With Stanislav there was scope for things to happen. There was the chance of a future. And the Pole, while being physical and showy as a gladiator, deferred to Dawn. When he barged his way into the crowd around Mrs White in the tea-tent murmuring *very good crumpet* and was frozen out, he allowed himself to be led off by Dawn without a single word of resistance.

Dawn and Stanislav were happy with each other. Amongst the other parents – farmers and country solicitors and gravel-pit owners – they stuck out as creations of a new time, the fusing together of fragments of a shattered world.

Daniel envied his friend.

In spite of present hatred for his stepfather, Bryant would let the Pole enter his heart, eventually. Even if he was ignored for a few more years to give his mother's new love room to breathe, there would be something to work on as a family.

Daniel's mother should meet a man like Stanislav, a man with all his imperfections on his head, perhaps many imperfections, and, in spite of herself, in spite of all her memories, do what Dawn had done, but do it with Mrs White's style.

That afternoon in the marquee he had watched the new vicar's wife become a potent force simply by being herself. Without effort, the woman had undermined authority, upstaged the rugby team and inspired the dreams of desirous men. He had never seen anything like it before, even in the musical at half-term in London. Mrs White's beauty had power.

With her dark, shining hair swept back from her face, her deep half-smile, her linen navy-blue suit tailored to the lines of her body and her high-heeled sapphire shoes, she had conquered. At the end of the proceedings in the marquee, Daniel followed her over the wet grass to the tarmacadam forecourt, fascinated. It was his first contact with the sublime.

He was stopped in his tracks when, in a natural gesture *ful of gras,* she took off her shoes because the heels were sinking into the rain-softened earth and gave them to her husband to carry. He accepted the task without hesitation, tucking the muddied shoes under his arm, even though he was having an important conversation with the chairman of the trustees on the crying need for a music department at the school.

It was the loveliest, most stirring evidence of true feeling between male and female Daniel had ever witnessed. The new vicar would do anything for his wife, anything. She would take off her shoes and walk over the grass in the midst of the most formal occasion. He would hold her shoes to his breast while talking to the mighty.

His mother could manage all that if she wanted.

After all, she was just as beautiful.

CHAPTER THREE

There were men who had courted his mother. He had observed the process from a distance, only becoming involved when the affairs began to be serious. Sat at the top of the stairs, he had often listened to long discussions downstairs between his mother and grandmother on the subject of re-marriage. These talks erupted into shouting-matches whenever his grandfather intervened from the depths of his armchair, pressing his rabid opinions home. Daniel heard the women tell his grandfather to shut up. He heard them tell him he knew nothing about relationships. He heard his grandfather tell them that relationship was the worst ship that ever sailed.

In the past, under pressure, his mother had allowed certain suitors close enough to her sons to see how they reacted. Daniel, ever hopeful, never disapproved, but John, younger by five years and possessing intuitive sensibilities verging on the supernatural – he was his reborn father, after all – inevitably let it be known that he was worried. There was something in each man that was not quite right. These rejections were backed up by the grandmother and grandfather for their own reasons, which, though not agreed upon, were the same in both cases. Neither of them could survive a marriage of such toxic discontent if the daughter wasn't there to draw off their poisons.

So men came on futile missions with their flowers and presents. This was arranged at times his grandfather wasn't at home. One solid, good-natured man, Norman, a shipyard foreman, who'd taken dancing-lessons in order to make himself interesting to Daniel's mother, turned up unannounced one Sunday hoping to take her for a walk. He came face to face with the beast in the back room sucking on a bottle of alcohol-based cough-mixture because he'd run out of Guinness. Pouring out a measure into an egg-cup he tried to force it on Norman, who declined. The beast then challenged Norman to justify his intrusion, his lecherous pursuit of a grieving war-widow, and poured contempt on the man's existence because he came from Birkenhead. Norman was so appalled by the experience he never saw Daniel's mother again.

Another, an inspector in the Palestine Police on long leave, bribed his way into John's good opinion with a donkey-engine that had been his own as a boy. It was too advanced a toy but his suit failed because he made no attempt beyond that to get to know the children, or make the donkey-engine work. The worst part of this attempted courtship came when his mother asked Daniel if he thought the man, with his dark handsomeness, looked like his father. When the boy confessed that he had no memory of his father whatsoever, she flew into a terrible rage. Later on, having worked out how few times Daniel had seen his father beyond the age of two because the man was in the Army, she asked for forgiveness.

Another suitor, Bill, a very good dancer with a winning smile and deep pockets who turned out to be married, killed himself when his offer to get a divorce was refused by both his wife and the woman he wanted.

Daniel's mother was amazed that she couldn't cry over him, even with the farewell letter in her hand. The telegram from the War Office five years before had neutralised all future bad news. Nothing could ever be as bad. But Bill's death by his own hand silenced all romance in her.

Even with all this history, Daniel never gave up the hunt for a new husband for his mother.

The main reason he had been so acquiescent about being sent away to school was that he'd stand a better chance of finding someone for his mother to marry away from Liverpool. Its postwar wreckage and misery promised little to anyone in quest of a new life.

Somewhere in the world there was a father waiting, a man he

would like, respect and look up to. His early experiences at Lord Mendora Land College had been disappointing. But Mule, Pacey, the Old Man and all the beating masters were as unrepresentative a sample of manhood as his grandfather. What had twisted them all out of shape was a mystery but he suspected it to be something to do with war.

When Daniel got low and his search seemed hopeless, he would conjure up a memory of his mother coming down the stairs dressed to go to a dance, jewels in her hair, Californian Poppy perfume following her out of the door.

In the year 1950, on October 7th at 8.20 pm, this vision was to be of use to him. He was up for what could be a beating and a half. A character-forming beating. A beating to turn a corner. A beating to redefine limits. A beating to remake a soul. A last-stand, grandstand beating. After this beating nothing would be the same. All risks would be taken with this beating, make or break. It was a beating to sort out the problem of Rogers once and for all. He had gone too far and taken Mule with him. They stood facing each other as though on an altar, trying to decide who was the sacrifice and who was the priest.

'Nothing seems to work with you, boy,' Mule said, staring at Daniel with his bottle-blue eyes and top lip trembling beneath his stiff grey moustache. 'I've gone as far as I can to understand your ways.'

Daniel stared back at him, seeing past the redemptory vision of his mother coming down the stairs to the patched elbows of the Mule's tweed jacket. This was the only man to equal his grandfather in generating revulsion within him. It was a power he resented, coming from a wreck, as it did. The smell of the killing-bottle for butterflies was in the room, overlying the Californian Poppy perfume in the boy's mind.

In the corner was a spare artificial leg, straps dangling.

'I've got to get through to you, somehow,' Mule fumed, almost moaning. 'It's essential.'

Daniel kept silent. If he spoke out of turn now he knew it could provoke Mule to madness.

'I notice you make no attempt to apologise. That's you all over.'

Daniel heard himself ask if that was what was needed – an apology.

'You haven't worked that out for yourself, you ignorant lout?' Mule raged. 'I trusted you, Rogers. In spite of everything, I trusted you, didn't I?'

It was a rhetorical question. They both knew there was not a shred of trust between them.

'Against my better judgement, I made you a house-captain.'

'I didn't ask to be made a house-captain, sir.'

'No one asks, one is appointed!'

'You told me it was because you didn't know what else to do with me, sir.'

Mule was very close to an insane outburst now, raising his heavy false foot and stamping. The stick was ready on the desk.

'D'you want to be expelled?' he fumed. 'D'you want to make your mother ashamed?'

'No, sir.'

'Then change your ways for her sake.'

'I will, sir. Can you say what's most the matter with me, sir?'

Mule eyed him, trying to ascertain whether there was any trace of insolence in this question. 'You're far too boisterous and rowdy' he said, continuing straight afterwards so Daniel couldn't query the analysis. 'If you don't change your ways and come to terms with authority, you will never amount to anything. You will suffer when you go into the outside world. As a house-captain you represent me, you are my deputy. I have to back you up at all times.' At this point he banged his fist down beside the stick and lost his balance for a moment, which made him snort. 'I have no option, boy. I must give one of my own deputies the severest punishment I can hand out, and it sickens me to have to do it.'

Daniel felt unusually calm. Mule's fury had been ignited when he had to sort out a brawl in the boot-room while everyone was putting their shoes away after inspection. Daniel had been at the centre of it, pushing and shouting with the rest. Every morning each boy had to present all three of his pairs of shoes to Mule and show front and back. No other master would supervise this ritual with its echoes of army life just as no other master would haul a boy out of the queue for breakfast for not saluting the picture of the King. The spirit of the boys when trapped in these archaisms was light-hearted. They obeyed but mocked the performance, which annoyed Mule.

'Why couldn't you think, sir, that as your deputy I was attempting to stop the fighting?'

Mule turned crimson. His eyes bulged.

'You dare lie so flagrantly to my face?' he bellowed. 'I can't believe it! I saw you! You were laughing and enjoying yourself!'

Daniel didn't care now. It wouldn't be six, it would be twelve, eighteen . . . Mule might even kill him, crushing his skull with the spare leg. This was the room of death. A thousand crucified butterflies stared at the ceiling.

He was in the hands of a madman.

'Perhaps you should have called in the Cosh Gang, sir?'

Their eyes locked. Mule had his stick in his fist, and he was shuddering with anger. He turned his back, shoulders heaving. Daniel thought he might be having some kind of fit.

'Get out, you vile, hopeless creature,' Mule hissed over his shoulder. 'I wash my hands of you!'

Daniel didn't escape scot-free. A more humiliating punishment was devised. Mule announced after dinner that Rogers had let everyone down, most of all himself, and had been demoted to the ranks. He was no longer a house-captain. Then he took down the board with the names of all the house-captains going back to before the war.

'His name will be removed from here,' Mule declared. 'I painted it on myself and I will see it erased.'

Then he thumped off with the board under his arm.

But no replacement house-captain was ever appointed. The board was never put back up on the wall but stayed in Mule's room, Daniel's name still in place. Also, he found himself leading his house into the dining-room as usual and onto the rugby field, and he was in charge of the house cross-country squad for the annual race.

It was then that his true punishment was imposed – one as strange and fitting as the supernatural birth of his brother.

While climbing over a five-bar gate during a cross-country run he put his knee on two rusty points of barbed wire. After the race he went to Ann Wood, the assistant matron, in surgery, and explained what had happened. Pacey was there, idling in the corridor, charming her because he had nothing better to do. He mocked Daniel for his concern over two tiny punctures.

'That doesn't look very serious to me, Mephi,' he drawled. 'I thought you were meant to be a tough guy.'

Ann Wood dabbed iodine on the tiny wounds and put a plaster over them.

'The barbed-wire was very rusty, sir,' Daniel said.

Pacey smiled, giving Ann Wood a wink. 'Your blood's so caustic, Mephi, no bacteria could live in it. Off you go, you're taking up too much of matron's time. There are others in the queue.'

In the middle of the night Daniel woke up in a high fever. His leg was swollen to twice its size. Cook was the duty housemaster. He immediately drove Daniel up to the school sanatorium, run by a wiry, no-nonsense ex-Indian Army male nurse, Joey Birch, who took one look at the leg and said there was no time to get Daniel to hospital. He would have to operate immediately.

Cook was uncertain, wondering whether he should consult a doctor first.

'It's poisoned and nearly into his groin. I've had to do this kind of thing before, so trust me, boy,' Joey said, switching his attention to Daniel only. 'I'm not allowed to give you anaesthetic but I'm sure you'll be brave.'

Cook stood beside Daniel, upset and watchful. When Joey took the scalpel out of the steamer, he took Daniel's hand. 'Mr Birch is very experienced,' he assured him. 'I'm sure he knows what he's doing.'

'I'm going in now, boy, if you want to look away,' Joey said.

Cook lowered his eyes.

Daniel gazed at the bloated leg. The skin was tight as a drum and his knee had disappeared in the swelling. 'I was alright before I went to bed,' he said, staring at the bright little knife in Joey's hand. 'It happened so quickly, sir.'

'That's dirt for you,' Joey muttered as he stuck the scalpel deep into the knee, slicing through from one puncture to the other. As the blood spurted, Cook groaned and let go of Daniel's hand, moving away. Joey gripped the ankle with one hand and the upper thigh with the other and drew both hands together with all his strength, veins standing out on his forehead. A fountain of yellow pus leapt from the wound followed by a lump. Joey picked it up in his rubber gloves and showed it to Daniel.

'That's the core of the germs, boy. You can see the little buggers moving,' he said, tossing the lump into a silver tray and doing another long squeeze of the leg. 'You should be alright now. Lucky you brought him up here so quickly, sir. He might have ended up with one leg like someone else we know'

White to the gills, Cook managed to frown disapprovingly. Joey's mention of Mule was done with obvious disparagement.

Daniel asked for a bowl to be sick in. This disturbed Cook as much as the operation.

'You're sure there's nothing else to be done?' he asked worriedly. 'The boy looks very rocky to me.'

'Don't worry, sir. It's all over. I'll give him something to make him sleep,' Joey said, removing the bowl. 'I've got it under control. I'll have to have a doctor in to see him tomorrow to check everything is alright.'

When Cook had gone, Joey came to the bedside with a bottle of whisky and two glasses.

'There's no one else in the san. I thought it only right you should have your anaesthetic, even though it's a bit late,' he said, sitting on the end of the bed. 'In the olden days this is all a soldier would get if he was having his leg off.'

Daniel took the glass. There was a quarter inch of golden liquid in the bottom. The smell was very strong.

'I'm not sure I can drink it, sir.'

'You should. It will help you sleep.'

Daniel drank the whisky down, feeling the fire in his gullet and stomach. His eyes watered.

'Is your family rich?' Joey asked, sipping from his glass.

'No, sir.'

'Then the school's lucky. You say you told the matron about the rusty barbed-wire and she just put iodine on it and a plaster?'

'Yes, sir.'

Joey pulled a face. 'I'd have been court-martialled for that,' he said sombrely. 'What did she think she was doing? Doesn't she know about dirt in a fresh wound? And there's nothing worse than rust.'

'It didn't look much, sir – just two little holes.'

Joey shrugged and shook his head. 'These young matrons!' he sighed. 'They know nothing. They only pick them for leg-over. Letting amateurs loose on young boys is cruel, but don't tell anyone I said so.'

Two days later Mule came to the sanatorium. Daniel sat up in bed, a pile of books beside him, his heart turning to ice as he heard the thump of the leg on the floor.

It was obvious Mule disliked Joey. Both men reverted to military relationship, officer and man. Mule told Joey to leave so he could talk to Daniel in private. Before he went, Joey gave Daniel a look and put a finger to his lips. This not only referred to Joey's loose talk during the night but also what the doctor

49

had said when he came next morning: how astonished he was that a trained matron, if she was, could be so neglectful.

'Let's see what you're reading, Rogers?' Mule said with a gruff attempt at bedside geniality, picking up the pile of books and scanning the titles.

'Mr Birch gave them to me, sir.'

'I wonder what kind of taste he has.'

Mule paused and put the books down. He was finding it difficult to getting round to saying what he needed to say.

'Have you any ideas about what you'll do when you grow up?' he asked, looking out of the window at the school dairy herd of Friesians spread out over a field.

'Write books, sir.'

'Any other options? You'll need talent, which you may not have, and authorship is a hard life.'

His eyes on the cows outside the window, Daniel replied: 'As second choice, I've thought about being a vet, sir.'

Mule bared his teeth in a soundless laugh. 'You'd like to look after animals, would you?' he muttered. 'Have you written to your mother about your accident?'

'No, sir.'

'What will you tell her?'

'I haven't thought about it, sir.'

'I see no point in upsetting her, do you? After all, you're better now. Mr Birch says that apart from your leg, which is mending rapidly, you're very healthy. No permanent damage was done.'

'I never tell my mother what she can't do anything about, sir,' Daniel said, 'it would only make things worse for her.'

Mule expelled his breath in a rush and turned for the door, swivelling expertly on his good leg. 'Good man,' he said with a fierce, bristling nod. 'Good man. I like that attitude. It shows there might be something worthwhile in you after all.'

When Mule had driven off, Joey came to dress Daniel's wound and give him an injection. There was whisky on his breath and his eyes glittered angrily. 'He wouldn't have come if the headmaster hadn't sent him,' he said bitterly. 'What such a man is doing as a housemaster, I don't know. Trouble is, Rogers, no one here knows what they're up to.'

He expertly rolled Daniel over so he could put the needle in his buttock and paused, letting out a whistle, the hypodermic poised. 'Wow, they've certainly marked you up here, boy,' he marvelled. 'Your backside looks like a tram junction. Who gave you these?'

'Oh, a few of them, sir.'

'I don't know how they get away with it.'

'They'll go in time.'

Joey laughed and stuck the needle in, 'You keep hold of that, boy. The buggers will all go in time. How many more years have you got here?'

'Six, sir, if I don't get expelled.'

'That's a long time – as long as the Second World War. D'you know what this place is? A refuge for old soldiers and second-raters is what this place is – but don't tell anyone I said so.'

Every Sunday afternoon after a walk around the school estate, all the boys of Junior House sat down together in the common-room to write a letter home. This routine task was supervised by a house master on the look-out for boys putting blank sheets of paper in the envelopes provided. There was something about receiving blank sheets of paper that cut parents to the quick.

Daniel was out of the sanatorium by Saturday, but off-games. He was also excused the walk round the estate. While everyone was out on the walk he sat in the common-room writing his letter home. By the time the rest of the house came back and joined him, his epistle to his mother was eleven pages long, spread out in front of him, and he was still writing.

Pacey was on letter-writing duty that Sunday. He stood behind Daniel, looking over his shoulder.

'My, my Mephi, you've got a lot to say this week,' he said quietly. 'Do you customarily compose such an epic?'

'My mother likes to hear my news, sir. She writes me a long letter every week and sends a parcel.'

'That's a credit to her, Mephi. I suppose you're the apple of her eye.'

Shutting out the sneer, Daniel bent lower over the paper, the pen only six inches away from the end of his nose.

'What are you telling her now, Mephi?'

'Would you like to see, sir?'

'What would a malefactor like you find to say to his mother?'

Daniel straightened up and held the sheet of paper above his head, offering it to Pacey who gave him a squeeze on the back of his neck

'Good Lord, I don't want to read your scrawl, boy,' he scoffed. 'It's just that I've never seen such industry from you, except in causing trouble.'

When the letters were closed, the envelopes stuck down, addressed and stamped, Pacey collected them so they could be taken to Mule for double-checking. The envelopes issued were of the cheapest sort and if a boy had put in a blank sheet of paper Mule could tell by holding the envelope up to the light. Daniel had written fifteen pages, on both sides. When folded they hardly fitted in the envelope. When he stuck it down, the bulk of the folded sheets inside made the flap start to come away. To hold it in place, he used a piece of sticky label.

On the following Friday, Daniel's parcel arrived, perfectly packed with a cake, honey, and chocolate, plus his mother's letter, written as ever in her clear, beautiful hand, and a pack of large, strong envelopes for his future use should he want to spread himself again. She thanked him for his letter, the longest she'd ever received in her life from anyone, including his father who'd written her hundreds. It had made her very happy to receive proof that he was settling down at school. She'd read it aloud to his brother who was always asking after him. At the end John had said it sounded such a good place where Dan was, he must go to school there himself one day. At the end of her letter she mentioned that the Post Office had re-enveloped his epic because the original had fallen to bits, and the address was not in his writing.

Daniel's epic was all about the countryside – the downs, the woods, the school farm, the animals, wild and domestic. He mentioned no human being in the closely-written pages, even to the point of excluding himself. His descriptions were of beasts and buildings, woods and trackways, hills and clearings, crops and gardens. These were all painstakingly objective and simple. He used colour and smell and texture, but extracted no meaning. Even the story of the recent RAF jet-plane crash on land adjoining the school estate made no mention of the pilot who had miraculously survived. However, even though his writing was purged of comment or romance, it seemed to his mother that the land he was living on was sustaining him in the way it had done when, straight after the war, to be independent of her parents, she took a job as a cook in a Cheshire country house, leaving broken, bombed-out Liverpool behind.

As a child, he had always played with toy farm animals. He had cows and sheep and pigs, chickens, turkeys and ducks, milkmaids, the farmer himself, standing with his stick, and his dog. There were tractors and trailers, ploughs and combine harvesters, and the farm itself, made of papier maché. When she read his long letter this memory of him at home playing on the carpet with his farm rose up to perfectly accommodate what she was being told. Without that memory to help her, she might have found the length and detail of the letter strange and oppressive because most weeks all she received was a single page to the effect that her son was alright and had played games of rugby and sung at village weddings.

Daniel's mother was no fool. She lived with her fingers crossed for her eldest son, unwilling to imagine his life at boarding school because it might be putting too much distance between them. She possessed enough good sense to interpret his letter as saying that the countryside was a buffer against any un-pleasantness in his daily life, and his love of the land was helping to keep him on an even keel. What she didn't know was how he contributed to that same unpleasantness by playing an active role in it.

CHAPTER FOUR

Cook was a strange man to watch – studied and slow in his movements, like a probing insect carefully feeling its way forward, or, just as often, backwards. When he was coaching cricket, every batting stroke he demonstrated was in slow-motion. Excessive caution marked everything he did, except the teaching of history.

Then the caution faded. He relaxed. He smiled a lot. The jokes came thick and fast. He was in safer territory. The dangerous lunacy of life was printed out in comprehensible form, fastened firmly in an epoch. Making time live again under his firm control was Cook's forte. His history teaching was many times more vital than his own existence, the validity of which he seriously doubted. History was his means of thriving in a world he found uncomfortable to live in.

Either in response to Cook's interest in him, or by natural inclination, or following his decision to find a father for himself and a husband for his mother, Daniel turned to history with such an appetite he became the best pupil in the subject in his class. He could communicate with Cook on a level above the heads of the other boys. They had conversations in class that made the others feel left out.

Cook gave Daniel books in advance of the syllabus, took him to ruins and museums. This preferential treatment was never explained or alluded to in any way. It was just there – like history itself, a part of its subjective interpretation, perhaps.

Three years in the Royal Navy at the end of the war provided Cook with a bond connecting him to all the other ex-service masters. He had that restraint, that sense of psychic imprisonment. But give him the past to roam in and he became a free man, full of radical opinions, daring to challenge establishments long gone, but still powerful in their influence on the living age.

He had gained a first class honours at Cambridge and been taught by men he considered great. One in particular was an austere, intellectual Benedictine monk driven out of his monastery for disobedience, but allowed to teach at the highest level. This rebel Cook venerated.

Cook's place of birth was a few miles to the east of Chesterfield – a farmhouse built in the shadow of an isolated high arch of ragged masonry, all that remained of a Praemonstratensian abbey. He showed Daniel a photograph. There was no need for an explanation of how it had affected him. This is what I am, he was saying – or all that remains of me in a time of destruction.

In every other aspect of his employment at Lord Mendora Land College Cook conformed, carefully establishing his base. It was his plan never to move. From here he would endure the present, master the past, and feel his way into the future.

His favouritism towards Daniel was noted. Such was the power of the Cosh Gang's prosecutor, no boy dared mention it – besides, it was not in the canon of boys's law to forbid the acceptance of kindness.

The other masters observed the phenomenon with incredulity. How could someone as difficult and violent as Rogers become anyone's pet? Pacey was a friend of Cook and he ribbed the history master for his odd fancy. Cook's answer was always the same – he wasn't in education to destroy what talent there was to find.

Although Cook's behaviour annoyed Mule, the senior housemaster had the sense to realise that here was a means of control. When expulsion of Rogers was recommended by Mule, the headmaster and trustees kept referring the case back for further efforts to be made. They obviously knew something Mule didn't, or the boy had enough sporting promise to carry him through all present trials to future glory. A belief or a hope that something could be made of the boy was alive somewhere in the system, but it somehow wasn't getting through to Mule.

Mule watched the relationship between Cook and Rogers closely making use of it when opportunity arose. As crises occurred – which they did frequently as the boy's energy-level rose even higher, backed by the young history master's quiet support – it was Cook who was called in to deal with it discreetly, on the side.

It would have helped Mule to entertain the thought that Cook was the only master in the school able to analyse what had happened to the soul of the Junior House. He had the intellectual power to place its corruption in an historical perspective. The greater world in its postwar torment was at Cook's elbow, as well as sympathy for Mule himself – one whose body and spirit had been deformed by that other war, the war to end all wars.

The only person the history master shared those insights with was Rogers, because he saw history alive in the boy.

His orphancy was history.

His violence was history.

His indignation at being displaced, beaten and persecuted was history.

Cook passed on his wisdom to his disciple in code, in humour, in secret. In return, Daniel opened up about his family, sketching in its class, its dockland origins, and the events that had rocked it over two world wars, much of it information gleaned from his researches using the cardboard-box full of family documents and letters during the holidays. He was aware that Cook was encouraging him to reveal this material for an historical purpose as well as to help him understand a boy in constant trouble.

Armed with his notes, Cook visited Goodboy Bluit to request sight of the file on Rogers so he could verify the family history and see if there was a pattern. The subject he wished to examine for his Ph.D. (should he ever get round to doing it) was the link between military conscription and the creation of the extreme radical mind.

'His file is out with the school solicitors at the moment,' Goodboy said gravely. 'You'll have to wait.'

'Is Rogers in that kind of trouble?' Cook asked, concerned.

'No, but we might be,' Goodboy replied. 'A local doctor has written to the Ministry of Education accusing us of gross medical neglect.'

Cook was silent for a while, looking out of the widow into the school transport yard where fifth-form army cadets were being given arms drill by Mr Hardwick, the dapper storeman who had served in the Durham Light Infantry. 'Litigation wouldn't help Rogers at all,' he said thoughtfully as the boys crashed the butts of their rifles onto the tarmac. 'We can make something of him, in time.'

'How right you are,' Goodboy said. 'I've told the headmaster the family would never sue, they wouldn't know how to start, but he's not convinced. However, you could say that young Rogers is now amongst the untouchables, but don't let him know.'

Cook smiled at the idea of anyone being untouchable at Lord Mendora Land College. Having progressed from the Royal Navy to his Cambridge college and from thence to Junior House he knew the many intricate ways a relentlessly inward-looking organisation with a purpose in mind can bring pressure on an individual and not leave any external bruises.

If after the Peterloo Massacre of 1820, guillotines had been erected in every major British city to work through the entire ruling-class and gentry, plus the worst specimens of the new industrial baronage, at the relatively low cost of some thirty thousand lives our country's political future would been much healthier. Discuss.

It was the monthly meeting of the sixth-form current affairs group. This radical proposition had arrived from an anonymous source, slipped under Maffer's door (legend had it the teacher had been at the siege of Mafeking, 1901 as Baden-Powell's water-boy), while the old master was developing wildlife films in the cellar darkroom.

'Do we want to talk about this?' Maffer asked, waving the note in the air after he'd read it aloud. 'The author once again hasn't put his name to it, but we can guess who it is, eh, Mr Gammon?'

Ronald S. Gammon smiled darkly. The sixth-form current affairs group was the only opportunity that ever arose for him to air his extreme socialist ideas without jeopardising his job. His rooms in the Cairns House where he was senior housemaster were lined with Gollancz Left Book Club volumes in their yellow jackets. What he was doing teaching Geography and Economics in a private school he didn't know. In bad moments he assumed it was where depression and an overpowering sense of futility had taken him. At the beginning of each week he felt suicidal. Although recognised by everyone as a brilliant up-to-date teacher, as a human being he was detested. The boys called him Les, from *Les Miserables*.

Cook had been invited up from the Junior House to participate in this month's meeting. Maffer skilfully used his little welcome speech to touch on Cook's deep knowledge of monasticism, hoping to steer the boys' attention away from Gammon's provocation.

'Am I right in thinking our nearest abbey to be Waverley?' Maffer asked Cook deferentially, slipping Gammon's note down the side of his armchair. 'Which order of monks was that?'

Gammon sighed heavily and sank back in the corner of Maffer's shabby hide sofa. He had a file for this current affairs group. Ninety of his radical political propositions anonymously put forward and never discussed were recorded there. It said a great deal for Maffer's loyalty to his superior that he had never notified the Old Man that there was a frustrated revolutionary on the staff.

'It was the first Cistercian house in England,' Cook said, 'if the boys were interested we could take the school lorry to the ruin and have a look around'.

Maffer raised his eyebrows and pulled at the long lobe of his projecting right ear. 'A history trip for current affairs?' he queried. 'That's going a bit far. Questions might be asked about that.'

'Do we believe the republican issue to be alive in Britain today? I'm not sure, myself,' Cook said with a show of solemn innocence. 'But we should bear in mind that we do have a Labour party with a manifesto that hints at opposition to the monarchy and the established Church.'

Maffer shook his head. 'The headmaster believes we should only discuss what's in the newspaper,' he said flatly, 'without showing any party or class prejudice.'

Gammon got his feet, muttering that he'd forgotten an appointment and had to go. Once his subversive item was read out each month and rejected as unsuitable – which he depended upon – Gammon always found a reason to leave, his honour as a socialist satisfied. He had brought a critical idea into the open. He had made the boys aware of alternative solutions. When they went out into the world as middle-class middle-of-the-road middlemen schooled for Conservatism they would carry infective spores of socialist doctrine with them.

Once Gammon had withdrawn, Maffer made no further mention of newspapers and encouraged Cook to give what was virtually a talk to the sixth-formers. While the history master did so, Maffer sat with his eyes closed, nodding agreement occasionally, going over in his mind the negatives he had to enlarge in the cellar darkroom.

Cook's lucid, easy-paced talk covered St. Benedict's Rule and the Cistercian variations of it. Everything was very clear in his mind on this subject because he had taken Daniel to Waverley in his car the previous weekend and walked through the whole of the ruined abbey with all its outbuildings, reconstructing the monastery in the boy's imagination. The speed with which Daniel had been able to mentally repair the overgrown wreckage and make the abbey work again had been remarkable.

Cistercians always built their monasteries in a remote valley close to a river. Sat on the banks of the River Wey where the monks had cut into the bank to make a channel for a water-supply into their kitchen, infirmary and lavatorium, Daniel was moved by the most powerful surge of confidence he'd felt since arriving at the school. Painful everyday questions that tormented his mind were eased by the settled stones of history – questions like:

Will I ever pass my probation?

Am I going to survive Junior House as a whole person?

Is this really supposed to be my education?

What do they want to turn me into?

Wouldn't I be better off living at home, even at the mercy of my grandfather and going to a grammar school?

In Cook he had a grown man whom he could respect. By Daniel's calculation the history master was nine years younger than his mother, which was nothing when her beauty was taken into consideration. Cook would be lucky to get such a prize.

Although her education had stopped at fourteen, his mother was no ignoramus. Outside her descents into burning grief, she possessed a natural refinement, a liveliness and a quick wit. Catch her on a good day and she was wonderful company.

Maybe she hadn't been to Cambridge, but she wasn't a nobody.

She could add up a column of figures faster than anyone. Her handwriting was super. As a dressmaker there was no one to touch her. She could kick higher up the wall than people a foot taller. He could see her in his mind's eye polishing several cups she'd won with Sonny for the slow foxtrot, the tango and the rhumba.

Here was a problem. The more Daniel thought about it, he realised that dancing was her love, a love that sustained her because inside the dance was the man once fitted to her body in the most perfect way, her beloved dancing-partner, the husband torn from her side by war. No man who couldn't dance would ever be of romantic interest to her.

Slow-moving Mr Cook, (Daniel didn't have to ask whether he could dance or not, the answer being obvious), would have to learn that art before they met.

Boys running away was a constant problem in the Junior House. Homesick *newts* shattered by initiatory cruelties fled into the countryside with no money, no preparation, and had to knock on the doors of strangers late at night asking to be taken in. Telephone calls would be made to the school. A master would be detailed to drive through the darkness to pick up the culprit. On his return, the boy would be flogged and put to bed. Even so, there were newts who ran away many times, always with the same result. The record-holder was Spew Robinson who made it to Peterborough seven times on platform tickets and was brought all the way back on each occasion by his grim-faced parent.

The head of the Cosh Gang himself, Judge Bryant, had run away three times in his first month, so when Mule broke the convention of pretending the vigilante group didn't exist and consulted him on how to reduce the very high number of new boys fleeing Lord Mendora Land College in the autumn term of 1950, three times the norm, he expected sound advice based on experience.

'Can you remember what was in your mind when you ran away, Bryant?' Mule asked.

'It's a matter of being very, very upset, sir – so upset you don't care what happens . . . ' the judge replied uncertainly.

'What was on your mind?'

'You don't think, sir. You just want to get away.'

This silenced Mule for a while.

'Are you saying that you didn't run away to get home?' he said eventually. 'You ran away so you wouldn't be here?'

'Yes, sir. One hates the place so much.'

'So did you only stop running away when you felt you didn't hate being here so much?'

'I didn't say that, sir.'

It was on the tip of Mule's tongue to ask why three times the number of new boys had run away this term, but he desisted. There had been several comments from visitors about the tense atmosphere. The term *neurasthenia* had been used by a parent removing a boy whose health had broken under the strain. Mule looked up *neurasthenia:* functional nervous weakness . . . includes paranoia . . . sleepwalking . . .

There had been a lot of sleepwalking after lights-out, but how could one tell if it was neurasthenia or simply boys wandering about misbehaving?

'Any help would be appreciated,' Mule said to Bryant, observing how the boy's right leg was vibrating wildly. 'You've been very successful at reducing petty theft.'

Bryant suffered from black moments. When a mood descended on him and he felt his soul swing downwards he was compelled to say whatever had to be said. On this day, no more than an hour before being summoned to Mule's room, three of the most disliked newts, ridiculous and puny in their submissiveness, had been put in their rugby kit, taken down to the enormous dung silo behind the cattle sheds and thrown in. Bryant had watched them crawl out, their faces masked in reeking slime. They had looked like exhumed corpses.

As one of them puked, Bryant had heard himself laughing. It had been a shock to him.

There, trapped in front of Mule, he felt a sudden friction. Two parts of himself were rasping against each other. All his living sensations tilted strangely and he became short of breath.

'Junior House should be knocked down!' he shouted in a great gasp, clutching his uncontrollable knee, reddening to the tips of his protruding ears.

Mule reared up and glared. 'That kind of talk isn't at all helpful,' he snapped. 'I didn't ask you here to listen to rubbish like that. Try to be of some use, boy!'

But Bryant was not to be denied. His tongue swelled in his head like a great beast coming out of a cave. 'Why should we have to put up with this kind of fucking awful life?' he shrieked. 'Kids who go to ordinary schools don't have to. Twenty-fours a day we have it! It's not fair.'

Mule got up, his cane-arm swinging ominously. 'Don't you use that gutter language in front of me, boy!' he said. 'I won't have it.'

Bryant was too far gone to be stopped. If Mule had threatened his life it would have made no difference. He took several deep breaths.

'If we have to come and be tortured, let it be when we're a couple of years older and we can take it,' he snarled, nostrils flared. 'We're only here because no one wants us! We're only here because our parents can't be bothered.'

'That's enough nonsense. Calm down . . . ' Mule said, holding down his anger because he could see the dangerous mental state the boy was in. 'You're very privileged to be here. I wish I'd had the same chances as you've been given.'

Bryant laughed, which set off more memories of the dung-heap in his head. 'And you're only here, because no one wants you!' he moaned aloud. 'Why don't you get out of this dump and make something of yourself? You don't teach us anything useful. What are you *for*?'

Mule's backhand blow sent the judge flying. Even then the boy refused to shut up, spitting out his execrations from the floor: 'You're not fit to look after boys! You're not fit to look after your fucking self! You should be in prison!'

The furious Mule dragged Bryant into the corridor by the scruff and left him there. Words continued to tumble from the boy's lips, as on he raged. 'See what happens when you hit me? Nothing! Nothing at all!'

When he closed the door on the noise, Mule was trembling so much he had to sit down. He could hear the imprecations still pouring out in the corridor.

Bryant was obviously in need of a psychiatrist. He would have to talk to the headmaster about it.

Mule looked at the clock on the wall. It was time for dinner. There were announcements to make. There were things to see to. He brushed his hair, changed his jacket and tie and cleaned his glasses. Five minutes later Mule was spruced up and ready to face anything. He'd been through worse times.

When he opened the door Bryant was still out in the corridor, curled up in a foetal ball, muttering incoherently.

'Get up,' Mule hissed, nudging him with his good foot, 'we can't have an important fellow like you down there in such an undignified position. What happens if someone sees you?'

The foetal ball tightened. 'Kill me if you want,' the boy groaned. 'I don't give a fuck one way or the other.'

'No more of this, please, Bryant' the Mule said with quiet anxiety. 'You must control yourself. I have to rely on you, remember.'

'The only help I'd give you is into the grave,' came the cold, bitter reply. 'I hate you more than anything.'

Mule stepped over him and thumped down the corridor. This could never happen in a well-run unit, he thought. I must rectify all faults, re-set my bearings. I've let things slide.

A few minutes later he was standing downstairs beneath the portrait of the King seeing that every boy saluted the monarch properly on the way to dine – not a cursory wave, not a dismissive flick of the hand, but a full-blooded quivering stiff hand to the temple, like his own virile salute as he brought up the rear of the column.

That night Bryant ran away for the fourth time. For a boy who had successfully survived the first year to run away in the second was unusual, especially one who had gained a position of authority.

He took all the money from the Cosh Gang fine box, walked to the next village so he wouldn't be recognised as being from the school, caught the bus to the nearby town and bought a rail ticket home. By the time he got to King's Cross the last train for Nottingham had left so he had to spend the night in the waiting-room, which is where the police found him, curled up in another foetal ball. When questioned, hoping to be sent north, he said he'd run away from home after an argument with his stepfather and was desperate to get back to apologise. By the time the police spoke to his mother on the telephone she had already been apprised of the fact that her son had run away from school yet again, which put her in a rage. The Old Man was contacted. Goodboy Bluit was sent to collect the runaway from St. Pancras police station and bring him back.

The conversation between Goodboy and Bryant on the train formed the basis of the boy's first attempt to write a horror story of his own in which a carriage full of passengers who detest each other never reaches its destination but goes on and on until they resort to cannibalism. 'Not an honest word passed between us,' he told C dorm that night after lights-out. 'Goodboy just kept simpering, like he does. He kept saying everything would be alright. He told me about famous old boys I've never heard of running the empire, and how I should want to be like them. What empire d'you mean, sir? I asked him. Satan's?'

While Goodboy was comforting Bryant on the journey he had had his own thoughts. In his long memory were lodged three attempted suicides from before the war when the school was an orphanage. He saw the confused faces of the children again. In his files were their photographs and records. Now and again he looked at them. He had no means of understanding their despair then. He had no means of understanding this despair now. All he could offer was a crinkle of the eye and a sad kind of smile.

The fact that Bryant wasn't beaten for running away was noted, and his power increased accordingly.

This appeared to be the end of the matter until one of the newts thrown into the muck-pile was taken violently ill in the night and had to be rushed to hospital. But no connection was made with Bryant and his guilt-ridden flight because at no time, even at his weakest moment, did the desperately sick new boy break the code and *split*. When tests identified bacteria only found in the faeces of cattle, the physician assumed it was a malfunction at the school dairy that must be responsible and the bacteria had got into the milk. As a result, the entire automatic milking and pasteurisation process had to be overhauled.

When the newt returned to the school, cured of a serious kidney infection, he was a different person – robust, cheery, hale and outgoing. He put his heart and soul into doing well at school, and being popular. Games he hadn't been able to play now came easily to him. His academic ability shot up. He made lots of friends. Most of all, he managed to please his fee-paying father, a trade diplomat based in Egypt in receipt of an education allowance, by extolling the advantages of life at the school. The father often told friends that sending his son to Lord Mendora Land College had saved the boy from being a totally wet, dependent personality.

Interviewed by a *Daily Telegraph* business columnist in later years, this same character proudly told the story of how he had been thrown into the dung-heap. 'It did me no harm to be made to realise I was contemptible, the lowest of the low,' he told the astonished journalist. 'It was my starting-point for the way upward, and look at me now. I'm a multi-millionaire for God's sake.'

When the editor saw the copy he struck out all reference to the incident because, in his words, he had serious doubts that any child could be treated that way and end up a sane, success-ful human being with normal responses. *This tycoon will need watching,* he scrawled in the margin of the story. *Let's hope he never goes into politics.*

In order to keep the boys actively burning off surplus energy, the school offered spare-time activities. There was a choice of what to do but no choice whether to have a spare-time activity or not. These took place on Saturday mornings after breakfast and continued until lunch. After lunch games took over.

Art with Mr Went, Young Farmers Club with the farm manager, Mr Joyce, Photography with Maffer, Life-Saving with Mr Grosmont, Scouts with Mr Dreed, Bee-keeping (spring and summer terms only) with Miss Broughton, and, recently, a new option, Music with Mrs White were all on offer.

There was only one piano in the school and that was in the gymnasium under the shadow of the ropes of Nuremburg. On the morning of Mrs White's first spare-time activity two-thirds of the school turned up, deserting their previous choices.

The Old Man was away in London for the weekend. His deputy was in the nearby town shopping with his wife. Aware that drawing this crowd was not to her advantage in the long run, Mrs White wondered whether to proceed or not.

The boys were quiet and biddable. They sat cross-legged on the parquet floor and waited. Mrs White was not unused to male attention and prided herself on being able to deal with it no matter what form it took. She decided she had to carry on as planned and sort out the numbers before next weekend.

Her lesson was on English song. The boys were asked to listen to several examples, which they did in complete silence, their eyes fixed on Mrs White.

After she had taken the last record off the gramophone she asked the boys what was the main characteristic of English song. Taff Jones, a lower sixth former who fancied himself, spoke up and said English song had no passion.

Mrs White agreed that English song had no passion. To further make her point she put on a record of Neapolitan song and asked if this was passion.

Jones spoke up again. 'Is there any difference between passion and emotional melodrama like that stuff?' he asked boldly, getting up on his haunches, eyes glittering. 'Can real love be expressed in any other way than physically? Even words are inadequate, compared to the real thing, wouldn't you say?'

Mrs White raised an eyebrow and slid a record back in its sleeve. She was unsure of what to say. Jones went back off his haunches and sat cross-legged, hugging his knees with satisfaction. He had accrued enormous kudos by this display of *audace*. It was as if an apprentice centaur had dared to interrogate Aphrodite herself.

Although the senior boys were marvelling at the bravado of Jones – amongst the younger boys there was now an indignant, sullen restlessness. They didn't like Jones putting Mrs White on the spot. She was above all that smart stuff, radiant in the lingering shadows of their much-missed mothers.

'What is love?' Mrs White said finally, looking straight into Jones' haughty eye. 'Who can say?'

'I'm sure you could,' he replied with a crude, neighing laugh.

Mrs White sighed bitterly and pointed to the door. 'Out!' she commanded. 'I won't have boys talking to me like that. What's the matter with you?'

Jones got to his feet, struggling to keep his dignity intact. He smiled, but it was fixed and void.

'I'm sorry if I upset you, madam,' he said hoarsely, 'it was the last thing I would ever want to do.'

As he wended deflatedly through the cross-legged boys, all kudos in tatters, he wondered what had come over him.

(Later, he admitted to being *smitten*, and a lesson being learnt. He promised himself that in future he would watch his step with women, especially if they bowled him over.)

Once Jones was out of the gymnasium, Mrs White smoothly moved on to Schubert's *Death and the Maiden,* (one of her favourites), then to the sonata form, (streets beyond her audience). But at the end of the session it was the questions raised about love that Daniel carried away with him. As he trotted down to the Young Farmers Club to feed his pigs he turned the power of beauty over in his mind.

He had seen Mrs White destroy an aspiring male's presumption with one blow of her sexual sword.

It was just like Judith cutting off the head of Holofernes in the Bible. One minute Nebuchadnezzar's general was lord and master, then down came her blade and the great man was gone. She'd made him nothing. It had been that quick.

These thoughts stayed with him as he mixed the meal and water in the bucket. Behind him he could hear the pigs battering their heads against the sides of the sty, squealing madly. Leaning over the wall he emptied the swill into the trough. As he watched the beasts gobble up their food he realised what good questions had emerged from the confrontation between Mrs Wright and Jones.

What is love?
What is lust?
What is beauty?
Who can say?

CHAPTER FIVE

The term ended only six days before Christmas. Daniel went home on the train and was met by his mother at Lime Street Station. She climbed up on the footplate of the engine and gave the driver half-a-crown for bringing him safely back to Liverpool, as she always did. As they walked arm in arm across to the tram stop a few streets away, Daniel noticed how pale and drawn she was. A peculiar nervous aloofness in her manner made him disengage his arm but she pulled it back.

'Let's have a cup of tea somewhere, son,' she said. 'I have to talk to you.'

Brought down to its essential elements, what he pieced together from his mother's scattered remarks, was that it would be better if he spent the whole holiday somewhere else. His grandfather had given refuge to a friend who'd been thrown out by his wife. This crony, a Mr Seyton, was one of his grandfather's drinking pals from the warehousing business. He'd been sleeping on the sofa in the front room for the last three weeks. The fighting and arguing between his grandparents was so bad, making the house such an unhappy place, to add Daniel to the mix was too dangerous.

'You don't want me to come home, then?' he said indignantly.

'I've arranged for you to stay with your Aunty Barbara.'

'I'm not going there, for a start. Listen, Mum, I can deal with anyone, anyone at all,' he declared. 'At school we learn that much. I'll be fine. What does our John think about all this?'

His mother grimaced. 'They make a fuss of your brother. He's their pet,' she said. 'I wish to God they'd leave the child alone. Please, Dan, for my sake. I can't stand much more of it.'

They were in a window seat of the café. She turned to the curtain and tried to hide her tears.

'You'd rather I came home, though, wouldn't you?' he whispered, reaching for her hand.

'Not to that house!'

'Perhaps this man will go soon,' Daniel suggested. 'He can't sleep on the sofa for ever.'

His mother described the routine. Every day the two old pals came home from the docks completely drunk. Dinner would be ordered for Mr Seyton – God With Us never ate solids – and a furious row would start in the kitchen. It rolled on until the men, having secured a morsel of something, retreated to the front room to continue drinking. At some point Mr Seyton would stagger out and piss in the garden because he had a bad leg and couldn't climb the stairs.

They called John in time and again to spoil him.

They found pretexts to get Daniel's mother into the front room so Mr Seyton could look her over. Seeing ahead to the post-divorce period, he would be needing someone to look after him.

'He's disgusting,' she said, 'I'd have to be chloroformed. I said to your gran, if Seyton's wife has got the guts to throw him out why don't you do the same? Throw them both out. I'll help you. Let them go and stay in a hotel. Seyton's rich! He's got his own business. But my mum'll never go that far. She shouts and bawls and complains but she won't take any action.'

'There are people like that everywhere, Mum. You have to work round them. I have a right to come home.'

'You sound just like your grandfather!' his mother blazed at him. 'He's always talking about his bloody rights! He has a right to bring home who he likes. Oh, yes – it's his house – which it isn't, it's rented – it's his money, his sofa!'

Daniel left her alone for a while and drank his tea. His mother had no idea what life had been like for him away at school over the past fifteen months. His reports had been bland understatements, not truthful records. Nothing his grandfather could do to him would be the same class of trouble as he'd been in down south.

In fact, he was more than ready for Mr Seyton.

'Mum, I'll stay in my room. I'll go out a lot. But I want to be with you and Gran and John for Christmas.'

His mother stood up, took the bill, went over to the desk to pay. Daniel remained where he was until she stalked out into the street without him. Picking up her coat, which she'd left behind, he followed her out, keeping well behind as she walked along the pavement until their tram came along and they both had to run for it.

When they got home his grandmother gave him his dinner early to get it out of the way before the men arrived. She always heaped his plate on the first day of his coming home.

'They don't feed you properly in that place,' she said. 'Get it down you.'

He was sitting with his brother reading comics when the key was heard in the front door.

'Here they are,' John said blithely. 'You can hear the bottles.'

Daniel didn't stand up when his grandfather came into the room. He deliberately waited to be told to get out of the armchair by the fire.

His grandfather looked at him through his large distorting spectacles, narrow head thrust forward, mouth askew. 'So you're back again, are you?' he slurred. 'Get out of my chair.'

Daniel carefully put the comics in a tidy pile, laid it beside the chair, paused, fixed his grandfather with a cool look, stood up and gave a sweep of his arm. 'All yours,' he said. 'Are you quite well in yourself these days, Grandad?'

'Don't talk posh to me. You can have the chair if you want. We're going in the front room anyway, so you can stay as you are,' was the woozy reply. 'But come and meet my friend first, and watch your manners.'

John was already in the front room unwrapping a small present Mr Seyton had brought him. The guest was disheveled and very, very drunk. He's younger than I expected and has more about him – but not a lot, Daniel thought as he stretched out his hand to shake. The man looked up with swimming blue eyes and sighed out the news that he had sons of his own and was missing them very much.

He hasn't had much sleep for a long time, Daniel reckoned, and someone should tell him that you don't cry in front of kids.

'Your little brother's a fine boy,' Mr Seyton said, ruffling John's black curls. 'Take care of him. He thinks a lot of you, you know.'

'I do,' John said, looking up at Daniel. 'We share the same room upstairs. His trunk hasn't arrived yet. I expect there'll be something in it for me.'

'So you're the future prime minister, Daniel,' Mr Seyton sneered mildly, abandoning his mood of self-pity and releasing a cloud of alcoholic vapour. 'Good man.'

'And what's your line of business, sir?'

Mr Seyton was taken aback by the directness of the question. He shook his head as if to clear it and smiled to himself before he answered. 'I import quality wine glasses, actually,' he said.

'How interesting, sir.'

'I've given your grandad plenty of different styles over the years,' Mr Seyton said, gesturing towards the display cabinet. 'As you can see, we go from champagne to balloon and tulip, liqueur . . . all kinds, but we only provide the best.'

In the kitchen the row started. Mr Seyton sat on the sofa and put a cushion over his head. 'Sorry, boys, but I can't stand this,' he sighed. 'I just need some time with a friend until I'm sorted out. I'll be gone soon.'

Daniel could hear exhaustion and desperation in his grand-mother's voice as she cursed and swore. She told her husband he was cruel and inconsiderate. She told him how ashamed she was for her grandson to have to come home from school to such a circus. She told him she was sick of having visitors and not being able to use the front room. She told him how hard she worked to keep a nice home for everyone on no money. She told him she knew he earned twenty-two pounds a week and gave her four. She told him no woman should have to suffer what she'd suffered for so long. All she got in return was a low, meaningless, pitiful mumble that provoked another yelling fit, then silence, followed by the clash of crockery. After a few minutes God With Us appeared in the front room with a small pork pie on a plate.

Daniel stood by the piano, hands clasped behind his back. He watched Mr Seyton slide the cushion off his head and accept the pork pie, murmuring 'You shouldn't have,' then sink back into the sofa, blue eyes awash with fresh tears. While Daniel was wondering if either of these men had ever been in love, his mother appeared at the door in her female magnificence, great eyes ablaze, and called her sons away.

It was the first time he was alone in the house since coming home. His mother was at work serving at the grocery shop up the road. His grandmother had taken John with her to the Co-op to crack jokes with the man on the bacon-slicer. His grandfather and Mr Seyton had gone to their jobs at the port.

When he went to look in the ottoman for the box of letters and documents, it wasn't there. He rooted all over the house, looking for it, with no luck. Sitting on his bed, he recalled his grand-mother appearing at the door, catching him with the box. She'd moved it deliberately.

The next day the railway carrier delivered his trunk from school. As he was unpacking it, he put shoes under the bed and hit something. When he investigated he found the box.

The next time he was alone in the house he pulled it from under the bed and spread the contents over the eiderdown. There were twice as many documents now, and lots of old sepia photographs. Some of them were of a well-built, striking young woman with bold eyes. He recognised his grandmother. In one of the pictures she sat with her beau standing beside her. Daniel stared at the elegant, poised young man for a long time, struggling to accept that this must have been his grand-father.

Although it was a formal photograph, the confidence and clarity of character shone through the Edwardian posture and absurd studio background. These were people of account, to be reckoned with and respected.

There were birth certificates for his mother and two aunties. He put them in date order. An extra one with the family name was for a girl he didn't know, Abigail. The father and mother were his grandparents. He had an aunt he'd never heard anyone mention. He found a death certificate for her. Pinned to it was a funeral bill, a newspaper cutting and a photograph with Aby written on the back in pencil. At the age of four Aby, a beautiful faery-child with a rosebud mouth and a mass of spun curls, had pulled a pan of boiling water off the stove and been scalded. Four days later she died in hospital.

That discovery was enough for one day.

What a blow that must have been.

He pocketed the photograph, put everything in the box and slid it under the bed. Then he went for a walk in the frosty park.

When he returned an hour later his grandmother was sitting in her straight-backed chair beside the stove smoking a cigarette. There was an anxious moment, brief and intense. As his hand went into his pocket to bring out the photograph, she started on her adventures while out shopping. A crowd had gathered at the Co-op to hear her news about her grandson who was home from boarding school; how tall he'd grown, how strong he was, how successful. Everyone had admired little John at her side who was, without doubt, the best-looking child in the area, and so like his dad. People hung about after they'd done their shopping, waiting for her to come into the shop and cheer them up. It was the same at the Saturday dance, the same on the chara when she went on a trip. Everyone looked to her for the comedy and high spirits. Her Burlington Bertie act in top hat and tails and clay pipe always brought the house down. 'I tell them we have no furniture at our house, we sit on orange boxes. We have no food but bread and dripping. Give me your dog-ends so I can smoke them in my pipe. They love that. That makes them laugh because they know I'm the most particular of housewives. My house is kept like a new pin. You can eat off our floor. My washing is the whitest in the street. My cooking is plain but the best, wouldn't you say, son? I bet you don't get chuck like that at school, do you?'

Her cigarette ash was long and about to fall off. She lifted her bulk off the chair and looked out of the kitchen window.

'You must be hungry,' she said, ignoring his stillness and silence and the hand in his pocket. 'Go and sit by the fire and I'll bring you something you like.'

At first he was unsure whether his mother knew about the transfer of the box to under his bed but the more he thought about it the more he realised it must be so. She cleaned the room – which was small enough – she made the two beds, she closed the curtains, she opened them.

He wanted to know more about Aby.

There was another Aby, his grandmother's elder sister who lived in a modern bungalow in a green suburb no more than half-a-mile away, who they never saw, but was often talked about. She was married to Uncle Dick, the managing director of the warehousing company that employed his grandfather, as well as an uncle and a great uncle.

When he was able to get his mother alone he showed her the photograph and asked for more information.

'Why are you always rooting, Dan?' she said plaintively, pushing the picture away. 'I don't need to look at that. Be satisfied with what you've got. Don't keep coming to me with it.'

'Were gran and her sister closer in those days?' he insisted. 'She never bothers to come here, does she? I don't even know what Uncle Dick looks like.'

'Are you surprised? Uncle Dick is your grandad's boss. He sees enough of him at work.'

'Why does he keep him in the job?'

'Families help each other out.'

Daniel recoiled. He went off on a historical digression, referring to lessons Cook had taught him on nepotism in the Church and feudal society, a tradition of corruption which had persisted to the present day in some walks of life.

This annoyed his mother.

'Is this kind of teaching supposed to be useful?' she said tartly. 'Every family helps each other. It's natural.'

'Even when they don't like each other? Even when they get given jobs they can't possibly do properly. Grandad is drunk every day.'

His mother's mood changed. She could see he was trying to find his way and she wasn't helping.

'I'll tell you this much, son,' she said, 'then you can leave me alone. Your gran lost her mind while Aby was dying. The four days while she lingered were terrible. Your gran got so bad she had to be put in a hospital so she wouldn't harm herself. That's when your grandfather was given his job by his brother-in-law – to help him out because he was very low; and that's when he started drinking.'

'We can say this is history, then, Mum?'

'It's not the Church and feudal society.'

Daniel grinned. He liked it when his mother was sharp. 'When he comes through the door tonight in his usual state can I say he's like that because of Aby?' he asked. 'Will that help me understand?'

'Oh, you do what you have to, Dan. I'm only trying to explain,' she replied, showing signs of tiredness, looking for her cigarettes. 'As far as I'm concerned it's a mess. I'm stuck in it, so is your gran. But you're different to the rest of us now. Since you went away to school you can see these things with a different eye. For your sake, I'm glad.'

The arrival of the school report had no terror for Daniel. He looked upon it as a fiction, a text with gaps left for parental guesswork, a cover-up that in no way reflected the real pattern of his life. For instance, the first subject listed in the report was Scripture. In spite of having a lesson with Henry Long once a week since starting school, no entry had ever been made on his report. It was left blank. The reading of the entire Bible meant nothing. Scripture meant nothing. It was the same with Mr White, the new vicar, the Oxford theologian. He talked a lot in class. He was obviously intelligent and knew what he was talking about but he also left a blank, which indicated he really had nothing to say about religion. It was the same with Music. There was a space for it, but no information. His voice, his days in the choir, being able to do it all by ear, were of no significance. The report showed the divided world he lived in – there was a side that was serious, and a side that didn't matter. And this sundered universe, perilously close to the madness of war, was ruled by the Old Man's ominous obtuseness in his comment at the end. *I am not altogether happy about his progress . . .*

Daniel's disrepect for any written word emanating from the school had begun with the arrival of his first report in which Mule wrote: *He has little idea what authority means.* When his mother tackled him he asked her just what authority did mean, which she daren't answer because she loathed all authority, especially the one that had killed her husband. From that time on she seldom discussed his report with him, but each document ended up in the box under the bed.

Special letters arriving from the Old Man complaining about his behaviour and threatening to remove him from the school were put in the box under the bed as well. His mother would choose a moment to refer to these warnings in passing, expressing hope that everything would be sorted out in time. The truth about Daniel's life away from home could not all be positive, she knew that, but he came back at regular intervals, seemingly healthy, upright and self-possessed, and said nothing to make her believe he was unhappy. When she asked him directly: are you happy at that school? he always looked her straight in the eye and said he was alright.

One item in his report for the autumn term of his second year got through to her, however, and she brought it to Daniel's attention.

'Who's this Mr Mo?' she asked. 'He's got a lot to say for himself.'

Mr Mo was Marcus Oliphant, the PT master. His comment was *could be more lissom*. This dismissive remark upset his mother far more than all the threats to remove him from the school.

'You're the child of champion dancers,' she said. 'You must be lissom. It's in your blood for you to be lissom.'

Daniel thought it a very odd thing for the PT master to write such a thing on his report. It gave him an uncomfortable feeling.

Oliphant was a perfect physical specimen himself, shaped like a human dandelion seed of ginger hue. He floated and skipped everywhere, always in a state of dynamic tension, leading a blameless, diet-conscious life, devoted to the physiques, game-skills and strengths of the boys in his care. With his fellow-Scot, the Old Man, he was responsible for carefully engineering into existence the perfect rugby fifteen each year until the public school fortress was stormed into surrender. To this end, every boy was measured, weighed and tested every term and the data pored over.

The tests Oliphant designed for flexibility were arduous.

Gymnastics were a strong point with the PT master and he could tie himself in knots like a fakir. Daniel had registered flexibility 9 on the 0 to 10 scale at the last examination.

'I think it's a mistake, Mum,' he explained. 'They get a lot of things wrong. There's a boy called Rowlands who comes right after me on the alphabet list and he's flexibility nil, completely rigid. I think the master mixed us up while he was writing the reports.'

'Lissom is a strange word for a man to use. Is this PT master a jessy?'

'No, Mum, he's not a jessy.'

'You can tell me. I won't be shocked. Perhaps there are a lot of jessies at your school.'

'You'd like Mr Oliphant,' he said, hoping to head her off.

'Why would I like him?'

'Well, he's always smiling. He thinks he's hard but he's kind. I'm surprised he's not married.'

'Are a lot of them single?'

'Half of them are.'

'How many of them are jessies?'

Daniel sighed, knowing he'd failed to sidetrack her away from that subject. 'You'd never know which ones are for certain,' he said with fake nonchalance. 'With some of them there's an edge. They have a way of looking at you.'

His mother frowned. 'I don't think I want to know too much,' she said finally. 'Touch your toes for me.'

Daniel did as he was asked.

'Now touch your toes and put the palms of your hands flat on the floor.'

He was able to do this with ease.

'Stay down there like that and count up to a hundred.'

All this was accomplished. When he straightened up his face wasn't red and his head didn't spin.

'Not lissom, eh? How dare he say that about my son. I'll write to him,' she said, doing a high-kick and striking the lintel of the door with her foot. 'We're all lissom in this family.'

So ended the last interrogation Daniel ever suffered at the hands of his mother concerning the contents of his reports.

There was always a Christmas party at the house. Even the unwanted presence of Mr Seyton was not allowed to interfere with that. Uncles, aunts and cousins came, and friends. By some alchemy of celebration, Daniel's grandfather managed to behave reasonably well at parties. He was benign, happy and even generous. The pain and evil drained out of him because his whole family were unarguably on his side for once, getting drunk along with him.

Daniel stood by the piano and watched his grandfather from across the smoke-filled room. It gave him an uneasy feeling, watching a mystery at work that went so deep. An anxiety began to gnaw at him. How would he ever be able to join in a party heart and soul as an adult? He would need to drink, but the rules were strict. His mother would never forgive him if he broke them.

He had a monkey mask hidden amongst the coats in the hall. Remembering how shy these parties made him, he'd hidden it there so he could make an entrance, do something to make a contribution to the fun without making too much of a fool of himself. As the oldest grandchild his dignity meant he couldn't play with his younger cousins in the next room. He was expected to be at the centre of the party as a witness but he felt now was the time to be noticed, not just talked about.

His grandmother had finished Burlington Bertie and was smoking a dog-end in her clay-pipe. Soon she would move into her Al Johnson mode and sing *Mammy* down on her knees in front of her husband. This was the high point of every Christmas party, in fact any party his grandmother attended. Daniel slipped out into the hall and put the mask on, then listened at the door as his grandmother went through her routine.

When it was over and applauded, he heard his grandfather order silence and toast his grandmother, using her name – a name he never used at any other time of the year.

'Raise your glasses to my Maud, the finest wife a man could have,' he always said. 'Happy Christmas, sweetheart. Spend this on yourself.'

Here she always took off her topper and held it towards him so he could unfold a big white five-pound note, wave it ostentatiously in the air, then press it down into the hat. The look on her face could be called a smile but to Daniel it was the grimace of a wounded clown. He hated that expression as much as he adored his grandmother.

As he heard the formula repeated, Daniel threw open the door and rushed in wearing the mask, waving his arms and gibbering.

Everyone recoiled in mock-horror. This was followed by mild laughter, but it wasn't of the right kind. It was uncertain, as though a stranger had entered, a trespasser.

He kept the mask on, staring through the eye holes, breathing hard. The laughter subsided. One of his uncles patted him on the shoulder as if to say – we understand. To cover his embarrassment, Maud put the top hat back on her head and launched into *Put Me Amongst The Girls*, twirling her silver-topped cane.

Daniel fled into the back garden. When his mother came out to find him she said nothing for a while, smoking her cigarette with her arm around him, giving a squeeze now and then.

'Don't take them too much to heart.' she said eventually. 'They'll find a way to include you in the fun one day.'

He started to sob.

'Don't do that,' she said sternly. 'You'll have me at it.'

'I don't belong here any more, do I?'

'Don't talk rubbish,' his mother said sharply.

'He treats my gran like a performing monkey,' Daniel groaned, 'and she just takes it.' He explained that it was the money, the five-pound note, that had provoked his stunt. The family's perilous economy was no secret. It was broadcast night after night during the shouting-matches he listened to sitting at the top of the stairs. His grandfather's contribution of four pounds a week was less than a quarter of his wages, the rest went down his throat. His mother made six pounds a week serving in a shop and earned what she could with her sewing-machine. With this amount the two women ran the house. Out of this they bought all the clothes he had to have on the two-page list from school.

'He gives my gran five pounds as if he was the emperor of China! And she accepts it like someone who sings in the street!'

Daniel fumed. 'My uncles stand there and watch! You and your sisters are the same! Why don't you all have a go at him?'

'It's not your business . . . '

'It is my business!' he raged.

'Your grandad doesn't have to support us. Have you ever thought what we'd do if we couldn't live here?'

'You could get married again.'

'I'll never get married again.'

'Why not? You could, easily, if you wanted to.'

'I wouldn't be as lucky a second time. There'll never be anyone but your dad.'

'But he's dead!' he howled, covering his ears. 'How can you possibly know you'll never fall in love again?'

'If you could be bothered to remember what he looked like, you'd know why there'll never be anyone else for me.'

'Then we're doomed,' he whispered.

'What d'you mean, doomed?' she said, lighting another cigarette from the one she had burning. 'We manage don't we? We get through.'

Daniel ground his teeth and wrapped his arms around his head. 'You're condemning us to live with a dead man for ever as if he were alive,' he groaned. 'It's always going to be like this.'

'What are you complaining about? Most of the time you're not here!'

He was trapped in his untold truth about life at school but he'd been able to speak one truth aloud that she had never admitted in his presence – Sonny was dead. Moving away from her he leant against the washing-line post, aware there was nothing else he could say that would help.

Inside the house they were singing. It had been discovered that Mr Seyton could play all the old musical hall songs on the piano. Glowing in his new popularity, rousingly applauded by his recumbent friend, he rattled through the favourites with verve. When Daniel and his mother came in from the back garden, *Let him go, let him carry, let him sink or let him swim, he doesn't care for me and I don't care for him* was in full swing.

Daniel's mother made him stand next to her and join in.

Singing was the right thing for him to do. He knew all the songs for certain, verse after verse. No matter what Mr Seyton came up with, Daniel knew the words. From early childhood he'd been with his gran at dances, whist-drives, chara-trips and parties. The others around the piano often faltered, not being able to remember the words, but he had them all. For one song there was only Mr Seyton, Daniel and his gran who could sing it right through, and Daniel put in such a good descant Mr Seyton stopped playing so everyone could hear. For the last verse they let him sing it by himself, and gave him applause which all the adults knew went straight to the centre of his need.

His grandfather, so drunk he was unable to stand around the piano, instead of joining in with the singing of old favourites, he confided in a pot gift-shop Bambi on a side-table, momento of some seaside holiday long ago. He had a relationship with this piece of bric-à-brac. Sometimes he didn't like the way it looked at him and he turned its head away. At others times, he found comfort in the sweet smile of the faun. With cigarette held between yellowed fingers, beaked nose shining, bulbous blue eyes doubled in size by the lenses of his spectacles, crystal bumper of dark navy rum at his side, he chatted to the hollow ornament. Out of nowhere a memory had descended on him through the clouds of drink, a passionate, life-and-death war memory of thirty years past – being saved from drowning in the Black Sea by the havildar-major of an Indian regiment.

'He took his turban off first,' he whispered to the Disney figurine, 'and he wouldn't take a tip.'

CHAPTER SIX

Cook put a note in his Christmas card to Daniel passing on news of the sudden death of Henry Long. This was a blow. He wrote a letter of condolence to Mrs Long. It was true that he had seen very little of his hero since the enforced retirement. When he had attempted to visit him Henry was always too busy writing his book to give him any time. It seemed the old shepherd had lost interest in what had been his flock. In Daniel's letter to the widow, he asked if Henry had finished his book before he died. He would like to read it. He didn't hear back.

In his Christmas card by return to Cook, Daniel wondered if Henry's great work would ever see the light of day. A New Year card back from Cook opined that if the books written by retired clergymen were laid end to end they would encircle the earth. There was a rumour in the village, however, that Mrs Long had looked at the manuscript of Henry's book and found it to be a cricket manual that might be worth something.

Another of Daniel's Christmas cards was from Bryant. It contained an invitation to go over to Nottinghamshire for a few days at New Year and stay at the Priory. This came just at the right time. Although the party at home was accounted a success, the period straight afterwards had been grim. It started with Mr Seyton's wife arranging for several suitcases and boxes of his possessions to be dumped in the front garden with a note that he might as well set himself up permanently with his new girlfriend. The allusion was to Daniel's mother. Denying that this relationship existed would be an admission that it was at all possible. Mr Seyton had to go immediately. But God With Us refused to budge on the issue. He would continue to give his friend hospitality, as honour demanded.

On the Saturday morning Daniel came down the stairs with his case, ready to leave the house to catch the tram to Lime Street Station for his train journey to Nottingham. Mr Seyton's baggage was piled in the coal shed, the men were barricaded in the front-room in the depths of hang-overs, his mother had gone to work early to get out of the way, and his grandmother was sitting in her straight-backed chair beside the stove smoking a Woodbine.

'I'm off now, Gran,' he said, giving her a kiss on the cheek.

'Give me my purse,' she said, pointing to a shopping-basket.

'I've got money . . . '

'I want someone in this family to have a good time over New Year, son,' she said, handing him a ten shilling note. 'I'll have all this sorted out by the time you get back.'

'What are you going to do?'

She stood up, puffing on her Woodbine. At sixty she was a heavily-built woman and strong, with plenty of stamina, born and bred in the terraced streets of Everton, which she remembered as a kind of paradise where neighbourliness and good nature thrived. Now she was forced to live in a characterless suburb that had as much sense of community as a taxi rank, spending much of her energy trying to kick some social life into it. For too long she had lived with a resentful, disappointed man. Service in the Great War, and life on the docks had beaten any good nature out of him. Tragedy had sealed his bitterness and weakened his will to live a healthy, normal life. He was a wreck, protected in his job by family connections, a family that detested him because he was such an embarrassment. But Maud had never given up on him. She had loved him once and that underpinned her patience.

When her temper was up she was a daunting figure. If it had ever come to a physical contest between herself and her husband he would never have stood a chance. She often told him during their interminable rows that a waft of her arm would give him pneumonia.

'What I'll do, Dan, is not for you to know,' she said. 'At your age you should ignore this kind of thing, otherwise you'll never want to grow up.'

Pity welled up in him. She was so proud and tough, this woman. With the little money she was given, she worked miracles. The house was kept scrupulously clean. She sent her man out every day in fresh clothes. Every night there was well-cooked food on the table which he consigned to the cat. Every night he came home drunk, mean and vile. He would never change now. In effect, she was a widow to the living dead. The only defence she had against despair with her lot was her comedy act and the presence of her daughter, another widow and fellow-sufferer.

'I don't know how you lie down beside him every night!' Daniel blurted. 'It's all wrong! You should have a better life!'

'Don't talk about your grandfather like that to me. You must have respect. You'll miss your train.'

He went out of the back door, banging his case into everything he could in his anger. On the tram going into the centre of Liverpool he wondered what she would do to get Mr Seyton out of the house. This engaged his mind all the way to Nottingham on the train.

On New Year's Eve his mother rang him at the Priory from a phone box to wish him all the best. She told him Mr Seyton had gone back to his wife, also that Bryant's mother, whom she had never even met, had written to invite her over to Nottinghamshire for the weekend, and to bring his little brother John as well.

The Priory stood on a three-acre site on top of a hill on the southern edge of the town facing the ruined keep of a Norman castle. The slope down to the castle was wooded. Wrecked lorries, vans and cars stood between the trees, kept for spare parts Stanislav might need at his repair garage on the other side of the town. There were tumbledown pigsties and stables, an orchard and an extensive formal garden much overgrown.

Every part of the building and sprawl of outhouses was in need of maintenance, having been neglected for decades until bought, somehow or other, by Stanislav and Dawn. It now housed more than twenty people altogether – including ten lodgers, mostly Polish miners with a Dutch East Indian and a Spaniard; Dawn's mother and retired miner father, and the illegitimate son of Dawn's sister; another sister and her husband and son in a separate cottage (all members of this family were *persona non grata* at this time and Daniel was under strict orders not to have anything to do with them. This prohibition was also in force against contacts with local girls who were, Dawn said, without exception, common).

It would be hard to find a better place for boys of their age to inhabit. In the first place, there was so much going on and so many people around no one took any notice of them. They were left to do as they liked, as long as they turned up at meal-times (provided by Dawn's indomitable bow-legged mother who baked and cooked all day) and bedtime. The castle grounds were open and not under care by the Ministry of Works. There were no custodians or wardens to interfere in games or stop them climbing on dangerous walls. The great fortress was, to all effects, a playground only separated from the Priory's land – another vast playground – by a minor road.

Beyond the Priory gates was the small mining town with its pubs and pie-shops and tanner-planks cinema. Dawn was in no doubt that with the purchase of the Priory went the acquisition of a certain status. Although the superiority of a second-hand car-dealer and boarding-house keeper to the general run of people was hard to define, it was there. They were not gentry, they were not *nouveau riche*, not any class previously known to the town. Despite being saddled with some old social pretensions – mainly on Dawn's part – they were new, alive, making do in grey postwar England with a fusion style all of their own.

New Year's Day, 1951, was bright and clear. The boys climbed the castle keep to the top.

Roman, one of the Polish miners, had challenged the boys to make the ascent and they had accepted. He had served in the forces during the war and now had to take what work he could find in England because return to Poland meant living under Soviet domination. The idea he might teach was at the back of his mind. Talking to youngsters he found easy. Back from night shift he'd breakfasted, spent three hours asleep, and now strolled through the Priory grounds with a pair of RAF binoculars. When he trained them on the top of the keep there sat the boys, true to their word. He was now honour-bound to join them.

The boys caught sight of him as he ran down through the trees. They watched as he hurdled the stone walls on both sides of the road, raced up the mound, then climbed the keep, sure-footed and fast. When he sat down beside them they saw he was hardly out of breath.

'Good morning, men,' he said. 'You kept your word. Is that what they teach you at school?'

Bryant said that they had kept their word to *him*. It had nothing to do with the school.

'You don't like this place Stan sent you to? Tell me about it,' Roman said, lighting a cigarette and sitting back, resting against masonry.

The boys were silent for a while.

'I won't tell Stan what you say. I'm interested in education, you see. In my own country I'm a qualified man.'

Daniel realised it was up to him to speak. His friend could get into too much trouble if Roman did let slip any criticism and it was reported to Stanislav and Dawn.

'The school gives a free education to boys without one parent, families in trouble,' he ventured. 'They send round a man to see how people live.'

'But education in this country is free anyway,' Roman pointed out, exhaling a plume of smoke. 'So why bother?'

'The parents of most boys at our school have to pay,' Daniel told him. 'We think they must be mad.'

Roman shook his head. 'Mad or not, there's more to this,' he said. 'This man they send round must be looking for a particular kind of trouble. What d'you think it is?'

Bryant said that from what he knew most of the boys on free scholarships lacked a father.

Roman congratulated him for working that out. 'So what is the school to you?' he continued. 'It is your father – what is called *in loco parentis*. This is pure politics. This is Communism. In the Soviet Union, (here he spat on the stones beside him) the state is everyone's father. Whenever an organisation takes over the function of the father look out for inhumanity, and in that I include all religion.'

Daniel drew in his breath. Here was a light shining. He felt as though the distance to the ground had doubled. Clarity came down on him in a shower. Alarmed at the strange exhilaration, hoping to remember every single syllable, Daniel listened raptly.

Prophetic energy was pouring out of Roman.

'Never mind losing fathers, I had a whole family once and I don't know where any of them are,' he exclaimed. 'I am a poet and I feel these things deeply. Dan, did you see me dancing with your lovely mother last night when the New Year came in?'

Caught off-balance by the switch in subject, Daniel could only nod.

'She can dance, but I can dance too, eh? We went well together. I think your mother likes me.'

Daniel nodded again, carefully.

'Watch this!' Roman stubbed his cigarette out and put the stub in his pocket. Then, on the narrow wall, with a drop of ninety feet on either side, he stood on his hands. 'Confidence, boys,' he said, upside-down. 'I know no fear.'

Mesmerised, they kept completely still.

'If I wanted to I could remain like this for an hour, but the breeze is a bit cool,' he said, slowly lowering his legs down until he was in an upright position again. 'Besides, I can't smoke that way up,' he laughed and re-lit the cigarette-butt. 'Control, control – that's all it is. But, boys, my life can't go on as it is. What am I doing digging coal? I'm a graduate of Warsaw University. I think I'll become a teacher and start my own school. Would you come?'

The boys swore they would leap at the chance.

'I would teach you how to be men. Come on, race you down. We'll go into the town and I'll buy Dan's mother some chocolates and propose marriage to her. What d'you think? Would I have a chance?'

'Oh, yes!' Dan assured him. 'Give it a go.'

'Good. That's useful inside information. And perhaps your little brother would like a lollipop? And you two? What sweets d'you like?'

'Liquorice Allsorts,' Daniel replied, his head in a whirl.

'Liquorice Allsorts it is!' Roman cried, jumping goatlike down to the next level place on the way to the ground. 'Let us achieve something today!'

The scene at the crowded Priory dinner-table could have taken place in the castle in its heyday. Unfortunately, it also reminded Daniel of meal-times at the Junior House. These blurred aware-nesses drifted through his mind as he watched Roman flirt with his mother under the eyes of twelve miners and Bryant's extended family. Daniel was amazed at his mother's skill in handling the situation. She laughed. She was warm. She was queenly.

'Roman only wants to marry her so he can be sure of staying in this country to work,' Bryant whispered at his side.

Daniel was shocked and insulted by the idea. 'Why did you have to tell me that?' he said.

'They're all looking for British women to marry so they don't have to go back to Poland. I reckon that's why my mother invited your mother over here, so Roman could have a look at her.'

Daniel furiously drove his elbow into his friend's ribs. 'Shut up!' he hissed.

'Roman is my appalling stepfather's best friend,' Bryant continued, edging away. 'They want to be partners. If Roman marries your mother the plan is you'll have to come and live here with this lot. What d'you think about that? D'you fancy living in a circus?'

'Why are you making all this up?'

'I'm not. I know them. Everything is business. Stan married my mother so he could stay in England,' Bryant persisted. 'He wouldn't have done otherwise.'

'The Poles fought on our side in the war. They don't have to get married to stay here,' Daniel muttered, keeping his eyes on Roman who was leaning close to his mother.

'You're wrong. D'you think even a Canadian, or an Australian can just come and work here? They have to have a permit.'

Daniel's optimism was dented.

'I don't believe it,' he said hollowly. 'No one would get married just for a permit?'

Bryant pointed at Stanislav and Dawn with his knife.

'I tackled her about it once. She got really angry. I told her she was just making do. Look at them. They don't belong together. They made a deal – and part of it was that I should be sent away.'

'Well, they seem happy to me. I think it's you who's got it all wrong . . . ' Daniel's reply tailed off as he watched Roman light his mother's cigarette with a smile that was too bright, too false.

The next morning Daniel's mother told him she was returning to Liverpool with his brother. He could choose whether to come home or stay another couple of days. The following week he was due back at school.

Disappointed and abashed, he decided to leave with her. On the train he waited to see if she would talk about Roman. When she did start talking it wasn't about him in particular but everyone at the Priory – the way of life, the place.

'I couldn't live like that,' she said.

John said he liked it there.

'That's because they made a fuss of you all the time. It wouldn't last once you started getting under their feet.'

Daniel read his comic for a while, wondering how he could bring Roman into a conversation without being too obvious.

'Mum, can you stand on your hands?' he eventually asked over the top of his comic.

'I used to be able to,' she answered. 'We used to tuck our skirts in our knickers and do handstands against the playground wall.'

'Not against a wall, Mum – with no support at all.'

'If someone held my legs for a moment I could do it.'

'With no one holding your legs.'

When his mother admitted that she couldn't quite remember being able to do that, but she might have had the skill at some time, he told her the story of Roman doing a free handstand on top of the castle keep.

Her eyes went hard and her lip tightened. 'What a bloody stupid thing to do, encouraging you to go right up there so he could show off!' she said under her breath. 'If he was here now I'd give him a piece of my mind!'

'No, Mum, it wasn't his fault. We were already up there. He came and joined us.'

'A normal man would have told you to come down.'

'D'you only like normal men?'

Until this moment Daniel had never been hit by anyone in his family. The thrashings at school were an oddity, freakish human behaviour indulged in by strangers who seemed part of another, inferior civilisation altogether. At home, in spite of the tensions and unhappiness created by his grandfather, a blow had never been struck. So the slap he received on the side of his head that day on the train came as a surprise, and he wasn't sure why he'd received it.

God With Us had changed. There was a different atmosphere in the house. Previously, it had been a matter of any given day being divided into two distinct parts – a good time when he was out and a bad time when he was in. Now his grandfather came in after work, said hello to Maud, kissed her cheek, then settled quietly in his chair to listen to the radio news with the cat on his knee. He chain-smoked but he didn't spit in the fire, he even came to the table to eat a bit of food. Another change was the yellow canary in a cage on a stand beside his chair. At times his grandfather spoke to the bird as if it could understand. What he said was trivial and silly for the most part. When the cat was on his knee he spoke to both creatures as though he was an intermediary there to keep the peace.

Daniel resisted the temptation to ask what was going on. It was obvious that, for some unaccountable reason, his grandfather was making a supreme effort to reform. The boy could only guess at the drama that had brought about this change.

In the context of this new era of peace he wasn't taken too unawares when his grandfather invited him to go fishing at West Kirby on the Wirral with one of his friends from work. It would be an all night operation because a baited stake-net would be used, driven into the sand at low-tide, left to be covered by the high tide, then recovered again at low-tide. They would sleep in the friend's van on the promenade.

Although pleased at the interest being taken in Daniel for once, his mother was unsure. He would get wet. If he caught a cold or a chill he wouldn't be able to go back to school on time.

God With Us assured her everything would be alright. The boy would be well looked after, kept dry and warm. It would be an adventure for him. The weather forecast was perfect, as was the state of the moon. They would catch a lot of flukes.

It came to pass exactly as described. There was no hitch, nothing untoward happened. The only beverage taken was tea out of a thermos.

Daniel's grandfather tucked him up in an army sleeping-bag in the back of the van, made him a pillow with a blanket, and the two men lay down on either side of him like guardians.

Before going to sleep Daniel conjured up the elegant young man in the formal photograph, the one taken in a studio with Maud in her bold, powerful beauty. He let that fade, replacing it with two pictures of the Great War soldier that were also in the box under the bed – one erect, standing beside his piece of artillery with his comrades, the other astride his horse looking down on the world like a conqueror. This is the same man, the boy told himself, eying his grandfather as smoked a final cigarette beside him before turning in. My gran believes he's still in there, hiding. Women can do that in their minds. That's why my mum still thinks my father is going to walk through the door.

At four in the morning he was woken and they went out over the sands to recover the net. There was a full moon over the three Hilbre Islands, its light twisting silver in the gullies. Daniel had never seen anything so perfect, or heard a silence so vast.

His grandfather praised the beauty of the scene as they walked along, speaking in terms Daniel had never heard him use before. An artist was striding over the sandbanks, delighted with life. He saw shapes, he saw movement, he saw meaning. He relished the salt in the air and the wind pushing the moonstruck clouds along. He talked about the stars and planets in space. He talked about the rotation of the earth. He talked about ships on the ocean and the ways of the tide. Most of all he talked about the wonder of light. At heights of his ecstasy he would suddenly stop and turn round, looking back to survey their footsteps over the moonlit sandbanks. Then this reborn man, this other force, this recreation of an earlier being, would resume his praise of nature, gesturing at the stars and the dark humps of the islands ahead of them, holding his face to the night wind.

It's as if he's drunk in a much better way, Daniel thought through his puzzlement. There's more to this than I've worked out.

When they reached the stake-net it was full, the flat fish hanging from every hook, twitching and shivering, white bellies shining. They filled two sacks with fish, took down the net and walked back to the van heavily loaded.

On the way back to the Birkenhead entrance of the Mersey Tunnel they stopped at a transport café and had bacon and eggs.

Throughout the trip God With Us was a model grandfather, solicitous, kind, touched by gentle philosophy, showing he could still find excitement in life. Although a couple of jokes were cracked about being henpecked and not being allowed into pubs any more, no attempt was made to leave Daniel sitting on a pub doorstep with a bottle of Tizer and a bag of crisps, his customary fate if he ever went out on the Dock Road with his grandfather. He was delivered back into the hands of his mother dry, happy, still aglow with revelations of what could be done with a man's spirit, and suffering only from a lack of sleep.

One sack of fish went off with the friend in the van. The other was carried into the house, taken upstairs and emptied into the bath. When Daniel looked in the bathroom some of the flukes were still flapping about. His mother tutted because she'd planned for Daniel to have a bath and now he couldn't.

While he was getting changed in his bedroom, a discussion was going on downstairs. It seemed to be under control but there was the threat of protest in his grandmother's voice. No one could eat so many fish. There was no fridge. The fish were all too small to bother with. They were stinking the place out. He heard his grandfather retort that if she didn't want the flukes she must get a cart and give them away to the poor or anyone who'd have them because he was going out.

A door slammed.

He heard his mother declare aloud what would happen next – the inevitable. There might have been a better way to deal with the fish. After all, it was good for her father to have a pastime. He should be helped. The women crossed swords, but lightly. They never fought out in the open but there were criticisms held in the sides of the heart if not the centre.

'You could have laughed at it, Mum,' his mother said. 'You can laugh when you want to.'

'I'd laugh if I didn't know we have to dig a hole in the garden and bury that lot,' came the reply, 'I can hardly put them out for the bin-men, can I?'

'You'll cook us a few for our dinner, surely.'

'You can if you like. I'm sick of the sight of them.'

Daniel was low for the rest of the day. The interlude at West Kirby was now a vision that had fled. He was living with people at war, people who should never have met, never have bred, never have been young together.

By the time he went back to school his grandfather had settled back into his old ways. On Daniel's last night at home he came in drunk and sour, as he had done each evening since the burial of the flukes. To make matters worse at this sensitive time, while the canary's cage was being cleaned that day, the bird had been let out to stretch its wings and the cat had killed it.

When his grandfather was given the bad news he went out in a fury to the coal-shed, got the axe and went looking for the cat. Daniel, foreseeing the reaction – it was so like Mr Seyton, this canary, it was virtually a metamorphosis – had the cat hidden in his bedroom. When his grandfather went down to the green-house looking for the culprit (one of its accustomed places of rest), Daniel ran down the stairs with the cat in a hessian sack and pelted to the tram stop. He caught a tram to Fazakerly at the end of the line and walked until he reached a farm where he pleaded with the farmer and his wife to take the cat and succeeded in winning them over.

When he got home several hours later his grandfather was sitting in his chair drinking Guinness. Beside him, perched side by side in the cage, were three blue budgerigars. While Daniel had been out on his life-saving mission, God With Us had gone up to the pub, found a man he knew who bred budgerigars, bought him a drink, gone round to his aviary, returned to the pub with the three birds, had several more drinks, then come home with his purchase. Shaking the budgerigars out of the container into the cage he had announced to his wife and daughter that these creatures – Shadrach, Meshach and Abednego – were the only friends he had inside his own house.

Before he went to bed Daniel approached his grandfather and told him that there was no point in waiting for the cat to come back because it was now in a good home where he'd never find it. The response was a strange, not unkind jeer.

'You know your own know.'

'What does that mean?'

'You know *me*. You know what I'd have done to that cat.'

Daniel was oddly moved by this admission. Although simple enough, it made him confront the importance he attached to his grandfather. From now on he would be able to talk openly to this man. Emboldened by this discovery, he asked why the budgerigars were named after the Jews Nebuchadnezzar cast into the midst of the fiery furnace.

'We both know our Bible, Dan,' his grandfather replied. 'What you read by choice I had knocked into me.' He paused, grinned bitterly, rubbed his eyes under the bottle-end spectacles, then lit another cigarette, staring at the flaming match. 'This house has been a fiery furnace to me for thirty years, son,' he said flatly. 'It won't change now.'

CHAPTER SEVEN

Daniel's trunk had to be made ready for the railway lorry to pick up two days before he travelled back to school. His mother was a superb packer. Every item was laundered, cleaned, and carefully folded into its space. The parcels he received at school were similar gems of the packer's art.

To interfere with the trunk once ready and labelled was inviting her displeasure but he took the risk, emptying the contents of the archive box under the bed on top of his things and sitting on the lid until he could snap the locks shut.

He couldn't bear to be away from family history for too long this time. Too much had happened. Via his growing knowledge of his grandfather he was touched by patrilineal magic. He must not lose contact with that sensation. There was construction work to be done on his real father, the forgotten man. Long silences over the dead must be broken, flatlands of time crossed. In order to reassemble his father he had to go deeper, but know roughly where he was going. He couldn't afford to get lost.

Cook was one of the masters detailed to meet returning boys at Waterloo Station before shepherding them onto the local train. He had no time to talk except to say how much Daniel had altered in such a short time.

'You've shot up over the holidays, Rogers,' he said with his shy, melancholic smile. 'Mr Oliphant might have to rethink his plans for you. I don't know that we can have someone so tall on the wing.'

January at Junior House was a mean, cold, overcrowded time. Nothing had changed except winter's savagery now revealed the true harshness of daily life under Mule and the Cosh Gang making all routines more of a punishment. The chore of tramping up and down the cinder track to the main school through wind and rain was a daily treadmill, lowering the spirit. Influenza struck the school. Snow and ice descended to make sport and outdoor exercise impossible. The rooms were fuggy and airless, the radiators madly hot.

Daniel kept his archive in a netting fruit bag he found in the kitchens while on washing-up duty. At first he had it in his locker but there was no room for anything else. There were cupboards and chests all over Junior House but not for boys to use. Eventually he was driven to ask Cook for help in finding somewhere safe and dry. He listened to Daniel's request with interest, head cocked to one side.

'So you're the family historian, are you?'

'Yes, sir.'

'What are you going to do with all this information?'

'I don't know yet, sir. No one else seems to bother.'

'People are like that nowadays. They want to forget the past. Who can blame them? My family is just the same,' Cook said with a shrug. 'We'll keep your documents here in my room. If you want to look at them you'll just have to ask me.'

Daniel was back within a matter of days. He had a free Saturday afternoon because the rugby game had been cancelled. Cook let him use the room while he was there marking history essays. They sat at opposite sides of the table, poring over their papers. After an hour he made some tea and gave Daniel a cup and some biscuits.

'What have you found today?' he asked.

'I've always been told that my father was six feet tall, sir, and a supervisor at Fort Dunlop tyre factory. His Army record card says he was five foot ten and a half and a labourer.'

Cook thoughtfully stirred his tea. 'Are you sure this research is going to be good for you, Rogers?' he said quietly. 'Do these details matter all that much?'

'He was a real person, sir,' Daniel said. 'No one in my family talks about him in that way. I know they make things up and exaggerate. I can't remember him at all because he went away to the war when I was two and only came home on short leave a couple of times.'

Cook sighed and shook his head. 'Don't expect your mother to dwell on the subject,' he advised. 'It's probably too painful for her.'

'It's not that, sir. She says I shouldn't have forgotten him.'

'Shouldn't?'

'Yes, sir. She gets mad at me. But I can't help not remembering him.'

Cook found the notion of blame preposterousness and said so. 'You can't be expected to *create* memory,' he said.

'If I learn everything about him it will be *as if* I can remember him, sir, and that might be enough.'

There was a knock at the door. Cook called out for the visitor to enter. It was Mule. He stared at Daniel who stood up and stared back.

Cook, aware of the mutual hostility, explained the boy's presence.

'It's a history project based on his own family. You know how people distort the past. Rogers wants to find the truth about his background – his father in particular. Would you like some tea?'

Mule came in and closed the door, his baleful blue eyes on the piles of paper, cards and photographs.

'Is this private tuition, would you say?'

Cook made no answer, only smiled in his apprehensive, guarded way as he poured another cup of tea.

Mule sat down, flexing his artificial leg. It made a series of clicks. He lit his pipe, staring at the archive through the smoke.

'I'll go now, sir,' Daniel said, handing Cook his empty cup.

'Don't let me drive you away, Rogers,' Mule breathed, sucking on his pipe. 'Continue with your important work. I have to discuss house matters with Mr Cook. It won't take long.'

'I've finished for the day, sir . . . '

'No, no . . . do carry on.'

There was steel in Mule's tone. Cook was as aware of it as Daniel was. They exchanged a glance. Daniel went back to the table and started looking at papers.

'What kind of people do you come from, Rogers?'

The question boomed in Daniel's head. He could see how anxious Cook was getting.

'Did you hear me, boy?'

'I heard you, sir. I'm just thinking about it.'

'Well, don't take too long. Most of us know the kind of people we come from. If we don't, there's something the matter with us, I'd say.'

Daniel stroked his throat. Inside rose a lava-flow of temper, his internal enemy. He was stemming it with difficulty.

'Mostly soldiers, sir,' he said in an odd voice. 'Soldiers like you were.'

Cook got to his feet in alarm. He told Daniel to put his archive away and go. Mule waved him back to his seat.

'Don't get in such a state, man. Nothing's the matter. Rogers and I understand each other very well. We're old sparring-partners. Tell me, boy – what kind of soldiers were they?'

'Let him go . . . ' Cook murmured.

'Soldiers *like me*, he said,' Mule went on. 'That requires explanation.'

'May we leave this, please?' Cook protested.

Mule sat forward and braced his shoulders. 'I hold what conversations I like with boys in this house,' he said, giving his shoulders an assertive shake.'

'Rogers came here to work.'

Mule said he was interested in what made a boy like Rogers tick. 'Don't deny me this one chance to understand. Let me follow it through. Now, Rogers – what kind of a soldier am I?'

'A wounded one, sir.'

Mule's mouth fell open a little. He blinked several times and snapped his mouth shut.

'You're one of my house-captains, aren't you, Rogers?'

'I'm not sure I still am, sir.'

'Of course you are. It's an experiment to see if having authority can make you understand the need for it. We haven't done too well so far, have we? But we'll plod on with it. Now and again I'll need to consult you on something important.'

'You want to talk to me, sir? Is that instead of beating me?'

'I haven't beaten you for some time.'

Cook spread his hands in a gesture of despair. 'Please, this is quite ridiculous,' he exclaimed. 'Running the house is hard enough without . . . '

'Oh, we don't run the house, he does, with his pals. Isn't that right, Rogers?' Mule cut in. 'I had a similar contretemps with his friend Bryant before Christmas, didn't I? He must have told you all about it.'

'No, sir, he didn't.'

'That's a blatant lie. They run the Cosh Gang and the Cosh Gang runs the house. That's what you think, isn't it, Rogers?'

Daniel was silent. The unwritten agreement had been broken.

'You see, Mr Cook? I asked them for help to solve a problem and they deceive themselves they're permanently in charge.'

Mule tugged at his grey moustache, eyeing Cook to see how he was taking this excursion into the murkier side of Junior House politics. He made the point that he'd asked the boys for help only as an alternative to bringing in the police. Now the thieving had died down, the arrangement was over.

'I want the Cosh Gang to stop. It was useful for a while but now there's no need for it,' he said, getting to his feet. 'I leave it with you, Rogers. Pass the word around.'

'Why did you need help in the first place, sir?'

'I didn't need it. All I was doing was teaching you to share responsibility. The thieving had got out of control.'

'But you can beat thieves like anyone else. What was so different? Beating solves everything, doesn't it?'

Mule's jaw dropped. 'Dear God, d'you hear this insolence, Mr Cook?' he said, swiping at his false leg with his pipe in fury, spilling his tea. 'Listen, boy, hundreds of boys have been through this house and been beaten and never complained. Most of them admit it was of benefit. I get letters all the time, thanking me for bringing them up with a firm hand. I made men of them. They're grateful.'

'You won't be getting a letter from me, sir.'

Cook sidled towards the door. 'I think you should go now, Rogers,' he said.

'No, let him stay. He doesn't worry me. I brought it on myself,' Mule quavered angrily, fussing over the spilt tea. 'I have to sort out this Cosh Gang business somehow. I don't mind swapping insults with the knave if he can help.'

'You'll have to accept that I've never heard of the Cosh Gang, sir. I don't know what you're talking about. It's not meant to exist.'

Mule drew a deep breath and sank his chin onto his chest, exhausted. 'I don't know what to do with you, Rogers. I really don't,' he sighed. 'You're unhinged, boy – but then, I'm no psychiatrist.'

'I'm not the one who needs a psychiatrist, sir.'

'Almighty God,' Mule groaned aloud. 'What have I done? I can't endure this. The headmaster will have to be told. Is that what you want, Rogers?'

'I don't mind,' Daniel replied, feeling stronger by the minute. He turned to his archive, shuffling sections of it around. 'I'm sorry leaving everything in a mess, Mr Cook, sir. I'll come back and put all my papers away later.'

Cook carefully guided him to the door. All the way across the room Daniel's eyes never left Mule's face. As he went he said: 'The worst day in my life was when I fell into your hands, sir.'

Once he had gone, Cook let Mule smoke his pipe for a while to get over Daniel's Parthian shot, which had been delivered like a curse. To cover this black period, Cook made neat piles of

Daniel's archive, putting the papers and photographs in a plywood box he'd found for the purpose.

'In spite of everything, including his terrible lack of respect,' he said to Mule, eventually, 'and I know he can be tricky, I say the boy is worth saving. We can do something with him, I'm sure.'

'I'm the best housemaster this school has ever had,' Mule declared mournfully. 'I've been told that many times. I've the knack of dealing with boys at this age. There are plenty who've been through my hands who look upon me as a father.'

'I know that's true. Perhaps one day Rogers will appreciate everything you've done for him.'

'I can't be two people at once. But I did make a big mistake allowing this Cosh Gang thing to happen. It was a weak thing to do. They have me cornered, I'm afraid.'

With some historical seriousness, Cook compared the state of affairs with the relationship between the Irish Republican Army and the British. 'When it chooses, the government deals and negotiates with the IRA. When it's a nuisance . . . well, out come the knives. But it can't be rooted out because it has become part of government. The cause has to disappear first. Then it becomes a criminal organisation, perhaps, then it dies a natural death . . . if you're lucky.'

'Oh, do stop talking bilge, man! This is a bad situation. I can't come out in the open and ban this nasty little Mafia. In my stupidity I created the damn thing! We've had a complaint from that Persian boy, Ashnar's father, that he was bullied with the backing of the staff. I've no doubt it was the Cosh Gang.'

'But bullying always has the staff's backing,' Cook observed mildly, a humorous light in his eye. 'We have to follow the pattern of public school life if we're ever going to achieve that status. We know about the levels of violence, the things new boys have to suffer.'

'Initiation of new boys isn't in the same class,' Mule muttered. 'That goes on everywhere. It signifies that they're joining a corps, a body of future men . . . as in *esprit de corps.*'

'You've obviously thought this through.'

'I have brooded upon it, many, many times.'

Cook left Mule to smoke his pipe while he made another pot of tea. When the older man's frustration had subsided, the history master put forward a suggestion: 'If we could settle what has been a fairly loose arrangement so far – leaving Rogers to me, letting me deal with him, especially on anything contentious or to do with discipline, I think I can keep him out of your hair for the next two terms. Once he's in a senior house, you can forget about him.'

'How will you hold that villain down?'

'Through history. He's very good at my subject. And he's ambitious.' He paused before making the essential connection with what was troubling Mule's mind. 'Meanwhile, I'll work on getting him to run the Cosh Gang right down before he goes.'

'You're asking me to admit total defeat,' Mule growled. 'If there are a lot more like Rogers on the way maybe I should retire?'

Cook smiled as he pooh-poohed the idea. 'If Rogers fails, the responsibility will be mine,' he promised. 'He's a very interesting test-case. In changing times, the school should be flexible enough to cope with him. Imagine the children throughout Europe now going to school – refugees, orphans, witnesses to the cruellest war ever waged. What can be the state of their minds? What can they believe in? Are they educable? What do we say to these children? The world's not such a bad place?'

Mule sat and thought about this for a while, pressing tobacco into the black bowl of his pipe. 'There is something in that,' he said eventually, 'and I do feel a bit left behind now and again. You know, Rogers really hasn't had it that bad. We've straightened out much worse cases over the years. I can give you the names of men in very high places I've had to bring to heel for their own good. The best of them admit it was the making of them.'

'The passionate loyalty of the old boys to you is legendary,'

Cook said with a winning smile. 'Ever since I came here I've been aware that you are the nearest thing to the living soul of the school.'

Appeased, Mule struck a match and lit his pipe, musing over the names of those who were devoted to him. When he thought about these boys he liked to gaze at his collection of butterflies, the lovely wings of the insects outstretched in an eternalised moment of flight. His nets, killing-bottles, stiffening solutions and pins had passed through the warm hands of more than a thousand boys very keen to get close to nature.

'Am I to assume you'd rather I didn't say anything to the Head about this Cosh Gang business?' Mule murmured, pointing with the wet end of his pipe. 'This is very small beer for me, actually. I've been through it all so many times I can't get excited about it any more.'

Cook lifted his head and grinned. Power had shifted. He chose the moment to ask, casually enough, whether Mule had known Rogers was in the room when he called in.

Mule sucked on his pipe, smiled, and had to admit this was so. 'Nothing much goes on in this place without my knowledge,' he said, brusquely tapping the metal joint of his knee. 'We have to keep an eye on favouritism. But now I understand why he comes to your room so much. It's for a good reason – and I respect your kindness to him.'

'Then you agree that someone like Rogers needs individual help?'

'I think I do – but it must be specific help.'

'And I am the one best placed to help him?'

'Well, I obviously can't do it,' Mule said with a curt laugh. 'He hates my guts.'

This is excellent, Cook thought. He's admitting his own incompetence. With Pacey at his side, Cook saw himself running the Junior House from now on – two highly qualified men with up-to-date ideas on education who would bring about great changes.

'It would be better all round if we kept everything amongst

ourselves,' Cook said, putting his hands behind his back and parking himself in front of the fire. 'Asking the headmaster to intervene would be too embarrassing. House discipline is our business. With intelligence and foresight we should be able to sort it out.'

With this deal settled, and Mule retired while still in office, Cook moved on to matters peripheral.

CHAPTER EIGHT

Events moved swiftly in the Junior House during the next week. The Old Man paid a rare visit and spent several hours in Mule's room. A sandwich lunch was sent up from the kitchens. When the Italian maid took the tray away she noticed the strong smell of whisky in the room.

Ashnar, the Persian boy, disappeared. The day afterwards, Cook was moved to The Elms, a rambling old house rented by the school opposite the workman's cottage inhabited by the widow of Henry Long. The history master lost his housemaster's allowance and the free board and lodging that went with that job. When this loss of income was queried he was told that his salary would be reviewed in March for the start of the new financial year.

Within ten days Pacey joined his friend at The Elms. He had been caught *in flagrante delicto* with Ann Wood by Mule popping in (with cushioned foot) for a chat about the prep supervision roster. Ann Wood was fired on the spot and a much plainer version of womanhood hired to replace her. In a stony interview with the Old Man, Pacey was advised that he was a bonehead and should, in future, find females who lived well outside the district.

The snow and ice retreated and rugby games were played again. Drafted to cheer along the first fifteen in a fogbound home match against Christ's Hospital, Daniel saw Cook and Pacey on the touchline standing close together like two people who needed each other's support. He sidled up behind them unseen until he could overhear their conversation. They were talking in awed tones about the political genius of Mule. Over twenty years at Lord Mendora Land College Mule had foiled plots against him by simply bringing in the Old Man, confessing his boneheadedness and throwing himself on his mercy.

Back in 1938 when the ferocity of beating at the school was reminiscent of the Nazi's treatment of the German Jewish population, (relatives of the Lord Mendora amongst them) there had been an uprising in the Junior House. Boys locked themselves in, broke windows and started fires in protest against the indiscriminate use of the cane. None of the grievances were examined. The ringleaders were severely beaten before being expelled. Immediately afterwards, the Old Man sent Mule on a paid holiday to the Isle of Mull and ran the Junior House himself so a standard could be set. When Mule returned from Mull refreshed, his confidence restored, the Junior House was handed back to him in a state of iron discipline. Mule, (always more under the Old Man's protection than the boys were) was told to be more vigilant in detecting troublemakers and never to keep a crisis to himself.

Remaining behind after a history lesson, Daniel asked Cook if his family archive had been moved to The Elms. Cook assured him that the precious documents were safe. He added that once the dust had settled, Daniel would be welcome to visit and resume his researches. But that would not be until after half-term at the earliest.

After another visit to London with Bryant during which he saw the musical *Annie Get Your Gun* and visited Bow Street magistrates court again, Daniel chose a wild March Sunday afternoon to go down to The Elms.

The great trees around the house were bending and creaking as he walked up the drive. Cook's car was standing outside next to a silver Aston Martin coupé, both vehicles plastered with wet leaves. When he knocked on the front door it was opened by a hard-faced blonde woman smoking a gold-tipped cocktail cigarette. From his experience of these things, Daniel could see that she was very drunk.

'Well, hello!' she said, looking him over. 'Step inside. I can't keep the door open or all the leaves will blow in.'

Once in the hall Daniel asked if Mr Cook was at home.

'I think he went out for something.'

Pacey appeared at the woman's shoulder.

'Mephistopheles, here?' he slurred, making a grand conjurer's gesture. 'Did I summon you up from somewhere?'

Daniel explained the purpose of his visit.

'You'll never find anything in this place,' Pacey said, leading him into a big sitting-room with a used lunch-tray in front of an open fire. 'We're living in chaos. Nothing has been unpacked.'

'If Mr Cook is out, sir, I'd better come back another time . . .' Daniel said, retreating towards the front door.

'You don't have to go,' the woman said. 'Sit down and talk to me.'

'He's not staying,' Pacey said. You don't know this evil fellow.'

'You should have at least one boy at your birthday party.'

'Not this one.'

'Does Clive teach you?' the woman asked.

Daniel shook his head.

'I couldn't teach Mephi anything if I tried. But he can have one drink. Ever tasted champagne, Mephi?' Pacey asked, picking up a bottle. 'Silly question. You probably had it with your mother's milk.'

'I'd like to be introduced, if you don't mind,' the woman announced, curling up at one end of a sofa. 'My name's Veronica. What's this *Mephi* he calls you? I've never heard that name before.'

'He is the Prince of Darkness, and no gentleman,' Pacey said, giving Daniel a glass.

'Come on, stop being smart with me. You tell me, Mephi.'

'It's another name for Satan,' Daniel replied. 'It's Mr Pacey's joke.'

'It's no joke. You're incorrigible.'

'Well, if Clive can call you Satan you must be very bad indeed. Come and sit beside me.'

'Oh, no you don't,' Pacey said. 'Drink up – then get out of here.'

Daniel drained the glass. The woman asked for his real Christian name. When he told her, she said she approved of the name Daniel. He was a Daniel. He looked like a Daniel.

'But you are certainly no Veronica, Veronica – she was a sainted lady!' Pacey declared with a chuckle, pouring the last of the champagne into his glass. 'Give her another name, Mephi. Take a good look and give me a name that suits her better.'

Daniel was not enjoying the trap he was in. If he made a run for it, once sober, Pacey would follow things up, somehow. The master's fall from grace at Junior House was general knowledge and the source of many jokes. Before he could go, Pacey would need an assurance that Daniel wouldn't say anything about what he'd walked into that afternoon.

'Gloria is a better name for you,' Daniel said boldly with what he hoped was a charming smile.

Pacey burst out laughing. 'Gloria, Queen of the RAF married quarters! Mephi, you're a diabolical genius! Where did you learn to flatter?'

The situation was saved by the return of Cook. He was not pleased to find Daniel in the house. There was a tension between the men. It was obvious that Cook disliked the woman. Before long Daniel was outside the front door with Cook pushing him in the direction of the gate and telling him quite fiercely not to just drop in when he felt like it.

As he was walking down the drive, the gate opened and a group of people entered carrying flowers, bottles and gifts. Henry's widow was there with a cake-box, and Mrs White with her husband drifting along abstractedly a few paces behind her. Mrs White's beauty glowed against the darkness of the wet elm trunks. Her black hair, blown by the wind, fluttered over her brilliant eyes. She was carrying gramophone records pressed against her breasts. Not English song, I bet, Daniel thought, fired up by champagne, imagining her dancing at the party. He stopped, unable to take his eyes off her.

A huge gust of wind bent the trees, sweeping a mound of dead leaves into the air all around him. Standing there in his grey uniform, all the party guests walked past without giving him a look.

What Daniel had wanted to see Cook for that day was to show him a letter he had received from America. When his father's father was killed near Arras in 1917, his wife, Marion, had left her infant child in the care of her dead husband's brother and sister and emigrated to New York. She had never seen her son, Daniel's father, again. After his death in Tunisia in 1943, she had entered into correspondence with his widow and sent food parcels for the rest of the war. She was very Spanish-looking and glamorous, survivor of an American divorce. There was a daughter of this second marriage, Betty, who went right off the rails, throwing away a top secretarial job in IBM to become the kept mistress of a Wall Street millionaire. He had set her up in an apartment on Fifth Avenue, bought her a pair of white miniature poodles and introduced her to his many friends in the film industry, including Richard Burton and Elizabeth Taylor, two staunch Britishers. When the millionaire died suddenly, Betty found herself dumped outside on the pavement with only her old IBM typewriter and the poodles for company. Deranged by this abrupt change of fortune she went to live with her mother and ate for comfort until she weighed twenty-five stone.

Daniel had gathered much of this information when Marion decided to return to Liverpool after a breach with her enormous daughter in 1948. She stayed at the house with the family for several weeks while she looked for a flat. Her flirtation with his grandfather was a wonder for Daniel to behold. She found her way through to the last remaining spark of maleness, never

114

failing to raise his spirits with her coquetry and clouds of perfume. But it was not to last. Marion suffered the same fate as her daughter on Fifth Avenue, dumped on the pavement with her luggage one day, a strident reminder from Maud of her betrayals as mother and mother-in-law ringing in her ears. Within a month she had shaken the dust of Liverpool off her feet and returned to New York.

Daniel worked out that there must be more to her story. He wrote to her asking for information about her early life and the marriage to his grandfather. When he walked down to The Elms on Pacey's birthday he had Marion's reply in his pocket to show Cook, hoping he might help to elucidate it.

43 Broadway,
Haverstraw, New York State,
914 HA. 9 5296
6th February 1951

Dear Dan – About your Grandfather. He was a wonderful man. When he was a young chap, he was the Captain's Tiger on the *Lusitania*. At the time the ship went down he was home with pneumonia. Heartbroken at losing his ship, he got straight out of bed and went down to the recruiting office in his pyjamas and joined the army. He joined the Liverpool Pals, that was what the soldiers called the regiment. It consisted of stockbrokers and the cream of Liverpool. The regiment was on Lord Derby's estate somewhere near Ormskirk.

While being witness for a girlfriend who was marrying a soldier I met your grandfather. He was the groom's witness. We decided on the spur of the moment to get married as well the same day even though we had only just met. At that time all soldiers could get married without any red tape. He was on orders to go to France, and had two weeks embarkation leave, but due to the marriage, was given another two weeks. We only ever had that one month together. I became pregnant straight away. I wrote and told him. He was in France seven months before being killed at the battle of the Somme. Whilst in training he was made a sergeant.

We spent the month we had together in my mother's home in Liverpool. We had many happy times together. This is as much as I can remember right now.

Love,

Granny

P.S. The zip code in my address is underlined because it is important you realise how it is part of the family history you are so interested in. The zip code system was invented by your Aunty Betty when she was at IBM and stolen from her by fellow-workers in her office. If she had patented the idea she would be worth millions.

It was another fortnight before Cook would pay him any attention outside history lessons. By the time he did so, Daniel had heard back from the Army Records Office that all personal information regarding his father's father had been destroyed by enemy bombing during the last war. There was some better news from the War Graves Commission however. They had a record of his date of death – 12th August, 1917 – number, 25533, rank of sergeant – and location of his burying-place: Plot 1, Row E, Grave 6, Red Cross Corner Cemetery, Beugny, Bapaume, near Arras.

Daniel had also ascertained from the school library that the passenger liner *Lusitania* was torpedoed by a German sub-marine off the south Irish coast in early May 1915 on her return journey from New York. The captain, (without his regular *tiger*) whose vessel was carrying 173 tons of ammunition as well as passengers, ignored British Admiralty advice to zig-zag every few minutes in this area to confuse U-boats, their lordships having been warned by the Germans that the liner was a legitimate target. Of the 1198 people drowned, 128 were US citizens. This indirectly contributed to the eventual entry of the United States into the Great War.

'My gran's memory can't be correct, can it, sir?' Daniel reasoned as he walked down to the village with Cook. 'What she says happened over seven months happened over two years and four months, which is four times as long, but the pregnancy works out because my dad was born on 14th April, 1916 which is about right if his father joined up in May, 1915 and was in training a month when they got married and then they had their month together.'

Cook nodded, swinging a stick he had picked out of the hedge.

'This is very close work you're doing, Rogers,' he said. 'Remember that the average person has a very poor recall of time past, especially detail. They can remember an event but not the exact context.'

'I wonder what she was up to in that lost twenty-one months?' Daniel mused. 'When her husband was killed my dad was fifteen months old. Had my grandfather, the sergeant with all his stockbroker pals, ever come back on leave and seen his son?'

Cook gave him a sideways look. 'Have you thought what it must have been like for a ship's steward to be chucked in with the cream of Liverpool?'

'That's right, sir – a ship's steward was all the tiger was. Quite lowly. But then, can we be sure about the cream?'

'Don't be too hard on your American grandmother's simple pretensions. With our sad class system, people end up like that, I'm afraid.'

Daniel wondered aloud how a true history could ever be compiled if allowances for pretensions, inaccuracies, gaps and lies were always being made and built into the story, the form of which might last for ever.

Cook laughed and twirled his stick, before slashing at the hedge.

'That's why history is an art and not a science.' Then he stopped in mid-stride and said abruptly. 'I hope all this digging around is helping you.'

'Oh, yes, sir! It's helping me a lot!' Daniel enthused, moving on to the questions he wanted to ask about his grandmother's letter: first, what was this regiment the Liverpool *Pals* – he could find no trace of it.

Was it the Liverpool Kings under another name? And wasn't the battle of the Somme over by the time his grandfather was killed on 12th August 1917?

'Rogers, with your talent for following things up, I'm surprised you haven't found the answers for yourself by now.'

Daniel looked away, hurt. It was tactless for Cook to high-light the boy's need to share. When he turned back, there were questions in his eyes for the older man: has your offer of help been withdrawn? Have you lost interest? Cook picked them up and felt guilty.

To cover his apparent insouciance, which he regretted, Cook confided that he would never be able to examine his own family background so thoroughly without encountering so much pain and shame it would reduce the happiness of all his relatives, including his own. *Digging around* of any kind was unpopular with his family – taciturn farming folk with a taste for endless in-feuding – who loathed meddlers and preferred to either let sleeping dogs lie or shoot them.

'So I'm quite jealous of your ability to walk where angels fear to tread,' he added. 'If I went as far as you do, my people wouldn't talk to me at all.'

Daniel felt some way encouraged to hold the young history master to his promises. After all, there was no one else going out of their way to help him stay on at the school. He explained, with an attempt at casualness, how he'd computed the total time the last two male Rogers had been able to enjoy married life before being killed.

'One month and two years. That's not long, is it, sir? It's not normal.'

'A meaningless concept,' Cook said, swiping at a tumble of old man's beard hanging out of a hawthorn and accelerating his pace. 'Don't use normality as a starting-point, whatever you do. After such a war as the world has just been through assume all family life everywhere to be in a state of tight-lipped torment. We are in shock and shame and we can hardly talk about it.'

Heartened by this advice because it decreased his sense of isolation, Daniel produced a postcard and trotted alongside Cook to hand it to him. 'I found this amongst the papers, sir.'

Cook had to stop in the middle of the lane to examine the postcard. It was a black and white photograph titled: *Lee Bay from Golf links, N. Devon*. On the reverse was written in pencil: *Where I used to go swimming.*

'That's my father's writing, sir.

A car came along and they had to move close to the bank while it passed. When it had done so, Cook handed the postcard back without comment.

'I think he was at that place on manoeuvres before being sent to North Africa with the First Army. One day I'm going to go swimming there myself.'

'Rogers, I think you should go back to Junior House or you'll be late,' Cook said, averting his face then setting off again at speed. 'Cut across the field.'

'But I've got a free afternoon, sir . . . '

'I can't have you getting into trouble because I've detained you. Goodbye, Rogers.'

Daniel stood in the lane and watched as Cook threw his stick into the hedge and, on a fine line between trotting and the Olympic walk, disappeared around a bend.

18th March 1951

Dear Mrs Rogers – Allow me to introduce myself. My name is Hugh Cook. I teach your son History at Lord Mendora Land College.

You will have noticed from his reports how Daniel does well in my subject. To further improve his ability I will, if you approve, offer him a trip to the West Country during the first week of the Easter holidays to do some historical research. We will leave from school at the end-of-term and, once our fieldwork is completed, five days should do it, I will bring him home to you in my car. This fits in nicely with a proposed visit to my brother who lives near Chester.

There will be no expenses for you to pay. It will be of great help for me to have a research assistant.

Please be so good as to write me a letter with your decision in this matter.

Yours sincerely,

Hugh Cook

The consternation this letter produced in Daniel's mother was pitiable. In one way it was a gift from the gods because her father had returned to his drink-sodden ways and Daniel would need to spend as much of the holiday away from home as possible. In another, it presented a high risk that Cook would encounter her father when he brought Daniel back. This chance could be lessened by offering to pick Daniel up in Chester. The darkest doubt lay shrouded in her ignorance of what went on at the school. For a master to take a boy away with him one to one meant an act of trust on her part. She could only give that trust if Daniel could assure her everything was above board.

She had never had to write a letter like the one she sent.

It took her several evenings to complete it – valuable time she needed to spend on her sewing to keep up her earnings.

The letter was put in Daniel's weekly parcel with his five-shilling postal order wrapped round a green and gold tin of Tate and Lyle's Golden Syrup, held in place by an elastic band.

On the day the parcel arrived – parcels were given out at teatime – Daniel had no time to open it because he had to attend rugby training and be measured again by Oliphant. He put the parcel in his locker. By Cosh Gang law no boy was allowed to have a padlock on his locker. To do so meant admitting defeat in the battle for honesty. When Daniel came in from rugby training and opened his locker the parcel had gone. Several witnesses queued up to tell him that Hepworth, a dyed-in-the-wool crazy thief (so much so that he was known as *Klepworth*) had taken his parcel and was at this very moment distributing the contents to everyone in the prep room.

Daniel barged his way through the crowd, pushed Klepworth to the ground, grabbed a handful of his hair and banged his head against a table leg.

'Choose someone your own size!' Klepworth protested.

'No one my own size has stolen my parcel,' Daniel said, kicking him in the ribs and grabbing another handful of hair and pulling him to his feet. 'Everyone who's got my stuff has to bring it back *now*, or else,' he threatened, gazing round the mob of boys. 'You lot should have stopped him!'

This turn of events had been anticipated by many in the crowd. All the edible contents they had got their hands on had been immediately bolted. Some articles were returned – a tube of tooth-paste, a roll of comics, and a tin of Tate & Lyle Golden Syrup with paper wrapped round it held in place by an elastic band.

'You're going to be tried for this crime, Klepworth,' Daniel said, violently shaking the culprit.

'I wish I had your mother, Rogers. I reckon you get the best parcel in Junior House. My parents don't send me anything.'

Klepworth had been beaten up so often he didn't really care what happened to him. With the excitement of his deed draining away, he slumped to the floor in a heap.

Daniel gathered together what had been returned and went to his locker. At least he'd got the comics back, and the syrup and the postal order. Sitting on a radiator by the window he read his mother's letter, which was in three parts. The first was for him. The second was for Mr Cook if Daniel decided to go on the trip. The third was for Mr Cook if Daniel decided he didn't want to go on the trip.

He had to make up his own mind whether to go or not.

His mother could trust him to take the right decision.

Set against this was the knowledge that she had no option

but to trust him because the alien world of Junior House was unknown to her and it was better kept that way. When he moved up to the senior school as a third-former, when life would improve, all being well, she could be let in on more of the truth.

Returning to the prep room he found Klepworth where he'd left him, still lying on the floor but no longer tearful, being stepped over and ignored by everyone who passed. Daniel pulled him to his feet and made him empty his pockets to see if he'd kept anything for himself.

'Don't beat me up again, Rogers?' Klepworth whined when a Mars Bar was found.

'Why must you steal?' Daniel nagged at him. 'You know it's wrong.'

Klepworth shrugged and felt at the lump on his forehead. 'D'you think I should see matron about this?' he said cunningly. 'You've given me a headache.'

'It's nothing. Don't sham.'

'But you're tough, Rogers, and I'm a softie. I'm sorry I found your parcel, but there we are.'

'Tell you what – I'll let you off this time,' Daniel said, putting a hand on the felon's shoulders. 'There'll be no trial this time, but just you watch it in future.'

Klepworth beamed. 'Thank you, Rogers. To be honest, I wasn't looking forward to it – not with my record. I always say you're not so much a bully but just someone with a bad temper that gets the better of him sometimes.'

'Is that what they call me – a bully?'

'You're in the Cosh Gang, aren't you?'

Daniel stared into Klepworth's moon face, searching for signs of insolence and found none. 'You can't help yourself,' he said after a while. 'You're a bit mad, aren't you?'

'That's what I keep telling my parents. Junior House is doing it to me, Rogers, and it's doing it to you. If they took us away from here and let us live at home we'd be in our right minds soon enough.'

CHAPTER NINE

When Daniel's mother was expecting her first baby she had wanted a daughter. Being a quick seamstress, in the first three months of her pregnancy she made a whole layette of baby clothes up to the age of one year. There seemed to be no point in stopping there so she went on to year two, then year three. When a boy was born the clothes for the first year could be used without arousing too much comment, but by the time Daniel was two, and stocky, people who knew his sex found it amusing to see him in skirts and a frilly sun hat. By this time his father was in the Army and unable to put in a word about proper male costume for his son. There were several photographs in the archive of Daniel dressed as a girl. He always understood the economic argument for using up the clothes and was strangely indifferent to the implications for his psyche – mainly because they never manifested themselves. What did interest him was whether the disappointment of having a boy affected his mother in any way. When he asked her the question directly in a letter from school she wrote back to say that his father's joy in having a son to succeed him did away with any lingering regrets of her own.

Daniel told this story to Cook as they walked round Stonehenge, having paused in the car journey along the A313 towards the West Country. The archive was in the boot of the car and that night over dinner in the *Flying Horse* near Padstow, at Cook's request, Daniel produced these bizarre photographic images of himself.

'I wonder how different it is being female,' Cook mused, cutting into a piece of cheese. 'We're always being told how differently they feel to ourselves, but is it the case? You're a good person to consult.'

'Why, sir?'

'Aren't the people most important in your life your mother and grandmother?'

'Well, there's my brother. He's important.'

'Not old enough to be a person, I'd say.'

Daniel frowned. Was his grandmother a more potent force than Mrs White? He had enough sense not to articulate the question in front of Cook, who was watching him with a sly, shy smile, though his eyes were sharp.

'Are you very close to your mother, sir?'

'Don't try to get out of answering my question.'

'I'm not, sir . . .

'What is a woman? What is a man? What powers do they have as separate forces, and in combination?'

Daniel protested that these questions were far beyond him. He could talk about beauty, but not power. Much of the power of women was mundane – when it came to beauty, they were a delicious mystery. He trusted that.

'Will you ever get married, sir?'

Cook glared, hardly able to believe his ears. 'What's that got to do with it?' he snapped. 'We're talking about you not me.'

Daniel held his spoon still. He was imagining this scene being replayed with Cook as his stepfather. One thing they would not be discussing (until much later in life) would be women. If Cook was ever his father and they were on holiday by the sea they would be talking about other matters altogether.

'This custard is slightly burnt, sir.'

The frown disappeared from Cook's brow. 'Shall I send it back?' he said, relieved the difficult moment had passed. 'You can always have the cheese instead.'

'Actually, I quite like the taste of burnt custard, sir. I got used to it at school.'

Cook laughed, saying he was not free to comment on anything as subversive as that.

The mid-April sea on the North Devon coast was cold. Breakers on the steeply shelving beach and rocks just under the surface made getting into the water a slow process. The offshore wind had a chill, cutting edge. A recent storm had ripped seaweed from its moorings. Banks of it floated in the surf, winding round Daniel's legs as he waded in. He shivered and wrapped his arms across his chest for warmth.

'Get straight into the water!' Cook shouted from behind him. 'It's the only way!'

Daniel raised a hand in the air, half-looking over his shoulder. As he did so, a big wave crashed onto his chest. He staggered, trying to keep his balance. The sand moved round his feet, sucked away in the undertow. When the next wave raced in he threw himself forward, breaking the crest. The cold hit his head like a fist of ice and he gasped, striking out to swim into deeper water.

He heard Cook cheering.

Using a strong crawl, he headed towards the calmer water beyond where the breakers began. As his face went under with each roll of his shoulders he expelled air through the salt water, thinking: This is where my father swam. This is what it felt like – the same cold, the same rocks, the same wind, the same weed.

A line of rock jutted out into the sea to his right, waves crashing over the top. He headed for the furthermost point as a marker for his swim. There he would turn and swim back to the beach, going in with the breakers. He felt the current and saw how it was slowing him down but he was a strong swimmer and knew he could make the distance.

By now the cold had left his consciousness. It was part of him.

The tight band of iron round his head had lessened its grip, though it still throbbed between his eyes. Swimming out further he stopped, turned over onto his back and floated, kicking the grey-green water into foam, looking up at the clouds, following a gull's white cross through the sky.

There were six names on the bird.

Names from the tiny crumpled photograph sent by the Army with *Baharine Farm, Nr. Madjez, (In the Cactus Grove), Map reference J. 5632* written on the back.

Names he knew by heart, like a poem.

He saw his mother's face pale with anger, berating him because he could not remember a thing about her man. Duck-diving, he plunged down more than the length of his body, groping for the comfort of the bottom. It wasn't there.

His blood was slowing in the heart-searching cold. Numbness penetrated his skin, thickened his joints. He stopped swimming and let himself drift into bladder wrack and flotsam, lying with his legs and arms outstretched like a star, feeling himself a fragment of a greater body blown apart, hanging on a cactus spine. As the current pulled him towards the rocks he saw Cook bounding over the gaps, waving his arms.

'Are you alright, Rogers?' he was yelling over the sound of the waves on the rocks. 'You went too far out!'

Daniel trod water and waved reassuringly. When he called out that he was fine it sounded as though his voice belonged to someone else.

'If you need help, I can't swim, I'm afraid,' Cook yelled, teetering on the edge of a black blade of rock. 'Please come out right away if you can!'

Daniel shook his head. 'I want to go back the way I came,' he shouted. 'See you at the beach.'

Turning away, he swam as powerfully as he could.

As his body turned and twisted he wondered whether the vision was something he'd induced.

Or had history given it to him?

As he rode the waves, his strength and speed through the water was exhilarating. When he was in the shallows and able to stand he discovered there was no strength left in his legs.

He had to stand still for a while in the breakers, waiting until he could come in to the beach without falling over.

Cook watched him, waiting with a towel, silent, indignant but respectful. He held the towel up for Daniel to wrap around himself.

'I thought you were swimming right out and never coming back,' he said. 'You wouldn't do that to me, would you?'

In spite of chattering teeth, Daniel grinned. Cook had confessed that he suffered from the teacherly delusion that he could read the mind of those he taught.

'No, sir. I'd never do that.'

'I was having nightmares thinking how I'd have to tell your mother.'

Daniel felt an urge to explain how he had two lives to lead – his father's and his own. There was no need to remember the dead man as he was. That other forgotten, fragmented self was incorporated into his own being. There were times when this powerful sense of proxy extended even further to include the lives of both his grandfathers – the living, wasted drunk and the dead tiger. He would fulfil their promise also – three men in one boy.

He eventually confided a fraction of this thought to Cook – saying he had a lot to achieve with his life and would never endanger it. The underlying vicarious theme of his destiny – a theme that often seemed preposterous even to himself – he left out.

There were times when, enclouded by religious dreams, he prayed to be released from the task of living out other lives. It was when he had a book in his hands that it made sense. That was what authors did. When he picked the huge Bible up off the church lectern, the weight was of authors upon authors upon authors all living out other lives.

Rubbing his hair and peering out from under the towel, he took long, shuddering breaths and ran around in circles for a while to get his circulation going.

'You're blue around the mouth,' Cook said, 'and trembling all over. I don't want you catching a chill. '

127

He produced a hip-flask of whisky from his coat pocket and gave Daniel a swig. The spirit flared down his throat. He realised how deeply cold he was, how remote his feelings had become. His reserve buckled. The desire to talk became as compulsive as the need to get warm.

'Was it a mad thing to do, sir?'

'Not at all. It was there to be done.'

'I wonder about myself sometimes.'

The history master sat on his haunches looking at him with curiosity. 'Stay as you are,' he said calmly. 'Don't worry about thinking yourself odd.'

Daniel laughed as he eased his shirt over his damp, chilled skin. 'I don't mind about that,' he said, teeth chattering. 'What I care about is whether I'm wasting my time with these thoughts. I reckon it all started when my brother was born and they said he was a reincarnation of our father. He looks like him, apparently. I don't. They gave him his name. Maybe I thought it was up to me to do something as well . . . I don't know . . . '

The cold shook him so hard he couldn't do up the buttons of his shirt. Cook frowned, wondering if he should help. As the teacher stood up and raised his hands to offer assistance, Daniel grabbed the pullover and dragged it over his head, leaving the shirt open underneath, cuffs undone.

'But he's just a little kid,' he blurted, folding up the wet towel. 'He isn't my father! They know that. What are they playing at? What's it going to do to him if he believes it's true?'

Cook suggested that as the younger brother grew up and the pains of war and loss receded, adjustments would be made and common-sense would come into its own.

'I don't know how you can say that, sir,' Daniel shouted, stumbling up the slope of the beach, shaking his head, shoes in hand. 'When has common sense won out? I haven't seen it happen yet.'

Cook followed in his footsteps over the belt of washed sand

left by the ebbing tide. He was enough of an academic to consider the question even when it came from a source as troubled as Daniel.

A time when common-sense had come into its own?

When it *mattered?* Think about it.

'The eighteenth-century Enlightenment!' he called out. 'Perhaps the Athens of Pericles . . . the Roman Republic . . . the Swiss Federation in the fifteenth-century . . . Let's see . . . What else is there?'

The figure ahead threw the shoes high in the air ahead and broke into a stumbling run to escape from the rest of the list.

Bad weather came in from the Atlantic overnight and the fore-cast said it would remain unsettled for the rest of the week. Because his car was a small Austin convertible with a leaky roof, Cook decided to cut the south-western tour short and retreat northwards to his family home near Chesterfield. As they were leaving the bed and breakfast Daniel asked if they could have a last look at Lee Bay. He wanted to find the exact spot from which the postcard photograph had been taken, identified on the card as from the golf links.

It was only half-past eight in the morning and no one was on the course, which lay on the southern side. The strong wind blowing in from the west combined with the running tide was creating a cauldron of spume below the coastal cliffs. Down in the rocky bay where Daniel had swum, high breakers rolled in crashing onto the beach below a road they would have to take northwards. It was a violent scene, the skies torn into strips of dark grey and azure, the ocean full of foaming energy. It satisfied Daniel to see it that way.

Cook asked if it was alright to move on. He seemed anxious about his car and the distance they had to travel.

Daniel had noticed that the teacher was a slow starter. When he met him at the breakfast table, apart from a terse greeting, there was minimal conversation. The man either sat and stared into his cup or closed his eyes as though in a trance. A creature of routine, he only came fully alive at nine o'clock – the time of the first lesson he had to teach.

After running the gauntlet of spray and the flooded road, at Daniel's request they took the back road to Ilfracombe then branched off from the coast and climbed to the top of Exmoor. Cook wasn't keen on the move but the choice between staying on the coast and being higher up was of no real relevance. The leaking Austin, buffeted by the howling wind, rain slipping through rents in the canvas hood, was the wrong vehicle for the conditions in both cases.

They stopped in a cleared area off the road sheltered by gorse bushes. As the cloud was ripped aside by the wind they could glimpse the great naked moor all around them. Cook sat at the wheel, a cloth in his hand, aimlessly wiping the inside of the windscreen.

'Don't you like wild weather, sir?' Daniel asked.

'Saw too much of it in the Navy,' Cook muttered, stuffing folded newspaper into a gap between the canvas and the body-work. 'It has a bad effect on me, I'm afraid. If it goes on and on I become quite depressed. There have been times when I've thought of emigrating to sunnier climes.'

Daniel could see the melancholy at work. The shyness and kindness were being put under pressure. Cook didn't want to be up on Exmoor in a gale.

'I was told a story by my gran about my father,' Daniel said brightly, wanting to alleviate the gloom. 'It probably happened while he was on Exmoor. Would you like to hear it?'

Cook nodded and tried to smile. 'That's what we're here for, isn't it?' he said curtly.

'It's vulgar, sir, but it made me laugh when my gran told it to me.'

'Vulgarity is nothing to a Navy man, Rogers. Go ahead.'

The story wasn't written down anywhere. Daniel carried it around in his memory with other fragments he'd scavenged.

This made the space in his mind left by not remembering the real man less painful. As he told the story, because he was nervous about telling it, he clutched the shaft of the hand brake for support.

'My father's platoon sergeant was a real tyrant, sir. All the men hated him. During the manoeuvres the battalion stopped for a rest and the sergeant went off into the bushes to have a . . . Are you sure you don't mind, sir?'

Cook raised his eyes to heaven and clutched the steering-wheel.

'Do get on with it,' he said. 'I'm not your maiden aunt.'

'Well, he went for a shit, sir. My father got a long-handled frying pan and followed him. He crept up behind the sergeant and slid the frying pan under him and caught what he did, then took the frying pan away. When the sergeant looked round to see what he'd done, there was nothing there. The sergeant had a nervous breakdown.'

Cook rested his forehead on the steering-wheel. A tremor passed through his shoulders.

'It shows my father had an imagination, doesn't it, sir?'

'If only Hitler had met him at the right moment in world history . . . ' Cook wheezed, wiping his eye. 'That's an excellent story.'

'All the other men in the battalion liked him. He had a good sense of humour, he wrote my mother romantic poems, he could draw pretty well, and he was a champion dancer. What I haven't got so far, though, are things that were *wrong* with him – apart from being pretty vulgar – you know, faults.'

'Isn't looking for those a risky business?'

'Getting my mother to talk about him in a critical way is impossible.'

'Need that surprise you?'

'If he had weaknesses, she would know better than anyone, wouldn't she? He must have had some. Everybody does.'

Cook started the engine. As he nosed the car out of the

clearing onto the road he glanced sideways at his passenger. Daniel's head was resting against the window and his eyes were closed.

The Austin broke down while they were staying at Cook's family home, a farm outside Chesterfield. The car had to be towed into the nearby village garage for repairs. While they were at the farm, snow came.

Cook's mother, Delia, a tall, broad-faced impressive woman with dark eyes and a strong, searching look, ran the farm with Albert, her younger brother. Cook's father lived separately in a room rented in the village and was seldom seen by the rest of the family.

It was clear to Daniel from the beginning that Delia viewed his visit with suspicion. He had no difficulty in working out the cause.

'Are you very, very good at history, young man?' she said to him over tea an hour after they arrived. 'I think you must be. My son wouldn't take such trouble with you otherwise. Not that I think history is much use to anyone.'

Cook made fun of the question so Daniel didn't have to answer it.

His customary passive calm had left him as they walked through the door on arrival, replaced by an uncharacteristic belligerence.

'What my mother is saying to you, Daniel, is, for heaven's sake don't be a teacher when you grow up . . . unless its maths or agricultural science,' he joked loudly. 'And whatever you do, don't go to Cambridge or you'll be corrupted.'

Delia kept her eyes relentlessly on Daniel, watching every move he made eating and drinking. 'D'you mind me asking how old you are, young man?' she asked.

'I'll be thirteen next month,' Daniel replied, meeting her eye.

'You're big for your age.'

'That's what I'm told, Mrs Cook.'

'I could do with you here on the farm. How are all your other friends? I'm sure you've got lots,' she said, not shifting her gaze. 'Met any nice girls?'

Daniel was about to answer the question as best he could when Cook took over because the question had actually been aimed at him. His bluff, deflective reply – that Daniel wanted to be a writer – was designed to prevent the probe into his private life. His mother smiled knowingly before releasing Daniel from her scrutiny.

'If you ever want a real job, young man, you know where to come,' she said, offering him another slice of cake. 'I could use a bit more muscle here.'

Cook showed Daniel the farm on foot, always returning to the great one-sided arch of the abbey west window, sketching out the ground plan of the monastery in the snow, describing the daily routine of the monks, ringing the bell for Terce, Nones, Vespers – replaying a childhood game, the one that had trapped his mind for ever. In contrast to that simplicity, his talk became deeper and more complex. If they were out for a couple of hours Daniel often came back having said virtually nothing because Cook never stopped talking.

On the day before the car was due back on the road and Daniel could be driven home, Cook took him on a long walk up the valley, talking incessantly about the beauty of time within buildings – how history is put upon the earth to be worn down and destroyed, though one fragment might be venerated for ever for what it *implied*, which need not be a truth.

They had ended up beside the broken arch again.

Daniel's mind was exhausted with trying to keep up.

'The structure that remains is not true history. It is not a record of what went before,' Cook stressed, gazing upwards. 'The whole of that structure was greater and more fulfilled than any mere remnant, but my arch is truer in its meaning as a *symbol* of a special power. What would you think that special power is?'

133

Caught on the hop, Daniel groped for something to say. He was tired and confused by Cook's perpetual ruminations. He eventually managed to scrape together the reply that the special power was the medieval Church, perhaps.

'Not quite – but close. The special power is survival, which you know all about. We could say that applies to the medieval Church in terms of the Papacy we have today – but is it the same organisation? Has it improved? Just because it survived doesn't mean it got better.'

Cook wandered up and down over the tussocky snow-clad grass, making a line with his walking-stick. 'When I'm under the arch I know for certain that at some time it must fall down. It could be now. I've stood like this so often, waiting for masonry to fall on my head. D'you know what I'm saying?'

'I think so, sir,' Daniel lied.

'It's been here for eight hundred years. When will be the moment of its final collapse? Why not right now? And why has it been left standing here when all the other stone was stolen?'

Daniel suggested it might be too difficult and dangerous to get down.

'No, I disagree. It was spared for a purpose. The respect we give a symbol of something we've lost – like this arch symbolises the peace those monks had, a peace I crave – is much more intense than the respect we would give the whole monastery if it were still here, working. It would be more like a factory to us . . . yes, a prayer factory, wouldn't it? '

'More than likely, sir.'

'Imagine it in its heyday. If we came upon it, we would look first for the betrayal of its ideals, its worldliness. But because we only have this symbol in a field with a couple of cows we think of spiritual purity first. Wouldn't you agree?'

'Yes, sir.'

'Such is mankind, Rogers.'

'Yes, sir.'

'A most peculiar animal.'

'Very peculiar, sir.'

Cook patted the stone of the arch. 'This is my archive, you realise,' he declared with an upcurving, slightly demonic smile. 'But to the rest of my family, who can be very mundane when they've a mind to, it's nothing more than a nuisance. They'd love to bring it down. But I've personally seen to it through a solicitor dealing directly with the Ministry of Works that they can't ever demolish it. There are laws in place for the preservation of ancient monuments in this country. That hasn't made me exactly popular with my family. In fact I've probably lost my inheritance because of what I've done. But it's worth it because I'm convinced that if the arch comes down I come down with it.'

During the car journey north to Liverpool Daniel contemplated Cook's forthcoming meeting with his mother. By Crewe he had decided that all thoughts of having the history master as a stepfather were futile. They would never get on. His mother had left school at fourteen. A first-class honours from Cambridge would never marry a shop assistant.

He was also aware that the more educated he himself became, the further he would be taken away from his mother – and this saddened him because they were bound together at the heart. Already there were issues not spoken about – assumptions made – secrets kept from each other. She was a little afraid of him because other forces were shaping his character, insisting he must change. An unspoken agreement existed that there must be two different spheres of influence if conflict was to be avoided. She had to trust the school and he knew only too well how untrustworthy the school was – but the school didn't trust his family because its untrustworthiness was the reason he was at the school in the first place.

There being no telephone at Daniel's house, Cook had sent a telegram to say he would be bringing him home to the door but couldn't give an exact time. In spite of providing the farm's address, no return telegram had been received so Cook had to assume the arrangement was acceptable.

When they arrived, a neighbour came round with a key to let them in. She said Daniel's grandmother and mother had gone down to the Dock Road police station to escort his grandfather home after a night in the cells for being drunk and disorderly. The neighbour added on her own account that this must be the last straw for her friend, Maud. After years of loyalty and enduring the man's selfish, disgusting ways, how could any wife tolerate this kind of public humiliation? The poor woman couldn't hold her head up in the street.

Cook's immediate reaction was to remove himself as quickly as possible and start on his journey to visit his brother. He allowed Daniel to make him a cup of tea before leaving. As they were sitting by the slacked-up fire that was burning in the grate, Daniel got up and went into the hall because he thought he'd heard a car draw up outside. He opened the front door. It was a taxi containing his mother and grandparents.

His grandfather's head was bent and he was groaning. The two grim-looking women virtually carried him down the path. They said nothing to Daniel, only looked at him with dead, disappointed expressions. Once they'd got the man through the door and closed it, they made him support himself by holding onto the post of the bannisters at the bottom of the stairs while they took off their coats. His eyes were enormously dark behind his spectacles, contrasting with the sweaty paleness of the rest of his face.

'What are you doing here?' he croaked at Daniel. 'I thought you were supposed to be at the seaside somewhere.'

'Hello, Grandad,' Daniel said coldly. 'We had to give up because the weather was so bad.'

'I've got recurring malaria from the Black Sea . . . '

'Sorry to hear that. Weren't you there a very long time ago?'

'Comes back every now and again. Your legs go. Would they listen? Would they buggery. Once a policeman never a man.'

The women pulled and pushed him up the stairs without saying a word. Daniel's mother gave him a look that told him exactly what he must do. Encountering Cook's car parked outside the house she had guessed that the worst case of embarrassment imaginable was about to happen. It had to be headed off. Daniel returned to the back room where Cook was already standing by the fire, ready to go.

'I'm sorry this has happened, sir. Thank you very much for the trip,' Daniel said, holding out his hand to be shaken.

Cook shook his hand and held onto it for a few seconds. 'See you next term, Dan. We've got plenty of work to do,' he said, 'plenty of places to go. I'll be on my way.'

Daniel led him through the kitchen and out of the side door so he wouldn't hear anything from upstairs. As the Austin drove off up the street it represented the departure of a particular kind of sanity – a kind he would only find at home with the aid of his archive (which was already back under the bed) and his constructive interpretation of it.

As the car disappeared around the corner, he realised there was an advantage to be found in Cook seeing the situation for himself – but the boy hoped it wouldn't set off a train of prejudice or charity that would distort their relationship.

CHAPTER TEN

The following morning Daniel was in his room playing with his brother when there was a knock at the door. His mother or grandmother would never have knocked so he knew it must be his grandfather. When he opened the door he encountered a half-dressed spectre of hurt and bad temper.

'Help me do up this shirt,' he muttered. 'I'm going round to the doctor's. You two will have to come with me. Your grandmother's out doing the shopping.'

As they walked round to the surgery, which was in the next street, the boys walked on either side so he could put his hands on their shoulders and shuffle along. Neighbours stared as they passed by and were cursed by God With Us for their nosiness.

'You don't put a sick man in the cells. What do they know?' he muttered. 'I've been treated very unfairly. The doctor will have to give me a note for the magistrate. If I get a sentence our ship will go down. I'll lose my job, you'll have to leave that school, your mother will get fired.'

John asked what ship was going down.

'The family ship, son. The whole family. If I'm found guilty we'll all be ruined.'

'Me as well, Grandad?' John asked.

'You as well. Your future will be under a black cloud.'

When they reached the surgery it was discovered that a locum was acting for the regular doctor. Daniel and his brother sat in the waiting-room on either side of their grandfather reading comics. When he was called to see the doctor they helped him to his feet and across to the door, then handed him over to the nurse.

Daniel heard raised voices in the consulting-room, then his grandfather came out coughing, eyes moving madly behind his thick lenses. 'He says there's nothing on my records. He says he can't give me a note just on my say-so. He wouldn't know a malaria sufferer from a man with the common cold, the daft get!'

'Don't be upset, Grandad,' Daniel said, helping him to sit down under the eyes of the enthralled waiting-room audience. 'We can sort it out.'

'I've had this condition since the end of the First World War! And he says there's no record! What kind of National Health Service is this?'

In a whisper, Daniel said that he remembered a letter that might be useful that was with a lot of family papers under his bed. His grandfather stared at him.

'What kind of a letter?'

'Why don't I run home and get it for you, then you can show it to the doctor?'

Daniel left the waiting-room and ran back to the house, went upstairs and searched through the archive. There it was – a faded, dog-eared note from the Tropical Ward of the Royal Infirmary from 1920, dated 16th July, signed by M. G. Thompson M.B, B.Sc. DT.M., confirming that Emmanuel Hughes had been in the hospital for four weeks as an in-patient suffering from malaria and now needed convalescent tonic treatment.

He ran back to the surgery and presented it to his grandfather who couldn't read it because he didn't have the right glasses on, so Daniel had to read it to him.

'He can't argue with that, can he?' God With Us cackled elatedly. 'That'll show him.'

When the nurse opened the door to the consulting-room again the yellowed document was waved at her. She read the note and agreed that the doctor should see it.

When the second interview took place, Daniel and his brother went in as well because God With Us had taken a turn for the worse and needed them by his side for support. The doctor, who was a young man not yet hardened, looked at the note carefully.

139

'With the best will in the world, this is thirty years old, Mr Hughes,' he commented, 'and it makes no mention of *recurrent* malaria.'

'That's the kind I have.'

'Had you been drinking? You've already been drinking this morning, I fear. Isn't that so?'

'The two young constables who arrested me were wet behind the ears, straight out of training school. In my job, I have to take a drink for business purposes. I deal direct with ship's captains and men from the dockers' union.'

The doctor reluctantly agreed to write a note to the magistrate's court to confirm that Emmanuel Hughes had contracted malaria while on military service in Turkey. A blood sample would be tested to determine whether the malaria was still present in recurrent form. If it was, the symptoms could be said to be very similar to that of intoxication.

'Will that do, Mr Hughes?'

'It'll have to, I suppose.'

While the boys watched with interest, a vein was found in their grandfather's arm and blood extracted to be put in a glass tube and sent to the laboratory. Daniel noticed how dark the colour of the blood was and the presence of foam on top. This blood was, in a fourth part, his own blood. It had the power to influence his future. It would affect him and he might not be able to do anything about it. If his father's blood was stronger and more dominant than his mother's, (she had the suspect blood of God With Us in her veins), there was hope Daniel would turn out to be more like his father – which made determining the dead man's true character even more important.

The lucky one was his brother, John, who *was* his father, supposedly. He had nothing to worry about because, if that was the case, he had by-passed his mother's blood altogether.

All this eugenical theory made Daniel wonder how free anyone was who was born into this world.

When the boys got back to the house with their grandfather he returned the note from the Tropical Ward of the Royal Infirmary to Daniel so he could put it back under his bed for safe-keeping. This act of trust from the titular male head of the family made Daniel feel he was finally approved as keeper of the archive and that was his function from now on, accepted by all.

In view of the doctor's note, the magistrate's court delayed the hearing until the results of the test arrived. When they did so, the presence of malarial parasites hidden in the blood was confirmed. But they had only emerged because the patient's immunity had been drastically reduced by excessive drinking. Faced by this conundrum, the magistrate – who had many cases to deal with that day, including twenty-three for drunk and disorderly – decided to dismiss the case. He advised the defiant accused, who was a hard-working and diligent super-intendent of warehouses recently engaged in vital war supply, (and a Great War veteran to boot, twice gassed, half his stomach removed, having served with his gun-team on the Western Front and in several provinces of the Ottoman Empire), to take a personal lesson from the test results and reduce his intake of alcohol so the parasites would not be aroused and come out of hiding at inopportune times in future.

A few days before going back to school for the summer term, Daniel asked his grandfather how the magistrate's court had worked out. He was grudgingly told the result, and advised never to trust a policeman. When Daniel raised the matter with his grandmother shortly afterwards, he wondered aloud how over thirty years when his grandfather had probably been drunk every day he had managed to be arrested on the only one he was sober. His grandmother got very angry at this, called him a disrespectful young swine, said she didn't like disloyalty in any-one, and pushed him out of her kitchen.

CHAPTER ELEVEN

On arrival for the start of the summer term – Daniel's last at the Junior House – he noticed a change in Mule's attitude towards him.

This new benignity was crudely acted out, and the origin of it was the Old Man.

Within a week Daniel had the motivation for the new initiative before him. After yet another strength–flexibility–stamina testing session Oliphant let slip that a major change in school sports policy had been decided during the Easter holidays. Frustrated by the obstacles being placed in the path of his drive for public school status, the headmaster had dropped all his ingrained north-of-the-border prejudice against cricket, the quintessentially English game. A drive had been initiated to put Lord Mendora Land College up there with the best. From now on cricket was to be as important as rugby.

'You're a natural fast bowler, Rogers,' Oliphant said, stretching the tape-measure across Daniel's shoulders. 'You've got the height, the physique, and the aggression. By the time you get to the fifth-form we want you bowling at high speed but with accuracy rather than your uncontrolled hurling of the ball.' He paused, studying a card from his files. 'That's what it says here. You're too erratic . . . too unreliable in terms of length and direction. There's also a note from Mr Cook who thinks you must learn to swing the ball away from the batsman. D'you know what he's talking about?'

Oliphant was even more of a Scotsman than the headmaster. Cricket to him was a waste of good exercise time. Fat, slow people could play cricket very well. It was more of a mental than a physical game and therefore not for him.

'Mr Cook has said that kind of thing about my bowling in net practice, sir,' Daniel replied. 'You have to shine one side of the ball on your trousers.'

Oliphant gave him a look shadowed with incomprehension. 'I'll be honest with you, Rogers,' he said with a tight little grin, 'that kind of technicality is a complete mystery to me.' He wrapped the measuring tape round Daniel's relaxed right bicep. 'But I can say, notwithstanding, that fast bowling is the one aspect of cricket that interests me. I approve of its full effort, its need for energy, fire and brimstone. D'you know what I mean?'

'Yes, sir, I do.'

'We believe your impetuosity can be harnessed. You're the only boy in your year we can make into . . . ' he consulted the card from his files again, *the pace weapon the 1st XI will need in 1955–6*. You should be flattered.'

'I am, sir.'

'Truly? You're not laughing at me?'

'No, sir.'

'I've worked out a training scheme for the physical development side. Mr Cook and Mr Pacey are the cricket experts and they'll help me with you. It's a pity we lost the Reverend Long when we did.'

'He was a very good slow left-arm spin bowler, sir. He got five for nineteen at Taunton.'

'So I understand. Mrs Long has been so good as to lend me the manuscript of the book he was writing at the time of his death, and there's an entire chapter on fast bowling, which, though not his speciality, he knew a great deal about. I showed the manuscript to Mr Cook and Mr Pacey and they say the ideas on fast bowling are revolutionary.'

Daniel commented that the ideas the Reverend Long had on most subjects were revolutionary if one could understand them.

'Don't be disrespectful, Rogers. He was a great loss to our little community – part of the mix that made it work so well.'

'Anything he ever said or wrote has my respect, sir.'

'Good. You should understand that height is critical for a fast bowler. In the next three years you must grow another four inches and we must make your arms as long as possible.'

Daniel expressed the hope this wouldn't make his appearance apelike because he was planning a career as an intellectual.

'Everything will remain in proportion,' Oliphant assured him. 'At your present rate of development we should, with a little encouragement, hit our target. Hold your right arm straight up over your head and hold the end of the tape.'

Daniel did what he was told. Oliphant stood on a box, reached up and drew the drum of the tape down to the ground.

'I note that you'll be thirteen in three weeks, Rogers,' he said.

'That's right, sir.'

'Today, the maximum height you could bring a ball down from is seven foot two and a half inches. By the time you're sixteen we want that to be at least seven foot eight inches. According to Henry Long's calculations that would mean you'll be capable – all things being equal – of bowling at a hundred and twenty miles an hour – which is forty miles an hour faster than my car will go.'

'That's terrific, sir.'

'It's all science, you see. I'll arrange for you to have cricket boots with extra long spikes for better purchase during a high-speed run-up. Your mother won't have to pay for them.'

'Thank you, sir.'

'The recommended run-up for a six-foot four bowler – your anticipated height – is twenty yards. You must accelerate from a standing start to deliver the ball when you're moving at . . . ' here he worked a small ivory slide-rule, squinting at the calibrated scale, 'twenty one point five miles per hour. That's a very good first phase for a hundred yards sprint. So you see how fit we have to get you in three years, Rogers.'

'Yes, sir.'

Oliphant put all his papers and tapes in a document case and held it under his arm, blue eyes bright, ginger hairs of his eyebrows and nostrils glinting. 'It's all very well to agree,

Rogers, but you have been a most difficult boy in your time,' he said. 'To be frank, you've come very near to losing your place at this school. I don't want to waste my life mastering a game I don't particularly like to no purpose. The headmaster wants us to *win*. Do we understand each other?'

Daniel looked at the ground to hide his smile. He liked the PT master. At times he had put him on the list of bachelor teachers he might try to interest his mother in. And there was a touch of Henry Long digressive magic there, a wandering, mildly troubled gentleness – a nature that wasn't quite certain what it was doing on earth. The two men could have been soulmates, but they hadn't even been friends.

'I will try to make my arms longer, sir,' Daniel promised. 'Perhaps if I hang from the wall-bars for half-an-hour every day that might help?'

Oliphant frowned and shook his head. 'You see what I mean? You're mocking me, boy. This has to be serious. It's part of your way forward. Take it!'

It was not a good early summer. On June 10th Daniel was under instructions to watch the First Eleven playing cricket against Charterhouse. After an hour of play, a snowstorm came in from the east. In their whites, the players on the field disappeared from view. The only contact spectators on the boundary had with the game's progress was audial – the sound of bat on ball, the fielding side's talk and smatterings of applause at the wicket. In order to let the game proceed the umpires told the bowlers to moderate their speed until the storm had passed. When the snow stopped falling and the air cleared, the spectators saw a slow-motion ballet, white gliding over white, on the new-fallen snow. The match should have been abandoned but the visiting team had come a long way and both sides, urged on by the Old Man sitting wrapped in a rug in the pavilion, wanted to play to a result.

Sheltering in the lee of the pavilion Daniel guessed, with the writerly part of himself, at the sermon Henry Long would have concocted out of the freak snowfall. The nub of it would go something like this:

Boys, because in cricket both sides wear identical white kit and cannot be told apart, the snow is telling us that in life it is, in essence, always the same team playing against itself.

We are all in whites at birth, only evil puts us in team colours. Love one another.

As the players made a quagmire of the wicket, he realised the full extent to which Henry's death had removed a strain of thought from Lord Mendora's Land College, and how much he needed to keep it alive. To survive the entrenched power structures of school life he must participate, taking advantage of whatever was offered, while keeping his mental distance. To find the meaning, and the depth of these advantages, he must not retreat. The Old Man thought of him in terms of a future being, not a present and abiding problem. That was the current in the stream he must steer along.

Mr O'Leary the groundsman strode out and told the umpires to stop the game before the cricket square he'd prepared for the summer was completely ruined. He did this without going over to ask the Old Man's permission. He was so incensed at the destruction of his handiwork that he couldn't trust himself to keep a civil tongue in his head.

The Old Man merely removed the rug from knees and went to the changing-room toilet. The players trooped off the field in good humour, basking in the strangeness of the whole event, which had created a light-hearted, friendly mood between the two schools. When the Old Man returned into the main pavilion he shook hands with the Charterhouse cricket master, shared a few wry comments on the weather, then took him off for a warming glass of whisky in his office.

Later on he confessed to Oliphant that he had been glad of the snow because it was common knowledge that the First Eleven was a weak team and Charterhouse would have beaten them hollow. This losing situation would have to be endured throughout the fixture list with wins only possible against Bedales and Frensham Heights, experimental liberal schools where sport wasn't taken seriously, and the summer after that wouldn't be any better. Important schools were already muttering about whether playing Lord Mendora Land College at cricket was worth the effort. The highly-trained team of 1955–6 would change all that.

Daniel found it difficult to sleep that summer. Having to be in bed at nine o'clock when it was still light, his mind often turned to what he was missing in the outside world. The noises of the dormitory didn't help. Twenty boys talking in their sleep, snoring, wanking, whispering, sliding around on blankets, pestering, sometimes drove him to go out for a walk in the middle of the night, especially in warm weather. He wasn't the only one to take this recourse. Other boys clambered down the same stout drainpipe, responding to the moon and stars, ready for anything.

The farm's eight heavy horses were on the brink of redundancy caused by the school's purchase of a fleet of grey Ferguson tractors. The horses had their summer pasture in a big field adjoining Junior House. Many of the boys were the sons of farmers and liked to show their power over animals. One night when Daniel was returning from a nocturnal ramble in the woods, he heard the thunder of hooves ahead. Emerging from the trees he saw the huge horses galloping round the field with half-a-dozen boys waving from behind the fence. When Daniel joined them he was told that Vorley was on the back of Old Fred, a peaceable Suffolk Punch who'd suddenly started a stampede. Vorley couldn't get off because the other horses kept running alongside. If he dismounted he'd be trampled.

Vorley went past, pale under the moon, legs sticking out virtually at right angles across the broad back of the great horse. He was sobbing and cursing with rage.

'They've been going round and round the field for ages,

147

Rogers,' one boy said. 'Can't you do something? You're his house-captain.'

The horses went past again, clods flying from their feathered hooves, whites of their eyes gleaming.

'They'll stop when they've had enough,' Daniel said off-handedly. 'It's Vorley's fault for showing off.'

They continued to watch, waving at Vorley each time he passed. Daniel recalled the boy's last exploit, performed in front of the whole house walking down for church – taunting one of the Friesian bulls when it was out with the cows, shouting and throwing stones at it. When the bull started to get annoyed, Vorley had swaggered up, kicked it on the nose and stood there, arms akimbo, cursing the beast as a coward. The bull had shaken its head, bellowed, then turned and fled. All the boys had applauded that day. Vorley claimed it was a deed worthy of the best Spanish matador.

Old Fred began to slow down, falling back from the lead until he was galloping alone at the rear. When closest to the fence where the boys stood, Vorley suddenly swivelled himself round and slid off over the horse's glossy backside. As soon as he hit the ground he ran to the fence and squeezed under the bottom railing, then lay in a heap on the grass, clutching his knees and shaking.

'Fucking stupid horse!' he seethed, teeth chattering.

'You won't do that again in a hurry, will you?' Daniel said, giving him a prod with the toe of his shoe. 'Even Old Fred knows a moron when he's got one on his back.'

'I'll show him!' Vorley snarled, getting up and shaking his fist at the dark field. 'No fucking horse gets the better of me!'

Daniel waited behind as the other boys accompanied Vorley back to the dormitory. There would be a queue for the drainpipe. He leant on the fence and watched the ghostly shapes of the horses move about the moonlit field. These were the descendants of war-horses. Cook had told him the story of Polish cavalry charging German machine-guns at the start of the Second World

War, thirty years after the petrol engine first appeared on a battlefield. Redundancy took its time. War kept its grandest postures to the bitter end. In the archive was a photograph of his grandfather in army uniform mounted on a horse called Charlie that had been shot from under him. He claimed to have wept as he sheltered behind the carcase, the battle raging around him.

Old Fred came and rested his jaw on a fence-post. He was a favourite with the boys. They brought him apples and biscuits. His neighs, whinnies, snuffles and grunts were a language they imitated at the fence while they gave him food. Vorley had probably got on his back while he was being fed. Even now, in the middle of the night, the old horse wanted something. Daniel tore up a fistful of grass and went over, holding it up to the velvety muzzle, copying the noises Old Fred was making.

Not sure why, he kissed the horse's cheek.

By some strange entropic energy – an equal and opposite force to that which creates passionate fads in enclosed societies – the Cosh Gang sank into obscurity, although it didn't disappear altogether. Bryant, the presiding spirit, concentrated his attention instead on researches into Red Indian culture and the Age of the Dinosaurs, and fell victim to glossomania, a mild pyschosis in which the sufferer is unable to stop talking. Being in lessons became an agony to him because he wasn't the one holding forth.

Eventually, Daniel was forced to avoid him.

The penny dropped after a while.

'Is our friendship at an end, then?' Bryant asked, catching up with Daniel during a walk up the cinder track to the main school one morning.

'Will I be given time to reply?'

'What d'you mean?'

'Before you need to start gassing again!' Daniel said, accelerating. 'Besides, I can't listen to you now. I'm running over some French oral prep in my head.'

'Come to London for half-term,' Bryant said, forced to trot to keep up. 'We can go and see *Irma la Douce.*'

'And spend three days having my ear chewed off? No, thanks.'

'Don't give up on me now, Dan, please . . . '

Something in the voice slowed Daniel down. He looked back and saw Bryant standing with head bowed, satchel between his feet. Other boys passed him, giving odd looks.

Daniel went back. 'What's this *don't give up on me?*' he demanded.

'I've got to see a psychiatrist in Harley Street on the Saturday morning of half-term. I've got an anxiety neurosis. Don't tell anyone, please. Will you come with me?' Bryant said, taking off his spectacles and cleaning them on the cuff of his shirt. 'Haven't you noticed how I've changed lately?'

Daniel frowned, picked the satchel up and hung it round Bryant's neck. 'We'll talk about it later, if you want. I've got to hurry.'

He ran off up the cinder track leaving Bryant behind. When he reached to gates at the top, he glanced back and the boy was still where he'd left him, standing with the sun behind him, satchel hanging over his knees.

Daniel walked back to him.

'Come on, we're going to be late,' he said, pushing him along. 'What are you anxious about?'

'Everything, apparently – but especially about losing my friends.' He moved faster now, striding out. 'They've been calling us Hitler and Mussolini, you know.'

'Us?'

'Of course. What d'you expect? It's Mule's fault. He made us do it and I've ended up with a guilt-complex. I'm finished with the Cosh Gang. Someone else can take over.'

The first bell for assembly started tolling. All the laggards on the cinder track broke into a canter.

On Midsummer's Day, Veronica, the Vampire squadron-leader's wife, who held a pilot's licence, took Pacey up for a spin in a light aircraft based at a club aerodrome. Accepting the invitation was a typical act of bravura on his part. He had ended their relationship only a week before.

Once off the ground Veronica flew the plane to the RAF aerodrome and dived it into the bedroom of her own house in the officers married quarters where she had lain with Pacey many times while her husband was out on night-flights.

Letters written to her parents, brothers and sisters, friends and her husband, telling them what she was going to do and why (her unquenchable passion for Pacey and her need for revenge) made it impossible to keep the story quiet. There were front-page newspaper pictures of the back half of the plane sticking out of the house. Reporters crawled round the school and village for days. In spite of the gates being closed and threats to prosecute newspapermen for trespass, virtually every boy in the school was collared by a reporter at some time, many of these newsmen being from other countries, attracted by the strangeness of the deed.

For the Old Man, it was the worst kind of publicity imaginable. However, his predicament touched the hearts of a few headmasters of public schools who knew him. They wrote and phoned, describing similar embarrassing incidents in the long histories of their famous establishments and how recovery had been achieved – mainly by sweating it out and not adopting a high moral tone. Because he managed to behave with dignity, and without condemning Pacey (whom he described publicly as *a talented and dedicated young teacher* and privately as a bonehead) the scandal actually consolidated his nucleus of support. What frustrated him was the time it would take before a full return to a sound reputation for the school could be made. It seemed to put his plans back five years.

Every response the school authorities made to the event was closely watched by the Press. The postwar British character was under scrutiny, especially in terms of the kind of people private schools turned out. When Pacey's parents announced that he would be buried at their East Anglian village church a dozen boys from the school were taken in a hired bus to attend and Daniel was one of them. Cook, representing the staff and the headmaster, was in charge of the party.

The journey started at the five in the morning with a packed breakfast taken on the bus. The funeral was due to start at ten-thirty. It was planned for the party to return the same day. Passing through Bishops Stortford, Daniel asked Cook if he would be allowed to read out a poem he had written for Pacey at the funeral.

'It will be the funeral service laid down if the Book of Common Prayer,' Cook told him. 'As you know, there's no room in that for personal contributions. But it's a very nice thought.'

'What about at the graveside, sir?'

Cook sighed. He was not looking forward to the funeral. As far as he was concerned, the parents would have been better advised to keep it private. As it was, they had done the opposite, sharing their grief. It would be an unholy, tasteless bun-fight, with the Press everywhere. 'I'll have to look at the poem,' he declared. 'If you do read it out, you should be aware that it will probably be reported in the all the rags.'

'I don't think anyone will take much notice of me, sir,' Daniel said, handing over a piece of folded paper torn out of an exercise book. 'It's a sonnet. We were told to write one for English homework.'

Cook read it quickly. *Mephistopheles Says Farewell* he murmured, half astonished, half repelled, trying not to smile. 'I suggest you say it in your head at some point in the proceedings.'

'Do you think it's any good, sir?'

'Oh, six out of ten, I'd say.'

'So you think no one else should hear it?'

'Oddly enough, Daniel, I think the family won't want to hear your homework today. They'll have other things on their minds.'

There was a huge crowd at the funeral. People stood in the churchyard during the service, or sat on gravestones. News photographers and cameramen were ringed along the churchyard wall. A pew directly behind the immediate family had been reserved for the school contingent.

When the Lord Mendora Land College school hymn, *He who would valiant be 'gainst all disaster,* came up during the service, the boys sang lustily in tribute to the one master at the school who had ever been a playboy.

CHAPTER TWELVE

Inspired by the glamorous death of Pacey, basking in the after-glow of the school's national fame, the boys romanced on a grand scale during a succession of heat-waves that summer. In the middle of the night when the returning Vampire jets flew in low over the school and woke the sleeping boys, it was the roar of the god of love they heard. The powerful winged force in the black skies demanded they should fall for any girl they could find. They walked and cycled miles from the school, searching villages and towns for someone to adore. If a boy got to know a girl she was asked if she had sisters and friends who might like to meet a passionate boy from Lord Mendora Land College where life was lived to the hilt.

Instead of teaching restraint, Pacey's extravagant end extolled a life of the senses. An exotic, purple tinge was put on his memory. In his short span he had experienced so much. He'd done it all. The lean and hungry boys, half-wild in their chains, burned off energy in sexual fantasies presided over by the ghost of a gentleman roué.

A favourite walk for the boys was to the down within the school estate, armed with a pair of binoculars or a telescope. From there the RAF officers' housing estate could be seen and the very bedroom window from which the plane had protruded.

It was said that the breeze passing through the silver birch trees on the summit of the down held traces of Pacey's fatal cologne, so well remembered from his classroom.

Under school rules, any friendship with a girl was strictly for-bidden. Incoming letters with local postmarks were opened. Boys caught talking to girls were beaten and gated. But still they sought beauty and destiny, going out into the surrounding countryside in the sultry evenings, pedalling miles to centres of population, idling on village greens, wandering through markets, hanging around housing estates, haunting the grounds of girls' schools, begging to be allowed into the magical aura of the other sex.

Two upper sixth formers were expelled after gate-crashing a party getting drunk on cider and pouring out their hearts to a couple of girls. A father complained to the Old Man and the culprits were expelled. They were eighteen and about to sit their Advanced Level examinations. Allowed to return to the school for this purpose, their papers were written in a converted cowshed attached to the farm manager's office.

There were girls at the school, however. They worked in the kitchens and laundry, cheap labour supplied by a reformatory in Winchester that operated a good behaviour day-release system. The Old Man had instructed the catering manager to employ only unattractive girls. The wages were pitiful but the girls prized the chance to get away from their penitentiary.

One sixteen-year-old reformatory girl called Marie got through the mesh by making herself unattractive for her interview, borrowing a friend's spectacles and slouching and messing up her hair. Her beauty was spotted immediately by the boys. When she was seen in the streets of a nearby town with a Teddy Boy there was much indignation. Everyone's pride was dented. How could she do this when she had the whole of the school to choose from?

Marie had fluffy brown hair, big brown eyes, a snub nose, a squarish determined little chin, and a lovely smile that came easily to her. She was tall, well-made, and moved with a grace that could suddenly snap into haughtiness. When she was overheard talking to another reformatory girl as they smoked a cigarette in the bushes by the kitchen back door, she surprised the boy eavesdropping on the conversation with the cultured musicality of her voice, which, he thought, sounded a bit French.

155

When Daniel was told this, he assumed she must have a story worth knowing. Marie's physical presence reminded him of the photographs of his grandmother Maud as a young woman. She had told him about her first job in domestic service. Her employer was a Methodist minister in Blackburn. A letter offering her the job of housemaid was in the archive. Daniel had worked out that his grandmother was only fourteen when the letter was written.

This minister used to molest her. One day she hit him so hard she broke his nose. Maud was taken to the police station. The minister claimed she had attacked him for no reason. She was given a warning by the duty sergeant, who was a knowledgeable man. He let the minister know he was on to him. This couldn't prevent Maud being sacked from her job and sent back to Liverpool.

Daniel watched Marie serving at the tables, speculating on her history. Why was she in a reformatory? Whatever conjecture he dreamed up, her physical charm and air of power and superiority strengthened the tale that was doing the rounds in his head. Forbidden to love whom she chose, she had set fire to the family chateau, killing both her parents and all the servants. She was only saved from the guillotine by her age. Escaping from a prison island she was picked up by a tramp steamer and taken to England where she was forced into petty crime.

That was the history he gave her.

As a house-captain he had to take his turn supervising boys on washing-up duty, working alongside the reformatory girls at the big wooden sinks. Some of the girls were chatty and cheeky, quite good fun, but none of them had Marie's authority – a potent blend of beauty and danger. Her refusal to speak even while working alongside the boys only increased the burning respect in which she was held.

Daniel thought long and hard on how he could break down Marie's defences and get her to talk. The more he watched and waited, the greater her influence became.

He decided to write her a poem in French and give it to her to see what would happen. Every effort he made to compose one was so bad he eventually decided to copy a poem out of a book he found in the school library. It was by Guillaume Apollinaire, the French text printed with translations into English on the opposite page. He noted where Marie hung her working apron and one evening slipped what he had copied (and signed as his own) into the pocket.

He was summoned to Mule's room the following day. Daniel had never seen an expression on the housemaster's face quite like the one he was wearing.

The piece of paper with Apollinaire's verse was put on the desk.

'Your work?'

'Yes, sir.'

'What d'you think you're playing at?'

Daniel didn't know how to answer that question. Bitter disappointment in Marie was uppermost in his mind. In spite of appearing to be a wild and beautiful criminal she was obviously as hidebound as the rest. Why had she reported him? Would a Teddy Boy have sent her a poem in her own language?

'My French is a bit rusty, Rogers so I've had this thing translated for me,' the Mule said, picking the paper up by one corner as if it was infected. 'In the first place, Mr Price, who teaches you French, thinks you cribbed it from somewhere. That you had the blatant gall to send it to a female employee in our kitchens beggars belief. What got into you?'

Daniel said he didn't know.

'*Let me love you and love you only a little,*' Mule said, reading from the paper. 'Can't you see that to use language like that to a girl in the kitchens is very unfair?'

'I suppose it could be, sir.'

'What will she think of us? This is a poem for adults, not children. Where did you steal it from?'

Daniel glossed over the plagiary and said he was hoping to

provoke Marie into talking to him. He was worried that she didn't seem to belong and might be unhappy in her work.

'Well, if she is, you've only made her worse. You'll come down to the kitchens with me now and apologise.'

'Yes, sir.'

'Will you and I ever get on the same wave-length?' Mule said, opening the door and leading Daniel out into the corridor. 'This kind of idiocy makes me wonder what goes on in your mind.'

'I didn't intend any harm, sir.'

When they got to the dining-hall, the Mule went into the kitchens and returned with Marie. Frowning from under a linen cap, she looked Daniel straight in the eye and folded her arms.

Her full attention was like a searchlight. Daniel was both dazzled and aghast. She narrowed her eyes and glared at him, then relaxed, raising her eyebrows. Was this pity or encouragement? He found her softened gaze exciting but unnerving. Was it a message? Did she regret reporting him?

When he apologised for sending the poem, his voice shook. He said he'd sent it because he thought she was lonely in a strange country.

'Huh!' Marie snorted dismissively, her eyes hardening 'Let me ask you something. Did I ask you to worry if I was lonely? I am never lonely. I have plenty of friends.'

'That's neither here nor there,' Mule interrupted. 'That will be all, miss. The boy's said he's sorry. Let that be the end of it.'

'I copied it from a poem called *Marie* I found in a book . . . ' Daniel faltered. 'I thought you'd like it.'

'Who cares what you thought?' she sneered. 'You're just a crazy person.'

'That's enough,' Mule intervened. 'Go back to your work.'

Marie lingered a second before she turned away, took the linen cap off her head, leant forward and smiling her lovely smile right into Daniel's face.

'There, is that what you want?' she hissed. 'Have it!'

Chilled, he stepped back, deeply shocked that she knew so much about the power of her smile.

Her artifice distorted the whole room.

His heart went numb.

'Such arrogance these damn females have!' Mule managed to splutter. 'Return to your duties, girl!'

Marie walked quickly away without looking back. Even now, in spite of what she had done to him, Daniel couldn't help admiring the bounce of her fluffy hair and the swing of her hips.

As Mule stomped down the corridor afterwards with Daniel by his side he did a strange thing. His hand went to Daniel's shoulder.

'I blame the caterer for taking her on. Anyone would have to be blind not to see how pretty she is,' he said, swinging his leg. 'A boy your age cannot fully understand such basic urges.'

'No, sir, we can't.'

'When you committed this blunder you were under the influence of . . . what shall we say? Growing pains? But, Daniel, we want no more poetry like that to anyone, if you don't mind.'

Daniel picked up on the use of his Christian name.

It was the first time Mule had ever used it to him.

'Lad, give yourself time to develop. Don't force the issue. Listen to those who know better. You have your whole life ahead of you.'

The effort of being studiedly sympathetic disturbed Mule's stride and he slammed his wooden foot into a skirting board and nearly fell over. His grip on Daniel's shoulder tightened until it was painful. Cursing under his breath, he took his hand away. 'Sorry,' he said, giving Daniel a watery smile. 'I thought I was going flat on my face. I should look where I'm going,'

Later on that day Daniel went to the library and read the translation of Apollinaire's poem again.

Masks become silent and
Music so far away
It is the sky singing
Let me love you and love you only a little
My unrest is delicious.

He confessed to himself that using the verse of a poem he didn't understand had been a big mistake. But although the complete meaning was miles out of his reach, it had obviously touched his mind when he first read it. He had pondered that first line. How can a mask *become* silent? Aren't masks silent all the time? He remembered the shock of the smile Marie had turned on – a mask speaking. When she stopped smiling the mask had fallen silent and devastated him.

Some sure instinct had led him to that book in the French Literature section of the library. Either by accident, or because all girls are the same, Apollinaire's Marie was very like her namesake. The poet's Marie must have smiled at him in that same way, stunning and disappointing him simultaneously, leaving his heart a wreck.

By the end of the week Marie had disappeared from the kitchens. The next time Daniel supervised washing-up duties, the other reformatory girls were hostile. They told him he should be ashamed of himself. It was entirely his fault Marie had lost her job. She was now cooped up all day in the reformatory. To punish him they were telling every boy who did washing-up duty the story of his stupidity, and how he'd been spurned. And no kitchen girl would ever talk to him again. And he should watch out for Marie's boyfriend, the Teddy Boy, who carried a razor. He would be doing something about the clot who'd got his girl locked up.

Daniel decided to ignore the opposite sex as much as he could. For now he would focus on what had saved him so far – history and sport.

News came from home that his grandfather had been told by the doctor that unless he stopped drinking and smoking so heavily and took some exercise and ate regular meals, he would be dead before he was sixty. He had very little strength left. Shortly before this bombshell hit God With Us he had been summoned to Uncle Dick's office and warned that because he couldn't climb the steps of a five-storey warehouse any more, he might be retired early

On the day he returned from the doctor's surgery the condemned man had thrown six full bottles of Guinness into the dustbin, borrowed several of his wife's Woodbines (Capstan Full Strength was out) and eaten a cheese sandwich. Four weeks later (Daniel's mother had bided her time telling him in case of backsliding, which had happened before now) he was still a changed man, visiting the homes of his other married daughters regularly, where he hadn't been for years, being amicable to his sons-in-law whom he'd held in contempt since their wedding-days, working hard in the greenhouse on a crop of tomatoes. All in all, the man was unrecognisable. To help him keep to his new regime and maintain hope in his heart, he had said several times that a visit to Daniel's school would be an inspiration for him to stick to his guns.

In the next letter his mother went on at greater length.

She struggled to describe in simple language the miracle of her father's rebirth as a lovable human being. *It's beyond me,* she wrote, *but we're all so happy it's happened and seems to be lasting.*

His grandfather had let it be known that he would like to take a look at the school, get the feel of the place, poke his head in the classrooms, talk to the teachers, stroll along the touch-lines, check out the dormitory our Dan slept in and the state of the kitchens. He had lived cheek by jowl. He knew the ropes, what was fair and good for young males. Though the chance our Dan had been given was a marvellous thing for the family, you had to watch it. His success at the school so far showed there was a strain of resolute character somewhere in his hereditary make-up. Perhaps this was the opposite side of the nihilism in his grandfather's previous nature? – that mysterious perversion of soul, powered by suffering. His own genius for self-destruction was in the process of transformation into a positive force through his grandson – but God With Us would like to know more so the family's future could be secured.

Desperate to encourage her father in his reformation – which was a truly wonderful thing to happen after so much pain and humiliation – Daniel's mother proposed to bring him to Founder's Day. Maud was no traveller (she had never been further than Blackburn) and would stay at home, keeping her fingers crossed that her husband would behave himself. If Daniel could find a suitable bed and breakfast in the village for his mother and grandfather to stay at, that would help – preferably not the local pub.

The news appalled him. The thought of his grandfather wandering around the school, reformed or not, was a nightmare. When he wrote to his mother the following Sunday he shared his doubts with her, disguising his true feelings. The trip would be expensive. They would have to pay for two rooms. The local bus service was unreliable. His mother didn't have to read too much between the lines to realise he didn't want them to come.

The answering letter was in his parcel when it came. His mother wrote that she had a right to visit the school, and a right to help her father.

She was hurt by Daniel's lack of enthusiasm. Dawn and Stanislav were coming down to Founder's Day by car and they had offered to drive over and pick them up at Rugby station and drop them there on the way back. It would work out very well.

Daniel prayed that his grandfather would have a relapse into his old habits during the next few weeks. If his mother came regardless, that was enough of a challenge. He would have to construct a glittering surface for her to look at, an ornamental screen that would cover the truth.

There was an advantage to her coming, however. Properly handled, it could further his schemes. He could introduce her to the bachelor masters – but not with his grandfather in tow. If he was with her, they'd run a mile.

Then a letter from his grandfather arrived, written in his large, exquisite copperplate hand. In the same envelope was a note from his mother telling him to keep in mind that it had taken her father two days to compose the letter, and it was, so he claimed, the first personal, non-business, written communication he'd made to anyone since the end of the First World War.

Before Daniel sat down to decipher the beauteous, almost illegible script, he prepared himself by summoning up one of his favourite archive items – the pencil message on an Army issue cigarette packet sent as a card from France after his grandfather had been posted missing with his gun-team for several days. Was this the other letter being referred to? Passed by a censor named Williams, it was dated 30th March 1918, and ran: *My Dear Wife, I am still alright. A letter will follow at the first opportunity. Em X.*

Daniel suspected that follow-up letter was never written. The cigarette packet had been sent after days of God With Us being lost in No-Man's Land, the fear of death working on him – much as it had after the doctor's warning.

Dear Dan – Your mother has shown me your reports and letters from the headmaster. I notice you are good at games and some subjects. What worries me is your attitude to authority. You are letting yourself down. This is something I know plenty about. When we come down to the school I want to speak to the staff. From now on I will be taking a fatherly interest.

Yours sincerely,
Grandad

Daniel went to London with Bryant for half-term. On the

163

Saturday morning, with Bryant's aunt in charge, they took the Underground to Oxford Circus and walked to Harley Street. While the psychoanalysis was in progress, Daniel and the aunt read the *Illustrated London News* in the waiting-room. When Bryant emerged from the consulting-room the tips of his ears were red and there were tears in his eyes.

Seeing his distress, his aunt, who was a tough Yorkshire woman who spoke her mind, wondered whether she should hand over the cheque Stanislav had sent her to pay the psychiatrist.

'He's supposed to sort you out, not upset you,' she argued. 'What's he done?'

'All he says is I need discipline,' Bryant sniffled. 'I told him that at our school I get plenty of discipline, thank you!'

'Well, I don't like the sound of this,' the aunt said, closing her handbag. 'You do need discipline. I could have told him that. If that's all we're getting for Stan's money it's a poor do.'

The aunt told the boys to wait while she went to the office to talk to the secretary. When she'd gone, Bryant described the strange procedure he'd been put through. 'He wouldn't let me tell him anything. All he wanted me to do was answer questions about my father. He never asked what it was like at school. At one point I told him I spend half of my time in one madhouse and then go home to another and he just ignored me.'

When the aunt returned they went for lunch in Piccadilly.

'You won't be going to see that man again,' she told Bryant as he ate chocolate pudding. 'I'll tell Stan not to waste his money. My opinion is you're idle, brainy, you make up problems for yourself, and you talk too much.'

'It wasn't my idea,' Bryant protested. 'I didn't ask to go. There's nothing the matter with me.'

'Stan was doing what he thought best,' the aunt retorted. 'He's prepared to pay for a quiet life. Your mother nags him about your relationship not working properly. You know what she's like.'

'I wish I'd never said anything to anyone,' Bryant said,

grimacing into his plate. 'Opening your mouth just isn't worth it.'

'If you write to your mother week after week telling her how miserable you are, what d'you expect? She wants to find the reason.'

That night she took them to see *Hamlet* at the Old Vic instead of going to a musical. In the interval she bought them orangeade. While they sucked on their straws in the foyer she suggested to her nephew that Hamlet's problem with his father, ghost or not, was a real one. In comparison to the great tragedy they were witnessing, and the psychological depths of the prince of Denmark's suffering, Bryant was having an easy time of it and should stop moaning.

'You boys without proper fathers should be very sensible and practical about yourselves,' she said as the first interval bell sounded. 'I know at your school there are a lot of you in the same boat and you talk amongst yourselves, but you should remember that pretending to have mental problems is un-manly.'

As they followed the crowd into the auditorium for the start of the second half, Daniel made the observation to the aunt that Hamlet was pretending to be mad.

'That's right, Dan – and why is he doing it?'

'To give himself time to work out how to murder the king.'

'Not bad. But you'll see the consequences of his pretending littered all over the stage at the end,' she replied. 'However, if he'd got on with the job and killed Claudius straight away, it would mean we wouldn't have a play to watch.'

Then this is a rule of human existence, Daniel thought, art comes first.

Back in their seats, he whispered a question raised by the aunt's strange reasoning: 'So is every life a play?'

As the curtain went up on Elsinore, her reply was: 'No one's ever paid to see mine.'

After half-term he went to Apollinaire again, poring over the strange thoughts of the Frenchman. One of life's great questions – the one raised at the Old Vic – might cast light upon another. It failed to do so. Seeking a few scraps of knowledge that might soothe his ignorance, he read the introduction to the translations for the first time. It said that Apollinaire had accepted the Great War as a magnificent manifestation of modern beauty. This disgusted him so much he took the book down to the Young Farmers Club and fed it to the pigs.

CHAPTER THIRTEEN

With only a few weeks to go to the end of term, the Old Man was pleased to get a report from Oliphant that Rogers was improving as a fast bowler. Keen and determined, the boy was funnelling all his frustrations and rebelliousness into the art – and it seemed to be having the beneficial side-effect of settling him down at last.

With Pacey gone – who had been the best cricketer on the staff – Cook and Oliphant were providing individual tuition, with Henry Long's manual always to hand. In its pages was a design for a contraption that *could* give a guide to bowling speeds. The physics master was inveigled into modifying the design into a workable machine – a plank wide as two full set of stumps and half again as tall, standing on a sensitive hinged spring. This was built by the fifth-form metalwork class. A good-length ball would knock the plank back against a calibrated scale fixed beside it. Although unable to give the actual speed of a delivery, a steady overall increase was determinable. The device, which was profoundly unscientific, gave some service until it fell to pieces under the bombardment. But before its collapse, Oliphant was able to give the Old Man statistics (the headmaster's special subject at Edinburgh University in the early 1920s) indicating that within three years the school first team would probably have, at one end of the pitch at least, the lethal pace it needed. There was still work to be done on accuracy but the speed was definitely increasing.

A note added to his report praised Rogers for his commitment.

Bowling faster and faster seemed to be important to him.

When he produced the occasional good ball it seemed to make him happy.

Absorbed in finding his way into this elemental skill, Daniel practised alone in the nets on the long summer evenings. To make things more difficult for himself, he used only one stump as his target. If he hit it – an infrequent occurrence – his triumphant yell could be heard throughout Junior House. In the common-room, boys reading comics by the open windows would turn to each other and say: *Rogers has done it again.* But long phases of inaccuracy bedevilled his efforts. He would run up to bowl telling himself this was it, the perfect ball, but his arm, eyes and brain conspired to make him fail.

Control and direction came in fits and starts. He could see no logic in how these powers came and went. One day he was synchronised, his body working as it should, the next day his bowling was all over the place. Sometimes he wondered if the stages of the moon had anything to do with it, or the dreams he was having. These were mostly about being chased or lost in a piled-up citadel of streets, corridors, cellars and halls, a dark ant-heap of a place, or falling off towers, pinnacles and precipices, suffering from paralysis, being shot or drowned, and attending several of his mother's weddings.

He noticed that he never dreamt about cricket and wondered why until he worked out that the struggle to master a skill was a dream in itself. People never dream about dreaming.

Channelling all the fire of his doubts and desires into the act of bowling the perfect ball, he drove wicketkeepers mad with wides and terrorised batsmen with bodyliners. He had to be warned by umpires against growling as he ran in to bowl, and giving war-whoops when he shattered the stumps. During one house-match, having been no-balled four times in one over, he lost his temper and threw the ball into a nearby copse. Both teams spent quarter of an hour searching the undergrowth for it, ruining the rhythm of the game. For this petulance Daniel had to pay the cost of a replacement ball and receive his only beating of the summer term, (his last at Junior House) administered quizzically by Mule who gave him two light taps of the cane.

A crisis came when Daniel knocked diminutive Wazz Burleigh unconscious with a bouncer, shattering his spectacles. Pieces of glass were hammered into the bridge of the boy's nose.

All the players, umpires and waiting batsmen ran to the fallen boy, leaving Daniel stranded in space. Burleigh's face was a mask of blood. The crowd turned and looked accusingly at Daniel. He turned away, walking off with his hands on top of his head. Someone shouted after him that Burleigh was blinded. Cook picked the wounded boy up in his arms and carried him off the field. The match was abandoned.

Matron had to take the slivers out with tweezers.

She said it was a miracle broken glass hadn't gone into the eyes.

Cook was horrified by what had happened, blaming himself for encouraging Daniel to be indiscriminately hostile as a bowler. *Have no mercy on the batsman* – was the dictum of Henry Long, a slow bowler with the heart of a fast one. But Burleigh was a feeble birdlike first year from North Wales, still in the throes of homesickness, who'd begged to be let off cricket.

Cook summoned Daniel to his room and told him that in future he should not bowl at top speed against short-sighted boys who were not good at sport but had to play it. Having been cold-shouldered by the entire Junior House since the game finished, Daniel was glad to agree.

That night he dreamt through the end of his father's life as it happened in Africa.

Lying in a sleeping-bag in the desert, the mysterious being woke for the last time, got up and did all the things men do when they get up. As he shaved, his face disappeared. Eyeless, he drove a lorry into a cactus grove. A cricket ball was fired from a mortar and hit the lorry. The explosion blew the faceless being into a fine mist. Afterwards, his face appeared in the sky as the sun, peppered with broken glass.

It was his first dream to include a reference to cricket.

The Old Man heard about Cook putting a restriction on the speed of Daniel's bowling and summoned the teacher to his office. He told him that parents paid for their child to be included in a healthy, competitive regime that mirrored the challenges of adult life. Just as no boy was sent to the school to be made weaker, no brake was to be put on Rogers. The aim of any fast bowler was to be as quick as he could. Anyone facing him could either learn to bat properly and defend themselves or get out of the way.

This vindication was to be passed on to Rogers in case the incident had made him lose heart.

Cook was not a man to challenge authority. His intense medievalism of spirit originated in the Platonic belief that the only hope for mankind was in a strong, sensible order backed by a hierarchical system led by an enlightened despot. To the young master, the Old Man was authority personified – tough, experienced, down to earth and uncommonly right in most things.

But this time Cook argued his case.

'Sir, with the greatest of respect,' he said bravely, 'with Rogers I believe it is *essential* brakes are put on him. His life will need to be one of continual restraint and containment.'

The Old Man fixed Cook with a cold grey eye. 'What a lot of interest you take in that boy,' he said with a mocking ring in his voice. 'Is he worth it?'

Cook faltered. It was an unfair question to ask – impossible to answer without betraying confidences.

The Old Man played with his paperknife, sliding it under the green paper of his blotter. 'From a position like mine it's very interesting to watch the patterns of friendship forming,' he said coolly, eyes fixed on Cook. 'I observe the shifts, the beginnings, the ends, the movements. You know what I'm talking about.'

'If he can channel his energies I'm convinced Rogers will come to something, and be a credit to the school,' Cook asserted, hoping to stop the Old Man's train of thought before he went any further.

Note was taken of the manoeuvre.

'Are you really the one to put the brakes on him?' the Old Man asked. 'Is that what you *want* to do? D'you think he'll ever come to anything, except on the sports field?'

'He can be guided, sir,' Cook replied manfully, 'and I think he's in the process of buckling down. My belief is he'll start to flourish once he gets to the upper school.'

'Is that so?'

'Oxbridge is possible.'

'To date, I have him down as bonehead and hothead combined,' the Old Man murmured, looking out of the window. 'He's given Mule a lot of trouble – more than we gamble for with the average scholarship boy. On occasions he's suggested to me that Rogers is deranged. How d'you get on with him?'

Cook said that he believed Rogers trusted him.

'No, no, I mean how d'you get on with old Mule? He hasn't got all that many years to go before retirement. Perhaps he's getting in the way these days? What d'you think?'

Cook found it shocking to be put on the spot by the Old Man who had acted so swiftly to defend Mule in the past. And it went right against the grain to be asked to criticise a colleague, especially a nominal superior. He had harboured doubts on the old soldier's suitability for the job of running Junior House – arguably the most important job in the school – finding his methods random, not thought through and old-fashioned, but had assumed, after his own removal from Junior House, that Mule's position was impregnable.

'We get along very well, sir,' Cook said carefully, 'though we are far apart in age and background. He was never trained as a teacher.'

'True,' the Old Man sighed. 'I'm wondering if he's too long in the tooth to deal with this postwar generation of boys. He's a piece of walking history. Besides, when it comes to education, the military prefer no mind at all. After a few years of peace, a war-hero with a butterfly-net and one leg runs out of his usefulness, wouldn't you say?'

Taken aback at the cruelty of the jibe, and that it was being shared with him at all, Cook found enough poise to maintain that any living examples of courage and sacrifice were useful in the bringing up of boys.

'To encourage boys to be cannon-fodder in the Third World War, you mean!' the Old Man retorted. 'Is that all we're here for? One day this school will change the English class-system from within. I'm biding my time, biding my time.'

Cook lowered his eyes. Was the Old Man a secret socialist? Or even an anarchist? To date he'd seemed to be the kind of normal conservative patriotic reactionary anyone could be comfortable with in a boarding-school staff-room.

'As a historian you'll surely agree with this,' the Old Man continued, leaning forward and squinting at Cook as though he held him in the sights of a gun, 'the English public school system and Oxbridge, as you call those places, have been run for centuries as quite immune from the country's laws on sexual behaviour. Why does this immunity exist? What is it for?'

In a torment of embarrassment, Cook mumbled that he wasn't completely sure how this state of affairs had arisen.

'I notice you don't deny the truth of what I'm saying,' the Old Man declared, triumphantly. 'Surely this corrupt old system has to go. Sex should be the same for all of us.'

Cook mumbled again. He said that as the Church from the beginning had authority over sex and education it was probably guiltier than most.

'Are you a religious man?'

'Yes, sir, I believe I am.'

'With such things still going on, are we living in a democracy or not? I want you to know how strongly I feel on this matter. I will not have it in my school.'

Feeling outraged but helpless to defend himself from any

more vague innuendoes, Cook firmly turned the subject back to Rogers. 'The boy is coming to terms with himself and the school, sir,' he said. 'The advantages he has here are sinking in. He's starting to enjoy life.'

The Old Man said he was glad to hear it. Every scholarship boy was an investment that had to pay off. They were bedrock on which change would be built. Suffering in family life plus knowledge and discipline at school were two ingredients in the cement of a strong character.

The Old Man moved papers on his desk as a signal to Cook that the interview was over. 'Tell me, young man,' he said as an afterthought, 'what kind of people does Nature best equip to bring up children?'

'Parents?' Cook ventured.

'Come on, historian!' the Old Man chided. 'Think it through. Monks? Nuns? The childless, of course! The rich have always known the answer. Send the troublesome creatures off to dispassionate experts whose minds aren't bent by parenthood. We're best at it. We have no blood prejudices for or against. Favouritism is foreign to a great teacher. Do you plan to marry at all?'

His mind reeling, Cook made an odd humming sound in the back of his throat, half protest, half plea.

'Is the idea repugnant?' the Old Man pressed on, his grey eyes mean. 'Not on the cards? You're not that way inclined? Would you ever contemplate having a child? Don't you realise it would do you a world of good?'

Cook's jaw sank lower and lower until he gaped in disbelief.

This was too much.

It was worse than the Navy.

He was no longer a free man.

It had always been his plan to get a job teaching history in a secluded, isolated, nondescript school incorporating a large estate of mixed pasture, arable and woodland, a river or stream, and an unchanged village with an ancient church –

Early English, preferably. It was to be a school that was as close to being a monastic establishment as possible. Here, he would give his entire life to living in the past. Lord Mendora Land College seemed to fit the bill exactly. Not lusting after fame, high status, or wealth, he only wished to serve people quietly in his own peculiarly medieval way. He did not want to work in the greater world and suffer its nonsense.

To bring his life-plan to fulfilment was a tall order but, until now, he had been optimistic that, in spite of a few hiccups, all was going well. He had been forced to compromise his dream by accepting the absence of a river, there being no surface water because the downland was based on very porous chalk. But at least three-quarters of his dream had been realised. Now things had changed, and, ironically, changed by moving in the direction of the past. The part of the Old Man's mind he had just encountered was Jane Austen, William Thackeray and Anthony Trollope rolled into one.

He had been ordered to get married if he wanted to keep his job.

When the baize-covered door closed silently behind him he stood stock-still for a full minute before finding the assurance to move. When he did so, he kept one hand on the wall.

On the way out he called in at the outer office where two female secretaries were working. He surprised them both with a winning, sexy smile and a vigorous, manly greeting – a marked shift away from his customary quiet formality.

The day after Cook's interview with the headmaster, Daniel received a letter from his mother informing him of a change of plan. Her father had persuaded her mother to come to Founder's Day, and they would also bring John, his brother, who was determined to be a pupil at the same school as our Dan one day. Stanislav had a small Mercedes bus in his garage at the moment and he would use it to get them all down to the school. Because Daniel's grandmother had never been to

London, they would travel to the city the day before, show her the sights and stay the night, then drive down to the school the next morning.

Receiving this news was like being in the path of an avalanche. When he complained to Bryant, his friend said that, as far as he was concerned, the prospect of the visit was so horrendous he planned to either sham an epileptic fit and be in the san until Founder's Day was all over, or run away again.

Daniel didn't make the effort to appreciate the huge improvement that had obviously taken place in the life of his family. All he imagined was the day itself. The balance between his two lives would be destroyed. Until cynical opinion from the staff-room percolated down to the boys, crediting the greatly increased attendance of parents at Founder's Day to Pacey and the school being in the news, it had never crossed his mind that this could be the reason his own people were coming.

When it did cross his mind, however, he felt better about the whole thing. In that kind of atmosphere, with love and tragedy in the air, his mother would be a natural star. Instead of being stuck at home sewing, or serving in the shop, she would meet a lot of people who would respond to her beauty.

When he wrote home that Sunday he let his mother know how glad he was that it would be such a family occasion, and a real lifetime adventure for his gran, and John. Now he would have to get down to finding bed and breakfast for four, not two.

Letters with a new tone began arriving from his mother in addition to the one in the weekly parcel. He noticed how she used the word *dear* frequently in the body of what she wrote, and the initial *Dear Dan* became *My dear Dan,* then advanced to *Darling Dan* as Founder's Day got nearer. An intimate as well as innocent woman, she extended the range of her feelings towards him, as well as asking more and more questions about his daily life. Daniel was disturbed by this change, anxious not

175

to be drawn into telling the truth about life at school, which he didn't believe his mother could possibly understand. It wasn't until he realised how similar in tone these letters were to a packet of thirty-two letters she'd written to his father early in their married life which his father must have kept *and returned to her,* that he became nervous.

Three months before the marriage, his father had been in a convalescent home in North Wales after a hernia operation. His mother and father had written to each other every day, but his father's letters were not preserved in the archive. In every letter his mother referred to items his father had written about – nurses and patients at the home, books he was reading, the catering, the weather. Why had his father given back the letters he had received? And what had happened to the ones he wrote?

There were flashes of thinly-disguised jealousy in his mother's letters: *'You do go on about this Deidre on night shift. Is she after you or something? Talk about having no social life, I haven't been out for a fortnight.'*

His mother's yearnings for her absent lover, and her imagination of future married bliss, were, as she expressed them, an odd mixture of Hollywood script romance, intense domesticity and the dance-hall. His father wrote her poems and sent drawings, which she referred to in passing, but whatever dreams he had on his side of the correspondence weren't mentioned. His mother had folded his father's dreams into her own. She dreamt for him.

The quintessence of this possession was in that word *dear.* It troubled Daniel so much that he looked it up in the dictionary and was amazed to discover its root was the Old High German for *glory,* and it had developed a lot of other meanings and lost the original. The primary meanings in use were *beloved* and *expensive,* and, from 1829, as a form of address when writing to anyone at all. Amongst the other meanings were *dearth, strenuous, hardy, heavy* and *grievous.*

Darling had emerged from *dear* after a journey through Old

Frisian, Dutch, and Old English. His mother had used *darling* quite often in her letters to his father, usually when she was planting ideas in his head. She would never call Daniel, *darling*. She would never do that, until now. But there was a more directly derivative word he feared, which was *dearest,* employed increasingly in her letters to his father as his discharge from the convalescent home approached.

Daniel noted with some relief that *dearest* did not appear in the dictionary. If his mother started using it and he had to ask her to stop, that would be the reason he could give her.

This oversight by the makers of the dictionary didn't prevent his mother beginning a letter *Dearest Dan* a week before Founder's Day.

Daniel noticed a coolness had developed in his relationship with Cook.

He had no idea what might have caused it. They saw each other often in history lessons and cricket coaching when Cook performed his functions with care and enthusiasm but the warmth had gone. He avoided any one-to-one conversations. He did not seek Daniel out. It seemed that the special interest had gone.

Unable to ask why, without looking an importunate fool, Daniel put the matter out of mind and spent more time with a gang of friends. The timetable for the last weeks of the summer term was much more relaxed, the weather was good, all the examinations were over, there was plenty of time for roaming the copses and downs. Except for the problem of finding somewhere for his family to stay – the village and the guest houses in the area were all booked up – and worrying about Founder's Day, Daniel's time was unusually free.

While on rambles with his friends, he saw Cook out for evening walks with several different women – assistant matrons, the bursar's clerk, a barmaid from the Cock and Dolphin pub at the school gates, and Mrs White. This last encounter, far from the school in a deep part of a copse, astonished the gang. Cook and Mrs White were in a sunlit dell thick with butterflies, a place known to be held sacred by Mule. They were sitting together on a fallen tree.

Cook was reading aloud to Mrs White from a small book. The look in his eyes when the boys came crashing through the undergrowth, alarming the host of butterflies so they rose in a gorgeous cloud of colour, was new to Daniel.

Here was a different man altogether – darkly primitive and guilt-ridden.

Cook snapped the book shut and got to his feet.

Mrs White stayed where she was and smiled.

'D'you great galumphing idiots have to make so much noise?' Cook remonstrated. 'You've frightened all the butterflies off!'

The gang fell into a sheepish silence, unsure what to do, but unwilling to make an immediate retreat. Catching masters in the act was a notable deed, and very useful. Besides, the swaying mass of brilliant butterflies around the splendiferous head of Mrs White had done its work on their souls. Although the boys could not put a word to it, they had looked upon pure ecstasy.

'We only came to see the butterflies, sir,' one boy said.

'Well, now you've seen them, and driven them off, you can go away,' Cook snapped.

Daniel admired the history master's coolness. He tried to read the title of the book in Cook's hand.

It had to be poetry.

'Go on,' Cook said, waving his hand. 'Leave us in peace.'

As the hand was lowered and held at Cook's side, by cocking his head Daniel was able to read the title of the book – *An Illustrated Guide to British Lepidoptera*.

His disappointment was acute.

The gang left the dell by a different path. As they went along, Daniel's mind was full of fermenting conjecture. If Cook was having an affair with Mrs White, could his mother compete?

Was she as beautiful? On the other hand, would she want to get involved with such a man?

Less than a hundred yards along the path the boys came across Mrs White's husband praying on his knees below a huge ancient oak. They stopped respectfully. He turned and beckoned them over.

'It would be appropriate for you fellows to help me out, if you don't mind' he said, holding up a wooden box decorated with Chinese characters. 'Let this be your good deed for the day. An old boy from the school died in Singapore a while back. He asked for his ashes to be sent home to England and scattered below this tree. He made a map.'

Reverend White took the lid off the box and put a hand in, bringing it out full of grey dust and scattering it over the dead leaves at the base of the tree. 'This place must have been important to him in some way,' he said. 'He'd like the idea of boys doing the honours. Don't be afraid.'

The gang was speechless at the sheer drama of the task, but no one wanted to be the first to put his hand in the box.

'He was a very successful man in the rubber business,' Reverend White explained. 'He must have spent many happy hours in these woods. I've had the box in my study for a few weeks and never got round to it. Come on, dig in.'

Daniel stepped forward and put his hand in the box. Reverend White nodded approvingly. 'That's the style, Rogers,' he said. 'Nothing to be afraid of.'

'This is all that's left of a man, sir,' Daniel said, feeling around.

'No, Rogers, I don't believe it is.'

Digging deep into the ash, Daniel felt something hard. He pulled out a small piece of bone and held it up.

'This bit didn't burn, sir.'

The other boys groaned in awe.

'I wonder which part of the skeleton it came from, sir.'

Some boys turned away, shocked by Daniel's boldness. He

179

feinted towards them, thrusting the fragment in their faces.

'I'd say the hardest bones are in the head, sir,' Daniel said, cupping the bone in the palms of his hand like a precious object and holding it towards the vicar. 'Perhaps you should give it a proper burial in your churchyard.'

Reverend White gave him an amused look as he made a hole in the leaf-mould with his heel. 'This is as much of a funeral as he'll get,' he said, pointing for Daniel to put the piece of bone into it. Then he covered the bone over with leaf-mould and stamped down hard. 'Don't want the fox to get it, do we?'

When every boy had dipped a hand in the box and scattered some ash, Reverend White asked them to spend a moment thinking about the man who had died so far away. When they had been silent for a while, he asked, rhetorically, 'Boys, when we can travel so far in our minds what are these great distances to us? This man spent most of his working life in Malaya, now his spirit is here, at rest. The days when we were truly happy are our true home. May God remember us, and preserve the power of human memory. Amen.'

The gang responded heartily.

Before returning to his wife, Reverend White thanked everyone for helping him. 'He will bless you,' he said. 'It was a manly thing to do for an old boy.'

As the gang continued its ramble, enthralled with the gruesome event, Daniel questioned the conclusions he had jumped to about Cook and Mrs White. It was a pity but it looked very much as though the three adults had gone out for a walk in the woods together.

Cook was still free and unattached.

A week before Founder's Day Daniel was in the village shop writing out a card to be put in the window advertising for accommodation for his family. The charge was two shillings, which he could ill afford, but the matter was now urgent. As he struggled over the text, Cook came in for tobacco. When he saw

Daniel, his manner was back to its old interest and warmth. When Daniel told him what he was doing, Cook told him to tear up the card he'd written and not to bother spending his money.

'They can stay at The Elms. Since Mr Pacey died I'm by myself in that big old place.'

'But there are four of them, sir . . . '

'Plenty of bedrooms.'

'Are you sure, sir?'

'It will be my pleasure, Daniel.'

'One of them is my grandfather, sir.'

'I look forward to meeting the old gentleman.'

'They haven't got much money, sir.'

'Don't be ridiculous! How could I possibly charge them?'

'But they told me to find bed *and breakfast*, sir.'

'D'you think I can't manage to give them breakfast?'

Stunned by the implications, Daniel rang his mother at the shop where she worked from the village phone-box and gave her the news. She didn't appear to be surprised.

'Mr Cook has been writing to me, lately, Dan,' she said. 'It will be nice to stay at his house.'

'What's he writing to you about?'

'About you, of course – long letters about your future and what we must do. He takes such trouble, son. I have to go now. The shop's full of customers.'

He felt anxious. What was Cook playing at? What *we* must do? What was all that about? Had he completely misread the man? Was he a predator? From giving the impression of not being particularly interested in women, the history master now seemed to be obsessed with them.

What worried him more was that Cook was already wearing the mantle of father, shaping the family's future. Daniel's imagination caught fire and blazed into acute anxiety. What if in one of those *long* letters, Cook had proposed to his mother, then he'd gone up to Liverpool and secretly married her. That explained the cool phase when Cook avoided him. He might have been nervous about whether Daniel would accept him as a father, wondering if he'd done the right thing. He remembered that Cook had recently gone away for few days and left his history classes work to do. That's probably when he had gone to Liverpool and married his mother.

The ramifications were serious. Could he stand living with a teacher?

From that stark consideration he progressed towards some honesty: If this is all in my imagination, and I know how that works, it shows how weak my position is. She still loves her husband *as if he were alive*. From now on, let that be enough for her. Her memories are so happy, they'll keep her going to the end. She'll die still married to him. It's a waste but there we are.

Whether he had ever *needed* a live father followed on from these thoughts. This was a profound shift. He'd never asked the question before. It struck him that having a father could be as thankless as being a father. People only said good things about fathers when they were dead. Was he better off being fatherless? Why have an authority figure when he had so many at school? Being educated was fathering enough, being dominated, bossed around, punished, beaten, brainwashed, insulted.

Look at his grandfather. He was a father. Look at all the men in the street at home who were fathers. They were a hopeless lot, trotting obediently off to work in their collars and ties like pharaoh's slaves, henpecked to hell. Look at the married masters with kids. They were a smug, sleepy, uninspiring tribe.

Calm down, calm down, he told himself. If they've gone ahead and got married without consulting you, this will need some handling. You can't go on like this, demolishing the past. A scene burst into his mind – he was setting fire to the archive. The record of broken, unlived lives blazed and went up in smoke. He was left with flakes of ash floating before his eyes and an acute sense of loneliness.

During bowling practice that evening, Cook told Daniel that he had secured a prize turkey for the visit of his family. Cook's brother, who had a farm in Staffordshire, was bringing it down. Live, it weighed twenty pounds, near enough. The brother had kept it in a wood so the Ministry of Agriculture inspectors wouldn't know about it.

'A turkey that big will take a lot of coupons,' Daniel muttered. 'Should I tell my mother to bring down all their ration books?'

'Don't mention that in front of my brother,' Cook said with a conspiratorial grin. 'If the weather permits, we'll dine outside. There's wine I brought back from the Loire. For dessert I'll make meringues in the Aga. It will be a banquet, my dear Dan! What fun, eh?'

And he paternally ruffled the boy's hair.

Dear. That said it all.

His heart sank at this stepfatherly outburst.

'Never seen my grandfather drink wine, sir,' he said churlishly. 'I'm not sure he likes it.'

'This is the best – which is what your family deserves.'

Cook's warm generosity confirmed his suspicions. And a twenty pound turkey was proof enough. They would probably make the announcement of the marriage over dinner.

There would be speeches.

Everything would come out into the open.

How should he behave, being the only one not to know in advance that those two were man and wife?

His little brother would know.

He'd probably been a page-boy at the wedding.

Because people in the street thought his brother was so good-looking, John had already been a page-boy a few times for weddings, dressed in satin and buckled shoes And he'd been paid for it. When Valerie, the shop manager's daughter, got married, Daniel's mother had sent Daniel a photograph of John in this poncey outfit, which she had made herself. His brother was smiling toothily over a glass of champagne, showing his dimples. Written on the back of the picture was: *He's the living image of his father.*

To think that Sonny could ever have looked like that had upset Daniel a lot. If his brother was ever unlucky enough to be sent to Lord Mendora Land College he'd have to give up doing that kind of thing – especially as his older brother would still be at the school.

'What does your grandfather habitually drink?' Cook asked. 'If my wine won't please him I'd better get something else in.'

'I think he only drinks tea now, sir.'

'Tea? Good Lord. The old chap has certainly changed his ways.'

Cook, never prone to over-familiarity before, was obviously in the family if he was talking like that.

Emmanuel, God With Us, that treacherous old two-headed bastard, was part of the plot. He'd taken Daniel's mother down the aisle and given her away. He'd worn a flower in his button-hole. He'd married his widowed daughter off to get rid of her and her nuisance kids. He could see the vile old creature smiling and sniffling at the ceremony, eyes full of crocodile tears behind his bottle-end glasses, wiping his great red shining beak of a nose with one of the crisp white handkerchiefs Maud sent him out to work with . . . Oh, God, God, the duplicity of the man! Poor Gran. What a life for her from now on. Now he'd return to being as bad as he liked, driving her out of her mind. He'd force her to commit suicide. She'd said that could happen if she was ever left alone with him.

His heart racing in a panic, Daniel violently rubbed one side of the cricket ball on the back of his shorts, trying to control his feelings. He forced his mind into an icy, calculating state. He became a cunning animal, searching hungrily for further proof of betrayal.

The ambush was carefully laid. Daniel's mother would definitely have written long, chatty letters to Cook (calling him *dearest*, no doubt) in return for the ones she received from him.

She might even have sent these letters in parcels, there were so many of them. If there was one major item of family news she would have covered more than once it was a recent dramatic change – one Daniel now craftily alluded to in his conversation with Cook.

'Didn't you know that my grandfather is supposed to have given up drinking altogether, sir?'

Cook's paused before replying. Daniel could see that this incredibly devious man had spotted the trap set for him. The trained historical brain that had studied the world's most evil men was working fast, composing a reply that would lead Daniel away from the truth.

'Then he'll have to share your dandelion and burdock,' Cook replied cheerfully. 'Now you've got a good shine on the ball, bowl me an outswinger.'

CHAPTER FOURTEEN

That night Daniel dreamt the dream of dreams. All the other classics he'd recorded – some with dialogue, music, and colours he could accurately remember and enter in his diary – were dwarfed by the beautiful intensity of this product of his mind under sleep.

In his dream, Mrs White was a butterfly and he was one too. Their faces were imprinted on their wings. They mated in flight, soaring through the air, and he came for the first time. Instead of this waking him, he pursued her through the dark air of a wood and did it again and again and again until his wings fell off. When he woke up in the glorious mess, he announced the good news to the whole dorm.

A history lesson was on his timetable that morning. Unlike many of the masters, Cook didn't let his pupils do as they liked just because it was near the end of term. Today he had them reading aloud from *Magna Carta* in a translation from its Latin text.

Getting back to originals in preference to summaries and commentaries was one of the strengths that had gained Cook his first-class honours at Cambridge. It could be said that it was Daniel's heroic reading of the entire Bible at the age of twelve that had first drawn Cook to the boy.

The history master's personal discipline was to saturate his mind with texts that had changed the world. Back home at The Elms a copy of Hitler's *Mein Kampf* lay on a beside table with a marker at page 421. He had started reading it on the first day of the summer term. Before going to sleep each night he read five pages and made notes. Beneath it *The Holy Kabbalah* waited to be read.

Form 2B was duller than usual this day. Outside, the sun was beating down, overheating the classroom. When the reading of the whole of *Magna Carta* was over, 2B had no questions to ask about the famous document. They'd forgotten the meaning of all the feudal legalese mugged up for an exam only two weeks before. The whole business of King John and his clash with the barons was irrelevant on such a lovely summer's day. More empathetic masters had moved their classes to the lawns outside the dining-hall and their relaxed murmurings were audible. Cook kept looking at Daniel with pleading brown eyes, asking him to come up with a question that would kick off a discussion.

Incensed by the way he'd been treated in the matter of the secret marriage – a ruse that had often cropped up in English history with dire results – Daniel kept quiet, avoiding Cook's appeal by looking past him at the cleaned blackboard.

'Have you nothing to offer, Rogers?' Cook said eventually. 'After all, this document is the foundation-stone of all our liberties and you are notoriously fond of yours.'

Daniel sat up in his desk. 'Would you read out the clause about the widow again please, sir?' he asked with measured but surly respect. 'I'm not sure I followed all that.'

Cook gave him a grateful smile. 'No widow shall be compelled to marry so long as she prefers to live without a husband; provided always that she gives security not to marry without our consent, if she holds of us, or without the consent of the lord of whom she holds, if she holds of another.'

Daniel nodded and looked out of the window.

'D'you understand it now, Rogers?'

'Yes, sir,' Daniel replied. 'A lot of *holds*. That's what threw me. Widows are very vulnerable, as my mother knows.'

Cook raised his eyebrows. 'Oh, really? The widows referred to here were once married to important landowners. The king looked upon the entire aristocracy as his national breeding-stock, not unlike plantation owners ordering slaves to mate in order to beget strong workers, and Hitler baby-farming Aryans.'

Daniel frowned, unwilling to wrangle further.

He'd made his point.

The bell went to end the period.

For the first time since he'd met Cook, he felt glad to be escaping from a history lesson. As he went past the teacher's desk, heading for the fresh air, he received an odd, perturbed smile and a mouthed, silent *thank you.*

Stanislav had the pick of many different vehicles for his trip to the south. The grounds of the Priory and the area around his repair and service garage were full of wrecks but there were machines of character still in working order. When the Polish miners staying at the Priory were forced to go on strike by the union, they had time on their hands. Instead of conserving their resources against the financial demands of a long and bitter dispute, they decided to have a holiday instead.

They would accompany their spiritual leader, Stanislav, down to Founder's Day. He was a man who had made a success of living in England. His business was thriving. He had married a well-spoken, genteel Englishwoman who adored him – and worked hard running a profitable guest-house and garage café widely known for its home cooking. His stepson was attending an expensive public school as good as Eton, mixing with scions of noble families. And Stanislav was still very much a Pole at heart who could hardly speak the English language. His example kept their hopes alive.

Stanislav allocated the Mercedes bus to his seven friends and did a lot of work on a Rolls-Royce Silver Ghost convertible that had been standing in all weathers under a horse chestnut tree. He was a good automobile mechanic with a feeling for the grand vehicles of yesteryear. The more he worked on the Silver Ghost, the more he loved it. He stripped the mighty engine down and rebuilt it. A complete respray was undertaken. The hood was replaced. Four new tyres were fitted. Every scrap of rust was removed. By the time the renovation was finished Stanislav had trebled the value of the car. When he got bored with it – which he would, eventually – he'd sell it to a lord or a film star.

The plan for the journey remained the same. They would drive across country to Rugby and pick up Daniel's family at the station. Grandfather and grandmother and John would ride in the back seat of the Rolls. By request, Daniel's mother would join the miners in the bus.

The arrival of the party in the classic motor – resprayed imperial purple, the hood and interior trim in beige – accompanied by a retinue of well-dressed, powerful-looking Poles in the Mercedes bus would impress the other parents and be a wonderful surprise for the boys. Dawn wrote to her son ordering him to be with Daniel at the school gates at two o'clock sharp on the afternoon of Founder's Day. From a map of the school sent with paperwork when her son was accepted at the school, she could see that there was a long drive up to the main buildings, perfect for making a grand entrance. For the occasion, she bought herself a white summer dress and a broad-brimmed beflowered straw hat with a lilac ribbon to tie under her chin.

Stanislav was measured up by a bespoke tailor for a new dark lounge suit to be cut in best Yorkshire worsted. At a bring-and-buy sale in aid of the striking miners, whom she didn't agree with *at all,* Dawn managed to find a tie that looked regimental.

She let the miners, her lodgers, know that Founder's Day at a topnotch English public school was a dressy affair and they must take their lead from Stan. No one must let the side down. One way and another the miners obtained or borrowed dark suits, white shirts, and black shoes, and ties close in design to the one Stan would sport.

At breakfast, before they left on their expedition, Dawn gave the Poles, including her husband, a pep talk. She trusted that they would behave like gentlemen.

Although Dawn was only a miner's daughter herself, (her father lived at the Priory, sitting all day in a straight-backed chair with a bottle of stout at his feet, silent victim of a rockfall)

189

marriage to her first husband had forced her up the social ladder, father-in-law being a successful auctioneer who had made justice of the peace. The parents were very certain who they were and what their daughter-in-law would need to be if she was to keep up. Dawn had accepted their schooling in the arts of self-belief and assertion and dominated her first husband accordingly. This was never difficult because the man was of a gentle, enquiring disposition, tending towards socialistic sentimentality, and he had delicate health. When he was killed on a train during an air-raid, it was only a few months afterwards that Stanislav appeared in her life. He borrowed an English language primer from the library where Dawn worked, and propositioned her at the counter with the first basic words he learnt.

The Old Man was writing his report to the trustees. It would be delivered from the platform in the marque erected on the sports field. The picture he must paint of the school's achievements in the academic year 1950–51 was already sketched out. Optimism had to be the keynote.

He had a friend, Maurice, who was staying with him at the house, a man of the theatre who was used to helping actors go over lines. Maurice was out in the rose garden, chatting with the Old Man's wife. A striking figure with two wings of white hair over a tanned aquiline face, one twisted, nut-brown hand always held against his upper breast – the result of a stage fire in Dorking – Maurice wore long summer shorts and a colourful Hawaiian shirt. His voice was deep and cultured, with an enchanting lisp. His piercing eyes were an intense black-brown, conveying a direct connection to a sharply sophisticated mind. Every autumn term he co-directed a Shakespeare play at the school with George Arnold, the senior English master. There was always a point in rehearsals – usually a week before opening night – when Maurice gave a passionate, tearful speech to the cast about the price of failure and the shame, the shame, oh, the shame, how he'd never be able to come back and do another play if this flopped – then he would faint and be carried into the open air by George Arnold who wore the same strange smile each year, a mixture of stoicism, tolerance and good humour.

Maurice saw to it that his friend, the reviewer from the local paper, understood the problems of an experienced professional (West End and Broadway productions listed among his credits) when working with boys who weren't used to freely expressing their essential selves through art. Regardless of these difficulties, the play was always declared to be a success by the Old Man days before opening night. Praise for Maurice's skill and dedication always featured in the report speech on Founder's Day, though he was never allowed to be present because he might alarm the parents with his exotic style of dress.

Every boy who was ever in a school play loved Maurice. He was a peacock, a fantasy, a deliverer from the intractable un-reasonableness of school life. During rehearsals the cast was invited, four at a time, to Maurice's home in Basingstoke where they were served tea and cakes by his dark, saturnine boyfriend, who never spoke a word. The walls were covered with photographs and posters of shows Maurice had directed on both sides of the Atlantic. He told stories about his triumphs and catastrophes and gave first-hand insights into the lives of great actors he had directed.

There was a mystery surrounding Maurice. No one at the school could understand how he could possibly be the Old Man's best friend – which he swore he was.

Maurice listened to the Old Man reading his draft of his report with every appearance of interest, then applauded good hand on bad hand, and made a few suggestions about delivery, pausing and emphasis. Each year he came to give his notes a few hours before the actual giving of the report in the marquee. He always concentrated on the sports section because he knew how important it was. Personally, he loathed games of any kind, but he was able, being a man of the theatre, to animate his creative self on any subject.

191

'Strength means so much to a strong man,' he said, with a proud gesture towards his thoughtful friend. 'Let's hear it in your voice, see it in your eyes, how you hold yourself. Mothers and fathers know the importance of health and fitness as the foundation of a successful career.'

The Old Man was listening carefully. He wrote *foundations* in the margin of the report.

The Old Man's wife chipped in to make the point, as she always did, that good, intelligent parents would be more concerned with the intellectual and cultural achievements of the school. 'What are you trying to produce here – civilised beings or hoodlums?' she said caustically.

The Old Man gave her a mean, withering stare. She was always uppity when Maurice was around, showing off as if she had a mind. He knew her limits – Rupert Bear, Sir Walter Scott and *Vogue* magazine. At no time in their thirty years of married life had he ever accepted her advice. Unlike Maurice, she knew nothing of real life, having never had a job in the greater world.

'It's a pity the rugby team did so badly this year. Would anyone notice if you jiggled the won and lost record and made it look a bit better?' Maurice asked innocently.

'The boys would notice,' the Old Man muttered. 'What I must talk about is the future. I thought my theme this year would be building on firm foundations.'

'Brilliant,' Maurice murmured.

The Old Man's wife hooted with laughter. 'What foundations? Face facts. The school's too small. A quarter of the boys are psychological casualties from broken families. The people who pay to send their children here are pretentious nincompoops. Get some quality. Put the fees up.'

'The board of trustees is bound by the will of the founder,' the Old Man snapped. 'We can't depart too far from what he laid down.'

'Which has been bent so much it's hardly recognisable!'

Maurice asked if he could borrow the speech so he could examine it in detail and wandered off while the couple squabbled. Three upper sixth-form boys were working out their last few days at school earning a little pocket-money in the headmaster's garden. They were weeding flower beds. When they saw Maurice coming over the lawn they threw their hoes and rakes on the ground and raced over with the wheelbarrow to offer him a ride.

'Boys, boys, don't neglect your work,' he said, ravishing them with warm smile, 'and I'm not yet a basket case, but as you're here, perhaps you can help me with something.'

Having ascertained that two of the boys were in the rugby first fifteen last season, he asked if they could tell him why the team had been so hopeless. The answer he received was simple enough – the talent and strength wasn't there in depth as it had been the previous year. There were a few good players but not enough to make a team. When this was added to the fact that the Old Man's coaching was desperately unimaginative because he didn't understand the game, and Oliphant didn't know a maul from a ruck, what chance did the team have?

Maurice was shocked to hear this. His friend, the headmaster, had the game in his blood. He had played stand-off for Edinburgh Somethings. It was obvious that not enough faith and energy had been given by the team. The boys must have let the Old Man down. 'But, my dear young lads, be of good cheer. There's always next season. Perseverance conquers all!' he declared, raising his good hand in an imperious gesture and stamping his foot. 'Remember your school motto!'

The boys were leaving in a few days. Scenting the approach of freedom, they were in hilarious mood, not ready to take anything seriously. The more Maurice ranted about school spirit, the more they laughed and teased him.

He became affronted. His eyes glistened. He tossed his long white hair. The crippled hand pounded his narrow chest. His dear, dear friend, the headmaster, was being crucified. The shame of failure was killing him. If this went on he would resign, or die. The school would lose an educational genius. Without the Old Man to inspire and guide it, Lord Mendora Land College would never fulfil its potential, up there with Eton and Harrow and the rest.

All three boys had been in *As You Like It*, Maurice's last school production. They had enjoyed his charm, affection, openness and tricks – and here he was delighting them once more. The wonderful old queen, forgetting where he was, and what the argument had been about, had slipped back into doing his number of despairing director again.

When he fainted in the middle of the lawn, they put him in the wheelbarrow and took him for a ride round the garden until he recovered. When he came to, all three boys marked how his dignity and poise returned on the instant, and his smile was for them.

'Dear boys, what thirsty work you've had' he said, brushing the dandelion parachutes seeds off his shorts, 'I see it is noontide. Let's go for a pint in my car.'

When Maurice didn't return to the rose garden with the notes for the report speech, the Old Man went to look for him. Encountering Fossil Tom, his full-time gardener, he asked if he'd seen Maurice. He was told that Maurice had gone off in his car with the three useless boys foisted on himself as helpers, and good riddance to them all.

In two hours the Old Man would have to stand up in front of the boys, parents, staff, trustees and governors and give his report. Without his notes it would be impossible.

'Any idea where they might have gone?'

'Your friend likes a drink as much as he likes boys. I heard mention of the Dove and Olive Branch,' Tom growled. 'The publican there serves kids from the school round the back, even though he knows it's against the rules.'

The Dove and Olive Branch was in a village five miles away,

situated in a narrow lane. When the Old Man arrived in his car he had to edge past a maroon Rolls-Royce convertible with the hood down and a small bus parked up on the verge outside the pub. Seated at a long table outside were eight powerful-looking men in dark suits, two brightly-dressed women and an old couple smoking Woodbines.

The Old Man parked his car in a farm gateway further down the lane and went round the back of the pub. He could see the colours of Maurice's shirt through the bushes as he approached and hear the laughter of the boys. When he suddenly appeared in front of them, the boys leapt to their feet, horrified.

Taking the report out of the breast pocket of Maurice's Hawaiian shirt, the Old Man expelled the three boys on the spot.

'Oh, no, no! Don't do that, dear friend!' Maurice protested 'It's my fault, not theirs! I brought them here for a fizzy drink after their labours in your garden. Please don't punish them so severely.'

'They know the rules,' the Old Man said grimly. 'They've been taking advantage of your good nature. Come on you three. I'm taking you back to your houses. I want you packed up and gone by tonight.'

One of the boys spoke up for the three of them in spite of his fear. All their parents were coming to Founder's Day. It was a big occasion for them. They'd been looking forward to it for weeks. They'd travelled a long way. For their parents's sake, couldn't the expulsions be for tomorrow when they were leaving anyway?

The Old Man didn't deign to answer. As he led them back to his car, he passed the publican coming out with a tray of eight pints of beer, three orangeades and a stack of sandwiches for the party at the front. The Old Man informed the publican as he passed that he would be reporting him to the licensing authorities.

'But we're all over eighteen, sir!' one of the boys said. 'We're allowed to drink by law.'

'Not my laws!' the Old Man declared, freezing him with basilisk stare.

Maurice remained where he was, heartbroken. He knew there was no point in pleading with his friend. When it came to discipline, the Old Man was adamant and immovable. Taking his drink, Maurice wandered round to the front of the pub. A group of handsome, very fit young men in dark suits were softly serenading an attractive woman in her thirties. Her eyes were dancing and there was a lovely, deep smile on her face. Fifteen years ago Maurice had directed a production of *The Student Prince* at the Palace Theatre, Watford with a tavern scene that was almost identical.

He sat down on a bench beside an old couple who were smoking Woodbines and drinking orangeade. He was anxious to forget the horrid scene he'd just witnessed round the back. It made him miserable to imagine the trouble the boys would be in once their parents found out they'd managed to get themselves expelled on their last day at school.

'What language are they singing in so beautifully?' Maurice asked the old husband. 'It's reminds me of Schubert but it's not Schubert.'

The man stared at Maurice through his bottle-end glasses, took them off as if he couldn't believe his eyes, then cleaned the lenses on his tie. 'That's Polish,' he replied. 'They're singing her love-songs. Where d'you get that shirt?'

'A US Army major gave it to me. From your cadences am I right in guessing you hale from Liverpool?'

'We do hale from there – and a great place it is,' the husband declared proudly. 'Where do you hale from?'

'Oh, outer Berkshire. Ah, dear old Liverpool – the Empire, the Royal Court, the Playhouse . . . great days, great days.'

'Do I take it you're a man of the stage?'

'Legitimate, you understand,' Maurice replied with a touch of *hauteur*. 'The last play I did in Liverpool was Bernard Shaw's *Man and Superman*.'

'I thought there was something about you. Me and the wife are music hall through and through, though I do like a bit of opera now and then. My name's Emmanuel, and this is my wife, Maud.'

They shook hands. Maurice rolled off his full name, Maurice Henry Garrick de Vigny, and said he was delighted.

'I met my wife at the Liverpool Empire forty years ago – a happy day for both of us, wasn't it, sweetheart?' the husband said beamingly. 'I'm taking her down to Founder's Day at our grandson's school where he's top of the form. According to the map, it's not far from here.'

'I know that school well. In fact, I've just come from there. The man who runs it is my best friend.'

The husband put the Woodbine out in the ashtray and cast an eye over Maurice, noting the rope sandals, the long, bell-bottomed linen shorts, passing through the jungle of the Hawaiian shirt to the wings of blue-tinged white hair. 'Have you had anything to do with our Dan, my grandson?' he asked. 'His name's Rogers.'

Maurice thought for a moment. 'I don't believe I have. What house is he in?'

'The Junior House.'

'Ah, that explains it,' Maurice said with a smile. 'The Junior House is for boys from eleven to thirteen. I only do my plays with seniors.'

The pain of the contretemps with the Old Man was easing under the influence of this warm human contact. Maurice liked these people. There was a genuineness about them, an open readiness. 'I'm going to get myself another drink. Is that gin and orange you're having? Would you care for a fill-up?'

The wife gave her husband a warning look. Holding onto his half-empty glass, the husband declined the offer. 'You're alright, Maurice. I'd like to but we have to move on. Besides, I can't drink much more of this stuff she's got me on. It's been nice talking to you.'

CHAPTER FIFTEEN

There was something in the outlook of the type of people who paid a lot of good money for their sons to go to Lord Mendora Land College that made them spend what was left over on cars. In the traffic jam backed up from the main school buildings down to the school gates and along the road in either direction there were Humber Super Snipes, Sunbeam Talbots, Aston Martins, Wolseleys, Bentleys and Lagondas, the whole luxury range of the British motor industry.

In the front passenger seats sat mothers in what appeared to be a uniform of straw hats and floral summer dresses, contrasted with the sartorial dark or light suits of their husbands. The parents sat and sweltered in the heat while one of the farm manager's underlings directed the queue of vehicles into the car park under the pine trees near the Scout Hut, shepherding each car carefully into place.

Dawn was fuming. By the time the Rolls reached the gates, her planned coup of having her son and Daniel ride on the running-board up the main drive had collapsed because the queue was hardly moving.

Daniel couldn't get over the sight of his grandparents sitting in the back seat of the Rolls smoking Woodbines. When he found his mother singing in the bus with the Polish miners, he was torn between filial embarrassment and pleasure at seeing her having such a good time. Roman told him that during the trip she'd received eight proposals of marriage.

'She is so proud, she is so beautiful,' Roman said sadly. 'She turned us all down but we will never give up hope. On the journey back she might accept one of us.'

Stanislav stood up in the driving-seat to see ahead. He sounded the horn in his frustration. The Rolls was starting to overheat.

Daniel's grandfather beckoned him to come nearer. He leant out of the back seat and put a hand on the boy's shoulder. 'What a night we had in Soho, son,' he said. 'Your grandmother had never been to a Chinese restaurant before in her life.'

At this point the Rolls boiled over. Stanislav cursed and turned off the engine. For the rest of the distance up the main drive the Mercedes bus had to push the Silver Ghost along from behind.

Walking beside the steaming vehicle Bryant whispered to Daniel that things couldn't be worse and he wished himself dead.

The headmaster's report was well received. The chairman of the school governors had a stutter but he waded manfully through his speech well enough. The guest of honour was a general with a red band round his cap and a red face to go with it. He gave a short address on how traditional values won wars. It was only when it came to the awards that there was a hitch. The winner of the short story prize was one of the boys expelled that afternoon. When no boy walked up to the platform, the Old Man remembered and quickly moved on to the next prize.

Bryant was relieved that his stepfather and the miners couldn't be at the ceremony in the marquee because they were repairing the Rolls in the shade of the pine trees by the Scout Hut. There was no jack in the boot so the miners had to lift the vehicle and prop the back axle up on a log. They did manage to complete the work in time to watch the Combined Cadet Force parade, however. Every one of the Poles had fought in the war. Three had been with the General Anders at the ferocious siege of Monte Cassino, remembered for its triumph of Polish arms and their terrible losses. As they stood watching the boys march past to salute the general on the dining-hall steps, the force of the image brought back how the misery and chaos of 1939–45 had begun – the invasion of Poland and Britain keeping its word, offsetting the shame of Munich by declaring war on Hitler's Germany. The miners didn't bother to disguise their feelings. They wiped tears from their eyes, lit cigarettes and puffed hard. It upset them to be dragged back to those times by fresh-faced children in battledress. At the end of the parade after queuing to kiss the hand of Daniel's mother, they said goodbye, and drove off in the bus to find entertainment elsewhere.

Stanislav and Dawn had booked a room in a hotel in a nearby town. A pilot in Stanislav's bomber squadron during the war was now a senior officer at the RAF base and they were to have dinner. After looking at the display of work in the gymnasium, they arranged to pick up Daniel's family at the church the following morning, then drove off, much to the relief of Bryant. Cook then ferried everyone who was staying with him down to The Elms in his car.

Daniel watched him carefully. The man had clearly been made jealous by the Poles. Cook had witnessed the way they had swarmed around his new wife and how she had enjoyed it. He could hardly bring himself to speak to her. Married only a few weeks and she was flirting already. Cook's apparent shyness was the paralysis of suppressed resentment. There would be trouble. Adulthood was full of such pitfalls.

How she shines in the old, gloomy house, Daniel thought, trailing around after his mother with luggage as Cook showed the way up to the bedrooms. I've never seen her looking so well. All the sadness has gone. She's alive again. It's wonderful to see her like this. This will be her home. I might be allowed to live here as well. But she shouldn't have gone ahead with getting married without telling me.

Cook opened a door on the landing and ushered God With Us and Maud inside, taking their case off Daniel and putting it by the double bed. They thanked him and said the room was lovely and they might take a nap after all the excitement. Cook told them where the bathroom was and closed the door.

This was a crucial moment. Cook opened another room and invited Daniel's mother inside, taking her case for her.

There was a double bed in it.

And red roses.

Daniel felt sick.

Red roses. Red roses.

What further proof was needed?

Not knowing what he should do, head swimming, heart beating, tears flowing, he ran down the stairs, through the front door and into the garden.

Passing through an orchard hung with fruit he came to the back fence of the property. Beside a hole dug in the ground he found a burly, bearded, middle-aged man with an unlit pipe clenched between his teeth plucking a turkey.

'You have to have somewhere to put feathers,' he said, pulling out a handful and throwing them down the hole. 'Who are you?'

There was never a better time for this question to be asked.

An ingenuous, dependable quality in the man made Daniel answer the question in full. He told the story of his last two years at the school, his divided life shuttling between two separate worlds, his persecution by sadistic, unhinged masters, his battles with his grandfather, and finally how his mother had betrayed him by getting married to his history teacher behind his back.

By the time he reached the end of his story, the turkey had been plucked clean and the hole filled in. The man stuffed his pipe, lit it, puffed away for a minute as though turning over in his mind everything he had been told, slung the dead bird over his shoulder by the neck and plodded through the orchard towards the house with Daniel, now silent and depressed, beside him, awaiting some kind of reaction to the story he had told.

'Well, it sounds as though it hasn't been easy for you – but don't lose heart,' the man said off-handedly. 'Are you coming to the cricket?'

Daniel gasped. He'd forgotten the single-innings match between the staff and a Junior House team that took place every Founder's Day. He was down to play. After asking the man to explain to Cook that Daniel Rogers had had to shoot off to change into his kit for the game, he ran off up the back lane, leaving his family to sort out the next few hours for themselves.

Because cricket wasn't played with any great refinement at Junior House, and Mr O'Leary, the groundsman, concentrated his efforts on the main school pitches a mile away, the Junior House wicket was made of concrete covered in matting. The theory was that this surface needed minimal attention, which was a myth in some ways. If the matting was damp it went slack and the ball skidded; if dry, the ball could lift atrociously, but there was nothing could be done about it.

Mule came out padded up, pipe clenched between his teeth for comic effect, and using a bat as a walking-stick. He was very sure of himself as a popular figure amongst the fee-paying parents. After taking his guard, he lifted the bat straight up behind him, and beckoned to Daniel, who was opening the bowling, that he was giving him a clear view of the stumps so he could do his worst.

By sharing his pain with the man plucking the turkey, Daniel had relaxed his hold on deep, turbulent emotions. Having put the story of his life together for the first time in a cogent form he now understood how severely he'd been wronged – and the man who'd done most to hurt him was there, staring malignantly down the wicket from under a ridiculously small yellow and green cap, bat raised like the cane that had done so much damage to Daniel's backside.

He started his run-up, tearing in as hard as he could, and thumped the ball into the dry matting halfway down the pitch. It climbed and whistled past Mule's left ear.

Mule remained with his bat in the air as if no ball had been bowled. He lifted his cap in a mocking salute. Laughter rippled round the spectators. Daniel walked back to the mark for his run-up, fuming.

His next delivery was a full-toss that struck Mule's artificial leg with a loud clunk. The ball shot off to the third man boundary. Going by the sound, Cook, who was acting as umpire, signalled four runs to the scorer.

'Get it right. Those are leg-byes,' Mule snorted.

The ball after that knocked the bat out of Mule's hand. The next ball hit him in the midriff and doubled him up. Taking his time, Mule stalked up the wicket.

'Tell him to pitch the ball up,' he said to Cook in a loud voice so Daniel could hear. 'The stuff he's giving me is unplayable.'

Cook shrugged his shoulders and said it was a matter of common knowledge Rogers could be erratic in the early overs, but he settled down once he was into his stride.

Mule returned to the crease to face the next ball. It was another very fast full toss that clipped his hip, swinging him round so he hovered over the stumps, nearly knocking the bails off.

He pounded up the wicket again.

'This is supposed to be a friendly!' he protested. 'He'll have to slow down.'

Cook told Mule *sotto voce* that the headmaster, who was watching, had been very clear on the subject of not slowing Rogers down. 'Why don't you retire hurt,' he suggested. 'That might be the best solution.'

'What, chased off the field by a boy like Rogers? Never!' Mule seethed. 'Thanks for your help, I must say.' Then he stumped back down the wicket twirling the bat like a bandmaster with his mace, and took guard again.

Daniel's grandfather sat in a deck-chair watching the game. The testy old member of staff who was taking a battering from Daniel out at the wicket and complaining so much was of particular interest. There was something about him that rang a bell.

Mule blocked a yorker that was going under his bat. The ball span and hissed on the matting like a live thing. He went to tap it away but the seam caught on the weave and shot the ball into his stumps, bringing the bails off. Daniel did a war-dance. Mule shook his bat savagely in the air, thumped it on the ground, and shouted at the boy to stop showing off.

That shout . . . that wave of the arm . . . yes, God With Us had heard that shout before, and seen that arm. When Mule stormed back to the pavilion and threw his bat up the steps, shouting, 'What a fluke!' he encountered a stooped, cadaverous figure in bottle-end glasses standing to attention.

'Hughes, C sub-section, 398 battery, Royal Field Artillery, reporting in, sergeant.'

Mule stopped dead and stared. Then he clattered up the wooden steps, sat down and started unbuckling his pads. 'Hughes?' he muttered, glancing up into the sunken, beaked face. 'Not Manny Hughes?'

'That's me.'

'I'd have expected that man to be dead by now.'

'Near enough.'

Mule beckoned him closer. 'Don't call me sergeant,' he whispered. 'I stayed on after the war and was commissioned.'

'They commissioned you with a leg missing? That must have taken some doing.'

Mule looked into the face of his comrade from the war of years past. Daniel's grandfather had been present when Mule's leg was blown off by a booby-trap in an abandoned farmhouse on the Asian side of the Bosphorus. They hadn't seen each other since their days in Allied occupation forces investing Istanbul in 1918.

'They gave me a staff job at Woolwich Arsenal. I eventually made captain,' Mule said with a tight smile. 'What have you been up to since those days we had together? What are you doing here?'

'Oh, that would take more time than we've got.'

God With Us remembered Sergeant McSweyn only too well. He knew the Army, even in its most purblind moments, would never have made him an officer. McSweyn liked to be called Mule after his victims, the stubborn animals in the gun-teams he beat so heartlessly. In the Royal Field Artillery he wore the nickname like a badge of honour, glorying in the conquest of obstinacy and strength that went with the label. It was true he could bend a mule's will to his own better than any other man in the company. Breaking an animal's spirit was his speciality. McSweyn was the mule-driver *extraordinaire*. He could bring a mule back from the edge of death to drag guns and limbers out of mud holes. He had a whip made of mule skin. As he flogged a team forward he cracked the same joke time after time after time after time. The dumb beasts were beating themselves. God With Us had seen full-grown mules on their knees, eyes rolling in pain, lungs blowing red froth into their mouth and nostrils, as they suffered under his blows. But whenever one died on him, he had wept.

Mule noticed the sadness in his old comrade's expression, lines of suffering and ill-health etched on the seamed, hollowed-out face, wear and tear on the spirit showing in the strangely distorted eyes – but a dim light left over from youth was still shining somewhere. Taking the elbow of his brother-in-arms, he steered him to a comfortable seat at the back of the pavilion.

'Let's sit here, have a smoke, and we'll go over some old times,' Mule said, taking out his pipe and tobacco pouch. 'It's been ages since I've been able to chat with someone from the old days.'

As they sat down together a loud cry came from the pitch.

'What's happened?' God With Us asked, peering out.

'Rogers has clean bowled the bursar,' Mule muttered. 'The poor old chap will be glad to get out of the line of fire.'

'Our Dan's got another wicket? I never knew my grandson could bowl so fast. He certainly gave you a peppering.'

Mule sat back. He slapped his good knee. Knots were being untied, mysteries explained. 'Rogers is your grandson?'

'He is, and I'm very proud of him.'

'I'm surprised you managed to have a family life, Manny. It must have interfered with your drinking time.'

There was a silence. The two men exchanged the glances of those who know each other's worst sides.

God With Us spoke first. 'I'll tell you something for nothing, *Mule*. Finding you here has put my mind at rest in a way. I've been worried about this place turning my grandson into a snob. To me a snob is the lowest form of life. But my grandson can't learn that with you on the staff. You've got nothing to be snobbish about, have you?'

'This school does not encourage class distinction, if that's what you mean,' Mule replied. 'The headmaster is hot on that subject.'

'That's not what I mean.'

Mule employed his blank, fixed stare. 'Then what are you saying?' he said coldly.

'I think you know.'

'I've changed a lot.'

'I'll ask Daniel about that and see what he says.'

Mule took a deep breath. 'As I said – I've changed. It was as if when I lost my leg that other side of myself went with it. Believe me. I'm a different man these days.'

God With Us couldn't hide the distrust in his expression. 'I hope you haven't been putting my grandson through it,' he said. 'He was sending that ball down at you with a message attached.'

Mule repeated his claim that he had changed beyond all recognition from the war years. Through the efforts of a senior Royal Field Artillery officer who was on the board of trustees, he had found a new life in education.

'I hope that giving the mules hell hasn't become doing the same to the boys,' God With Us mused, lighting a cigarette. 'You get to know someone over three years, war or peace. I'm trying to think of the advantages my grandson might have gained by being here, in spite of you. Getting away from my influence is one of them – but I'm not sure that your influence will have been any better.'

Lionel stood behind the Old Man's deck chair at the side of the pavilion. He had caught an early train from Waterloo, put his bicycle in the guard's van, got off at the nearby town, then pedalled the seven miles to Lord Mendora Land College through the lanes.

He had hidden his bicycle behind a hedge and spent the morning wandering around the estate, looking at the neo-Georgian buildings, the well-equipped farm, the distinguished old manor house, the pastures and copses. No one challenged him. Being Founder's Day there were plenty of strangers around.

This is all so fine, so beautiful, he thought. If my grandfather could only see it now he would be halfway to being satisfied that the terms of his will had been kept. It looks like the best orphanage in Britain. How sad that it isn't.

Lionel's father had been left nothing in the will. He had crossed his father too many times. He was a godless agitator, an intellectual left-winger. He had a police record. He had got divorced. He had offended in every way a Jewish son can break the heart of a Jewish *paterfamilias*. At the age of fifty-one, Lionel's father had cut his wrists, defeated and worn-out by politics, marriage and the onerous disappointments of broken dreams. All this would have been understandable and bearable if only the terms of the will had been kept to. If Lionel had been able to make this visit and have the satisfaction of knowing that the good his grandfather had intended, and sacrificed his son for, was being realised, there would have been no need for revenge.

But this was not what it was meant to be. It was three quarters of the way down the road to becoming like all the other charitable school foundations in England since the fifteenth century – taken over by the sons of the wealthy and built into a bulwark of the ruling class. The English who had honoured his banker grandfather by allowing him to buy a baronage and call himself lord, had corrupted his great act of charity.

Lionel knew all this first-hand because, as a boy who had lost his father, he had attended the school on a free scholarship during the transition time when its constitution was being eaten away. His mother had managed to wangle his free place out of the trustees before she died, arguing that as the grandson of the founder he had a right to it. Within five years of leaving he was as extreme in his socialism as his father. This school, and hundreds like it, were dividing the nation. There would never be a just society if private education was allowed to continue.

In his jacket pocket was a copy of a statement giving the reasons for his action. He had posted the original to the *Times Educational Supplement* that morning on his way to Waterloo.

Sitting in the marquee during the proceedings that afternoon he had noted how no reference whatsoever was made to his grandfather's wishes. The man and his dream did not merit a single mention. And there was no act of remembrance, no praise for the thought behind his gift, no prayer for his soul, nothing.

Lord Mendora, Sidney James Alexander, had a thing about orphanhood. The only child of wealthy, pleasure-loving parents, he was brought up by servants. Educated at home, mainly in the kitchen and scullery, he ended up loving the butler and the cook more than his mother and father. From this formative experience emerged his political philosophy – the idea that a country should be governed by an oligarchy of orphans trained from birth by the lower class to govern, inculcated so strongly with the principles of public service that they could never be twisted or bent into superiority.

His deathbed table was littered with notes that had to be made by solicitors into a cogent will he could sign. They were pragmatists who hammered his vision out for him – something that might work. At the end he lay, furred up with useless wealth, wanting to do good, his soul turning against him because he'd left it all so late. He was like a man crushed between two railway waggons full of gold who remembers to write his will before the bumpers are pulled apart to let him die.

But now it was the corruption that mattered; the sinking of ideals into the establishment marsh, deepening and darkening the compromise, keeping the political swamp saturated. And the man who was going to take this process as far as he could, dragging what had been the best orphanage in Britain into this bog, was less than ten yards away.

Since he left the school, Lionel's tussocky hair had gone completely white. His physique and robust health had been a gift of his seven years at the school, but all that had sadly declined under the strain and worry of his political frustrations. After the war so many changes had seemed possible. The new Labour government had set about rebuilding and restructuring the nation. If ever there was a time for the abolition of private education it was then, and Lionel had not only worked hard for it, he had genuinely expected it to happen. But by 1951 he knew that the English would never go that far. The separation of social classes was essential to the spiritual health of this conservative, deferential nation. Even those who stood up for equal opportunity secretly believed that meant the opportunity to join the privileged class. Every parent with left-wing views insisted upon the right to by-pass them when it came to the education of their children.

There would be no new Jerusalem.

The old one, in its ruin, would have to do.

No one was able to recognise Lionel, the first boy from the school to win a place at Oxford, even those teachers who had taught him. The slight, washed-out, bushy-haired nervy man wearing sunglasses, hands in the pockets of a cheap suit was the antithesis of the confident youth who had left the school. Lionel enjoyed that anonymity. The radical change in himself meant a lot. He had escaped. To return in such a transformed state was important. It was physical proof that he had freed himself.

Today he was on his own, cleansed and oathed.

He didn't applaud when a batsman made a good shot or a

fielder a good catch. Intent on his own volcanic thoughts, he spoke to no one. Now and again a spasm went through his wasted body. What he feared was being declared unfit to plead to the charge of murder. That would be too humiliating. At times he had held that to take another's life was larceny as well as murder, an act of terrible theft. History demonstrated that if this was the case the world had been governed by thieves from the very beginning. Without the theft of life no great empires would have arisen, no heroic wars ever been won – nothing would have been achieved.

Lionel would live for the sake of his trial and condemnation. Then, from the dock, he would have the opportunity to propound his principles inherited from his father and grandfather. For Lionel believed, in a phrase of his father's, that equality, freedom and justice were pillars of a lost temple sunk in the desert of modern life.

He would read out the list of the charity schools corrupted into pluto-colleges over the last five hundred years and ask why everything is taken away from the poor and given to the rich.

He owed his father and his grandfather that much. In his speech he would demand that the school change its name, dissociating it from his family altogether.

The Old Man got out of his deck chair and turned to go to the pavilion changing-room. 'Lionel!' he said as soon as his eye fastened upon him, immediately seeing through the changes with his piercing grey eye. 'How good of you to be with us on Founder's Day. Why didn't you let me know you were coming? I'd have had you up on the platform by my side.'

And he put out his hand.

CHAPTER SIXTEEN

Dinner in the garden at The Elms was a muted affair that evening. Embarrassment at being trapped together in the aftermath of an act of bloody violence, not knowing how to think and feel together because they were from separate worlds, prevailed. To have been able to divide and deal with the hideous incident privately would have been better, but there was no way this could be achieved. No other accommodation was available to Daniel's family.

Cook was dealing with two catastrophes at once. As well as the outrage at the cricket field, his brother had told him that Daniel believed there had been a secret marriage – his mother was no longer Mrs Rogers, she was Mrs Cook. The boy was nursing a huge psychological wound as deep as the one Lionel's razor had made in the Old Man's wrist.

No opportunity had yet presented itself for Cook to take Daniel aside and talk some sense into him. Everything was in such a cloud of chaos, denials in this charged atmosphere were futile, rendered so by Lionel's act of vengeance. The attack at the pavilion dwarfed all other concerns and, at the same time, made everyone feel completely useless. Over the years mentally deranged old boys had returned to the school in various guises – often to reunions to restart old friendships because the real world had proved too alien – and they had behaved oddly and badly enough but no one had ever tried to dismember the headmaster before. But within the act was a rationale, a substantial cause. Lionel believed charity, that greatest of human virtues, had been betrayed. That is why he had slashed the Old Man's wrist.

No one in the garden that summer evening was in the mood to work through political arguments. Instead, they sat in shock remembering the bright leap of arterial blood. They ate the twenty-pound turkey as if going through a Christmas that only recalled Herod's massacre of the innocents.

Everyone, that is, except God With Us, who'd seen everything in his time – all forms of wounding, bloodshed and maiming. As the veteran, the survivor of the trenches and his own delin-quencies, he was the only one who was relaxed, feeling at home in the aftermath of such horror. Everyone else was glad that the responsibility for filling the void with words had been taken up by another, even though it was this garrulous, pontificating old man. They kept quiet and let him have the stage.

With the flames of the fire round which they were sitting reflected in his bottle-end glasses, God With Us saw no reason to spare his audience the full force of his pessimism about the future of the human race.

'Man will destroy himself,' he said, pouring himself another glass of Cook's Vouvray, 'and I'm not sure that's a bad thing. We've had our chance. If there's anything left after we've ruined it all, let one of the other life-forms have a go. I've always admired the ant, myself.'

Daniel sat in a glum, bewildered silence, ignoring his grand-father (he'd heard it all before) struggling to bend his mind back to the tragedy. Lionel's attack on the headmaster had coincided with an appeal for *leg before wicket* off his bowling. If the batsman had been given out, his bowling figures would have equalled Henry Long's five wickets for nineteen runs at Taunton. But the match had been abandoned with the decision still up in the air, and he was denied. Cricket was all he could think about. To dwell on that at a time like this? What kind of a mind is that? After all he'd been through, holding himself together, believing he had some mental integrity, he was appalled to find himself so shallow.

If life was to be this random, one unsorted, deeply-delving, wild thing on top of another, Daniel might not be able to stand it. There must be certainties somewhere.

His grandfather took him by the arm and pulled him a few yards out of the firelight. 'Tell me about *Captain* McSweyn,' he said. 'How does he treat you?'

'Mule?' Daniel replied. 'He's alright, I suppose.'

'Mule? You call him Mule?'

'Everyone calls him Mule. He doesn't mind. That's what he likes to be called.'

God With Us put his hands to his face as if holding his head so it wouldn't fall off. 'The conceit of it,' he muttered wrathfully. 'Mule running the lives of young kids! Don't hide things from me. I knew him in the Army and he wasn't alright then.'

'He's alright,' Daniel repeated, his mind distorted by mayhem, bowling figures and marriages.

'People don't change that much, son. He's no captain. He was a sergeant. You can go to prison for impersonating an officer.'

'He's alright, Grandad. What does it matter? Leave it, please.'

'He should have the sack. No kid should have to live under someone like that.'

'I'll be in the seniors next term. We won't have anything to do with each other.'

'What about the kids who come after? What about your own brother if he ends up coming here?'

Daniel's face was impassive. He made no attempt to answer. His grandfather's concern had no real depth to it. The clown has no power to change things. He's there to be laughed at. 'John won't be as difficult as I've been, perhaps,' Daniel said after a while, edging back to the firelight. 'Besides, that's years away. By then, Mule might have retired.'

'I hope so for our John's sake,' God With Us muttered.

Maud was sitting on the end of the bed where John was sleeping. It had taken him a long time to drop off. Apart from the boy, she was alone in the big, old house, having volunteered to baby-sit while all the others went to the pub. Daniel had returned to the Junior House for his last night in that place.

As she watched the sleeping boy, Maud knew that she should have followed her instinct not to come on this trip.

In spite of all its problems, life was safer at home.

You can keep London and you can keep Blackburn.

Her husband had broken his promise and was drinking again. But then, this had happened so many times it wasn't worth getting upset about. He'd go on the waggon again, and fall off, get on again, and so on.

By the end of the night he'd be regaling the crowd in the bar with his four stories distilled from the dark wine of war.

The gun-team sacrificed in the fog.

The horse, the beloved horse, shot from under him.

The amazement at the size and beauty of the mosque of St. Sofia.

The life saved by the havildar-major who'd left his turban on the beach.

The recurrent malaria caught from the Black Sea might be mentioned in a tirade against all policemen, as might his opinion that the British should have been fighting with the Germans against the French.

Good luck to them all having to listen, and God help them.

She lit another Woodbine.

Before going out to the pub with the men, her daughter had been acting strangely. Maybe there was something in Dan's suspicions about her and the history master, whom Maud had quite taken to. He seemed a kind man, a thoughtful sort who might make her happy inasmuch as she could ever be happy.

She dwelt on this for a long time, grappling with her conscience, the ash on her cigarette getting longer and longer.

Not wanting her daughter to marry again was selfish – she knew that.

But if she ever did, and Maud was left alone with *Manny* . . .

No, no.

Anything but that.

To escape from the thought, she went back again to her

daughter's odd, skittish behaviour – strangely over-excited for her. Maud couldn't work it out until she realised that by being close to the crime on the cricket boundary – the headmaster's arterial blood had leapt yards to splash her – her daughter had been confronted by the first real act of violence she'd ever seen.

So many years of being haunted by the carnage in the cactus grove, dreaming it out in detail, imagining her love blown to smithereens, blood showering the earth, had suddenly shrunk to this one sharp moment.

It must have pierced her.

Gone right to the heart, to the quick.

Poor girl. So many years of grieving.

So much madness.

So much *waste*.

The ash fell off the cigarette onto the bedspread. Absently, Maud brushed it off.

She looked at the stub, which wasn't worth smoking.

Lying down beside the sleeping boy, she lit another Woodbine.

The editor of the *Times Educational Supplement* read through Lionel's letter, intrigued. The subject matter was not new. The rights and wrongs of public versus private education had tormented British politics for long enough. What interested the editor was the underlying analysis of charity in education and what appeared to be its inevitable perversion once quality was created and the rich went in pursuit of it. The letter contained a number of warning references to an act of political violence about to happen. He asked his secretary to keep an eye on the news and to get some reliable historical background.

'Did you know that Harrow was founded by a yeoman for the education of poor children in the town?' he asked the secretary as he went over the material, 'and Charterhouse for poor but scholarly boys . . . Christ's Hospital to take all the fatherless children and other poor men's children off the streets and give them shelter, food and schooling . . . The list goes on and on.

215

This fellow has a point. All our best public schools appear to have been stolen from the poor but it's far too late to do anything about it.'

West Kirby, the Wirral coast of Cheshire, Four Winds Guest House. 14th August 1951.

Daniel's mother had saved up enough for a week at the seaside. The room was in the attic, but there was a window overlooking the shore.

After the first two days, they were lucky with the weather.

Daniel's mother checked the times of low water, took a packed lunch from the guest house for the three of them, then set out to walk the mile to the three Hilbre islands while the tide was out. They were the first on the sands, following the edge of the tide as it withdrew ahead of them, leaving newly-washed sandbanks behind. Some of the gullies were still deep in places so they had to find safe crossings.

The salt air was bright. Under their bare feet the sand was ribbed and firm. But, afraid of being caught on the islands by the returning tide, they had come out too early. There was too much water still draining from the banks, which slowed them down.

The last time Daniel had been out here in the vastness was with his grandfather when they went stake-net fishing for flukes overnight. He kept the memory at bay because these days his grandfather's good intentions had completely collapsed and he was back in his old routine, destroying himself.

The mother was quiet, going over in her mind how easy it is to make mistakes by replying to advertisements in the newspaper. The guest house was cold, drab and disappointing. The landlady had no idea how to treat her customers, especially children. The packed lunch would be mean and skimpy. By the end of the day the boys would be starving.

John called Daniel over and held out his hand so he could be in the middle, between his mother and brother. They walked abreast, John insisting that their footprints be in perfect parallel lines. This was his game.

The three islands in the Hilbre group are outcrops of new red sandstone, a soft sedimentary rock shaped into strange, flowing forms by the sea and wind. Daniel's mother wondered which they should head for first, all three lying in a line. John said they should go to the little one first, then the middle one, then the largest.

Daniel's mother paused and looked back towards the shore. No one else had set out to walk to the islands yet. Since they had started out, clouds had piled up in the west. She felt nervous about her decision to set out so early. Had she got the right information? The weather forecast was good, according to the landlady.

Daniel could see his mother's anxiety. Instead of calming her fears he found himself embarking on a conversation that would take her mind off the danger. The enormous space they were in between earth and sky freed him from sensitivities he had learnt to follow with his mother. He asked her, over John's head, if she thought she would ever marry again.

She laughed. John, parroting her, laughed as well.

Daniel mentioned the Poles. According to Bryant, every one of them had proposed to her during the night out dancing in Soho. This was true, his mother replied, her head held high, and she'd told them that they were all so handsome it was impossible to choose between them.

John laughed again, pulling at their hands, then broke away to run over a wide stretch of flat sand that stretched into the glimmering distance.

'Is there really no one good enough for you on earth?' Daniel said lightly, putting his hand round his mother's small waist. An immediate erection shocked and appalled him. He went to take his hand away but his mother covered it tightly with her arm and deliberately bumped into his shoulder.

'Think about your own life, son, she said.'

217

He hardly heard what she said. What kind of an animal am I? he asked himself. Can't I distinguish between a woman and my own mother? He didn't feel ashamed, though. He nearly told her what had happened, but decided not to. What could she say? It was Nature and Nature was stronger than thought.

He managed to extricate his hand and walked a yard apart from her, concentrating on the horizon. He forced the erection back to where it came from by will power, still amazed at his response to the contact. For a while he remained silent, seeing himself as two different creatures, the animal and the civilised being. Both of these loved his mother in their different ways.

'Mum, d'you realise I'm nearly as tall as my dad now?' he said as they walked along.

She shook her head and laughed at him. 'No, you're not. Your father was six feet tall.'

'I've seen his Army record book. He was only five feet ten and a half.'

'Then there was something the matter with the tape-measure.'

'You should be able to remember how tall he was, Mum. When you're walking alongside me does it feel the same as it did when you were walking alongside him?'

She made no reply.

'When I was inside you, did you go dancing?'

'Of course I did.'

'That explains it.'

'Explains what?'

'Me. It explains me. All the different dances you did.'

His mother said she'd no idea what he was talking about.

'My dad was a bit of a borrower, wasn't he?'

His mother hesitated, frowning across at him. 'Who told you that?'

'Grandad.'

'He always paid back.'

'After I was born he put on quite a bit of weight, didn't he?'

'Did he? I can't remember.'

'You can't remember how tall he was, how heavy he was . . . '
Daniel mocked, surprised at the sharp edge in his voice. 'There's
a photograph of him holding me in his arms on the promenade,
somewhere. At first I couldn't recognise him, his face had filled
out so much.'

'I must have a look at that photograph.'

'I think he looks rather fed up.'

'Let's leave this, son . . . I can tell you're upset about something.'

'I'm not at all upset. D'you realise you never told me my dad
was dead? People in the street knew but I didn't.'

'I must have told you,' she protested. 'I must have!'

'No, you didn't. When the telegram came and everything
happened in the hall and you and my gran were holding on to
each other, I asked what was the matter, and you said, *a friend
of your dad's been killed in the war.*'

'I couldn't have said that.'

'You did. Those are the exact words.'

'I must have been protecting you.'

Daniel was silent, staring at the ribs in the sand as he walked
over them.

'You were only four, Dan.'

'Is there an age when we can be told the truth?' he said
indignantly. 'We know about death at four. That's the age when
we know we're going to die one day.'

His mother gave on odd little laugh. 'You seem to know a lot
about it,' she said huffily.

'All I can think is, you didn't really believe he was dead,' he
went on, anger still thrilling in his voice, 'but by the time you'd
accepted it, you'd forgotten the lie you'd told me.'

His mother raised her chin, shook her head, and walked faster
to get away from him.

The time had come for Daniel to bring things together as much
as he could. As they walked along over the sands there was

nothing left to say on the subject of his father. Nothing would change his mother's heart. She understood what her son had been revealing to her but felt no responsibility for the way she felt. Her loss would remain her defining moment. But, in truth, in spirit, she was no widow. The man had never died.

For his brother's sake, Daniel broke his silence on what life was like at school. Now he was free of the Junior House he could talk about it. In the senior school he would be a third-form nonentity. There would be three years of relative anonymity and quiet because all eyes were on the sixth form, his included. He wanted to do well. That would help him to survive. With this knowledge, he had the security to tell his mother that he wasn't sure his brother would be happy at Junior House.

He waited for a response. His mother kept walking, head down, dark hair blowing in the offshore breeze.

'You know our John wants to do everything you do.'

'He wouldn't if he knew the truth.'

'Is it any worse than what he'd have to put with at home?'

Daniel couldn't quite answer that. John was now a very small figure ahead, almost lost in the sparkling air. Daniel imagined him as a new boy being tormented and brutalised in a world of enemies. He'd get kicked around.

'We get the cane a lot, Mum,' Daniel said carefully. 'We get beaten for anything at all. It's their answer to everything.'

'They shouldn't do that!' she exclaimed. 'No one's told me.'

'Why should John have to go through it just because I did?'

His mother was quiet for several paces. 'You managed. Why shouldn't he?' she said after a while. 'He can do what you can do.'

This set Daniel back. His mother could see he was shocked.

'He'll need to be toughened up,' she said. 'Men need to be toughened up. I'm not sure that will happen if he stays at home.'

'Everyone hasn't got to be tough. Perhaps I needed it. My brother is different. He's got a different nature.'

'He won't be happy if he doesn't follow in your footsteps. You know why he thinks that way. You're all he's got in the world of men. If they take him, and Mr Cook thinks they will because he's your brother . . . '

'Did he say that?' Daniel enquired, surprised.

'They think a lot of you. They think there'll be as much good in our John as they've found in you.'

'Good? You could have fooled me, Mum!' he laughed.

'Hundreds of boys go through the hands of those teachers. They know what they're doing. Our John will have you there with him for a couple of years. You'll be able to look after him.'

Daniel turned his head away. That was a job he didn't want.

Father, husband, lover was for later on – much later on – with new people in a new time, a free time he would make for himself.

He left her, running off after his brother, his reflection passing over the blue sky in the pools of standing water. Ahead of him was a gully full of fast-moving tidal water rushing out. As he got closer he saw John squatting down on the edge of it looking at worm casts in the sand.